Peter Wild is the editor ⟨...⟩ Disease. His award-winni⟨...⟩ *Journal*, *Big Issue*, *Word Riot*, *Pen Pusher*, *Dogmatika* and many other places. He lives in Manchester with his wife and three children.

Perverted by Language

Fiction inspired by The Fall

Edited and introduced by Peter Wild

With thanks

[signature]

[signature]
Mackenzie

MANCHESTER
INTERNATIONAL
FESTIVAL

[Serpent's Tail logo]

Best wishes, [signature]

For Gary Ramsay

A complete catalogue record for this book can
be obtained from the British Library on request

The right of Peter Wild to be identified as the editor of
this work has been asserted by him in accordance with
the Copyright, Designs and Patents Act 1988

First published in 2007 by Serpent's Tail,
an imprint of Profile Books Ltd
3A Exmouth House
Pine Street
London EC1R 0JH
website: www.serpentstail.com

Designed and typeset at Neuadd Bwll, Llanwrtyd Wells

Printed in the UK by CPI Bookmarque, Croydon, CR0 4TD

10 9 8 7 6 5 4 3 2 1

Contents

Introduction by Peter Wild

I first heard The Fall twenty-one years ago. It was 1985. I was twelve or thirteen. A few of us were meeting up round my mate Dan Thomas' house. Dan was always robbing music off his older brother. That was how we'd all been introduced to the music we were into, everything from The Brilliant Corners through to Jonathan Richman. But – on the day in question – Dan wasn't playing The Brilliant Corners or Jonathan Richman. He was playing The Fall. More particularly, he was playing 'Bend Sinister'.

When I arrived, a song called 'Bournemouth Runner' was just starting. I don't know if you know 'Bournemouth Runner' but it starts with a foreboding bass-line, insistent and repeated over and over (The Fall, as I was to come to learn, are big on repetition). It could be the soundtrack to some low budget '70s Brit horror flick. There's a whispered and slightly menacing slurred vocal, too. That first time through, I reckon that I probably didn't pay all that much attention until about one minute in when everything stops and a voice – the voice of Mark E. Smith – yells, BUT THEN I TOOK A CHASE AFTER THE BOURNEMOUTH RUNNER! A drum is slammed four times in short succession. He shouts BOURNEMOUTH

RUNNER again, and C-C-COULD DARE and then the song races off in a completely different direction, all powerhouse drums and chintzy synth. It was at this point that I said to Dan, What's this? – and Dan (I remember this really clearly) replied, with a kind of smirk on his face that you'd associate with the bestowing of a great gift, This is The Fall.

And so it began. My obsession with The Fall. I can't think of a single other band I was listening to in my teens that I'm still listening as intently to now. Part of that is due to the fact that many of the bands I was listening to in my teens (The Smiths, The Chameleons, Joy Division) are long since gone. And part of it is down to the fact that The Fall continue to put out new material just about every year. The Fall are not like half a dozen bands that spring to mind, trading on former and diminishing glories. The Fall are constantly moving forward. But even that is only one of maybe five hundred things that make The Fall so interesting. I remember catching the band at the Free Trade Hall and marvelling at all the people on the stage, at the noise they made, at 'US '80s–'90s'. I remember, some years later, catching The Fall as part of some dumb festival in Heaton Park, Mark spitting out 'Idiot Joy Showland' wearing a leather jacket that barely concealed a gun and shoulder holster. I remember dragging an extremely reluctant girlfriend to a Stockport Townhall Fall two-nighter once (she hated almost every second). I remember celebratory BierKellar gigs. I remember a revelationary Glasgow show on the Fall Heads Roll tour where they encored with 'Carrier Bag Man' (to this day, my wife's favourite Fall song). Like Peely said, the thing about The Fall is that they are always different and always the same. That has almost become a Fall cliché now. But like all clichés there is a lot of truth in it.

Perverted by Language: Fiction inspired by The Fall sprang out of this. For years, I'd thought that a person could write a great novel/

collection of short stories using Fall songs as titles. For some years I'd kicked around the idea as something I could do myself. Midway through 2005, though, a buddy (Gary Ramsay, the fella who this book is dedicated to) and me decided that we'd start up a publishing house. I won't bore you with the long and the short of why, but 'The Fall book' (as we quickly started to call it) was one of the ideas I brought to the table – only it wasn't a book of my short stories or a novel, it was an anthology of short fiction by a bunch of writers who all dug The Fall in one way or another. I jumped in commissioning and I got some pretty damn great contributors, I think you'll have to agree. (Certain people on the wishlist slipped through the net – it would've been great to have Magnus Mills writing 'Container Drivers' or Sarah Waters doing 'Spoilt Victorian Child' or Sara Gran doing the aforementioned 'US '80s–'90s' – but you can't have everything, right?) The publishing house idea fell by the wayside (as these things are occasionally want to do) but the book survived (thanks to Pete Ayrton and Serpent's Tail).

So. Here it is. *Perverted by Language: Fiction inspired by The Fall.* As I sat down to write this introduction, I listened again to 'Bournemouth Runner' and I caught a bit of lyric I don't think I'd paid attention to before (to my shame). Towards the end of the song, in between the hectoring yelps of 'Bournemouth Runner!', the wonderful and frightening Mark E. Smith says, *Calendar! I've forgotten the date! No plot!* You're welcome! If anyone needed an introduction to the band that clocked in at just under ten words, there it is. The same also applies to this book:

Calendar!

I've forgotten the date!

No plot!

You're welcome.

Bingo Master's Break Out
Niall Griffiths

Ethel poured sweet and milky tea from her cup carefully into the saucer and sipped it, making a loud 'shloop' noise.

—Aaaahh.

Arthur stirred sugar into his mug of overbrewed orange Tetley's, three spoonfuls, and gulped at the drink as if it was beer and he a much younger man. He opened the KitKat that Ethel had bought him and separated the fingers and laid them out on the tablecloth pointing at the brown sauce bottle but he didn't eat any.

—We have to do summat, Ethel love.

—So you keep saying, Arthur dear.

—It can't go on like this.

—What's to be done, though?

—He's ruining tradition, that bugger is. That's what he's doing, he's trampling roughshod all over our tradition. Mine and yours, Ethel love. No respect these days, that's the bloody trouble.

—Trouble, yes.

—No spines. No backbones. Thinks he can just come along in that bloody shiny suit of his and his, his…

Arthur made a gesture with a shaking hand at the back of his own head. His liverspotted fingers trembled at the creased nape of his own neck.

—Ponytail, Ethel said.

—That's it, aye. Bloody ponytail on a man for Pete's sake. Never seen the bloody likes. And he's up there on that stage, bold as bloody brass, a caller in a ponytail. Never seen the bloody likes. Would never've happened in my day. Wouldn't've been allowed.

Ethel pursed her lips and shook her head. —My Bert would've been up on that stage with a pair of scissors quick smart, I'll tell you that for nowt.

—Yes but that's just it, isn't it? Nobody cares any more about what your Bert would've thought. Or my Tabitha, God rest her soul. These people today, they don't give a fig any more for us old folk. Not a bloody bit. We're nowt to them, us old 'uns. Doesn't matter that we've been going to the same bingo hall for nearly fifty year, that means less than nowt to them buggers. Everything for the young 'uns, that's what it's all about these days and I'll tell you for why; cos them's the ones bringing in the money, that's why. Oh aye, money's what it's all about these days, Ethel love.

—Money, yes. Nothing for us old 'uns.

—Now don't get me wrong.

—Oh I never would, Arthur.

—I'm all for the young folk coming to the bingo.

—To the bingo, yes.

—Breath of fresh air, that's what they can be. But it's when they start neglecting us old 'uns, *that's* what gets my goat. We're the ones who invented the bloody game, aren't we? Easy and relaxing, that's what it was, and if you were lucky you got a bottle of Scotch or a meat platter or a weekend in Blackpool but the night out, that's what was important, wasn't it? That's what mattered to us, the night out, nowt else. Cup of tea and a roll and you'd all sit together and have a laugh and a few games and then a bag of chips for the tram home and it was never about the winning, was it? The night out, that's what it was all about. For us old 'uns.

—You never did get that weekend in Blackpool, did you?

—Not once in nigh on fifty year of trying, no. But that's not the point is it, Ethel love? Didn't matter if all's you ever won were the gardening gloves in fifty bloody year of trying cos it was all just about the night out. Now, tho, it's all competition, isn't it? Win this, win that. It's all about who can win the most. You see them all, the young 'uns, not a chuckle out of them, like their bloody lives depended on it, bloody desperate for that last bloody number. And tell me this, what was ever wrong with just shouting 'house'? Why did they see fit to go and change that?

—House, yes.

—Trendy. That's what they're trying to make it. Bingo! Trendy!

—Trendy, yes.

—And it's not just the bingo, y'know. It's not just about *him* with his shiny suit and his, his…

That fluttering hand again at the base of the wispy-haired skull.

—Ponytail.

—That thing, yes. It's not just about that. It's everything that's gone wrong with the bloody world; all tradition ignored, us old folk just thrown to the side. On the scrapheap, we are. At our bloody age. All tradition, all heritage, it's all thrown to one side to make way for someone's daft bloody idea of what's new. Pen and pad not good enough any more, everything has to bloody bleep and flash and make some kind of bloody pointless bloody noise. Everything's so *loud* these days, isn't it? Why does everything have to be so loud? And electronical. Not good enough unless you have to plug it in. What was wrong with pen and pad? The game of bingo today is unrecognisable from what it used to be even *five* bloody year ago.

The rot's set in, Ethel love. And everybody's too bloody scared to make a stand. Except me. And you. We've had enough, haven't we, Ethel love? Had just about enough, oh yes.

—Enough, yes. Ethel sipped again at the tea in her saucer. Shloooop. —But what are you going to do, Arthur dear?

—*We*, Ethel love. What are *we* going to do.

She looked at him, across the table, over the teas and the KitKat fingers and the cruet.

—Don't be frightened, Ethel love. Everything'll work out fine. We'll be heroes, we will, bloody heroes. I'm working on a plan.

—Plan, yes.

She just looked at him there across the table, saucer held delicately beneath her whiskery chin. Arthur finished his tea in one wet gulp then looked around for the waitress to order another mug but she was openly flirting with a spotty youth in a baseball cap and she was wearing an obscenely tight black top that exposed some of her midriff and the top of a tattoo peeping up over the waistband of her trousers. A tattoo. On a girl of her age. Now what sort of signal does that send out?

The rot has well and truly set in. Tut.

—Here's our chance to make just a little bit of difference, Ethel love. Before we go, like. Pop our clogs. Not getting any younger, are we?

—Go, yes.

The next night, in the bingo hall which doubled as a nightclub on Saturdays, they went to take their usual seats at the front facing the podium and handy for the toilets but found that table occupied by a quartet of young women wearing very little and reeking of perfume and already half-drunk, to judge by their raucous cackling. One of them had hair like the comb of a rooster, standing up and just as red. Arthur gave them a hard and disapproving stare but they gazed blankly through him as if he had no more substance than smoke, which was only to be expected. He was going to say something to them, he was going to give them a piece of his mind in a short lecture about tradition and respect but Ethel whispered to him to save his breath and led him by the elbow over to another table on the left-hand side of the hall, still on the first row.

—*That's* what I'm talking about, Ethel love. No bloody respect. Did you see the way they looked at me? As if I wasn't bloody there. My Tabby'll be spinning in her grave. In my day you gave up your seat for your elders and betters, and you got a clock round the ear if you didn't. No two ways about it.

—About it, yes.

—The whole bloody world's going to the dogs. Young women, behaving like that! All gone to cock it has.

—Cock, yes.

—But we'll shake them up tonight, Ethel love, won't we? Arthur rubbed his hands together briskly in anticipatory glee. Sound of sandpaper on old, dry plaster. —By God we will, yes.

A steward handed them a personal keypad each and unsmilingly wished them good luck and they placed those unfamiliar objects on the table between them and sadly regarded them as if they were relics of some dead love. Arthur muttered something about pen and bloody paper but his words were drowned by the abrupt and too-loud playing of Eminem's 'Lose Yourself' and a roar from the crowd as The Caller, in all his ponytailed and shiny-suited unloveliness, took the stage. The cheers grew yet louder as he began to slide and shuffle across the stage in a kind of dance, his teeth gleaming out of his sweaty face, his ponytail resting on his shoulder like a squirrel whispering in his ear. The crowd appeared to love him and he did too.

He slid up to the microphone and the music and cheering died and he began to speak:

—Ah welcome one and all to all you wonderful people, the young and not so young...

Did he nod his head here at Arthur and Ethel? Arthur thought he did, yes.

—...clever and not so clever, hopeful and not so hopeful, straight and not so straight oo missis, man, woman, in between, whatever, equal opportunities gamesmanship only here ladies and gents and a special prize tonight of a weekend – dirty if you want it – in Blackpool, and we all know you do! Now ladies and gents excuse me while I give me balls a shake oops pardon!

—Poofter, muttered Arthur.—Bloody nancy boy.

—Only a-joking of course of course, no balls these days it's all done by our random number generator or Reggie as I call him which is funny cos that's also the name of the feller who used to jiggle me balls oops pardon! No, moving with the times here lazengenmen, moving with the times, oh yes. No further ado and eyes down for a full house!

All over the hall, people switched on their personal keypads with a succession of bleeps, excepting Arthur and Ethel who looked across the table at each other as The Caller began to call out numbers. Two old friends, Ethel and Arthur; Arthur had been best man to Bert at Ethel's wedding to him and had fought alongside him in France, holding him sobbing under shellfire. Ethel had nursed Tabitha all through her illness, the uterine cancer that would eventually kill her, had never left her bedside, had held her hand at the very moment of her passing over. They communicated all these experiences to each other there in that bingo hall with the table between them with their fading and red-rimmed eyes, Arthur and Ethel did, the two old friends, as the ponce with the ponytail flung numbers out into the intensely quiet and expectant hall:

—Two metabolically challenged people, eighty-eight...So Solid

Crew's seconds to go, twenty-one…Finbarr's favourite, sixty-nine fnaarr fnarr! Oops pardon!

Arthur let this nonsense go on for some time as the tension in the hall built up and up and the air pulled tighter around his face and then he nodded at Ethel and as one they both began to shout out random numbers:

—Seventeen!

—Thirty-nine!

—Four thousand one hundred and sixty-two!

All eyes in the hall suddenly on them with an almost palpable weight. The Caller looked down at them from his dais with a bemused half-smile on his face that glistened like wax under the overhead fluorescents.

—Twenty-six!

—Four!

—Do we have a problem here, my friends?

Power surged through Arthur. It propelled him upright. Ethel, too.

—Aye, son, you do. Two old folk who will not take it any more, that's the problem you've got. Near on fifty bloody year we've been coming to this bingo hall, week in week out, rain or shine, and I've never heard such…drivel. Tripe. You're changing it, son, and not for the better neither. We want it back the way it was. I'm making a public bloody complaint here I am. And no one's going to stop me.

A grumbling began somewhere in the crowd and began rapidly to rise into shouting but The Caller called for hush.

—No no, let's hear what these fine senior citizens have to say. Let's listen to their grievances. Never know, we might learn something, eh? Let them impart their wisdom. Would you two like to take the stage?

Security began to move from the back end of the hall towards the podium but The Caller shook his head at them and they stayed put, eyes like drills. The Caller watched fondly as Arthur and Ethel, hand in hand, slowly mounted the five steps to the stage and doddered over to the microphone and he stood aside for them, making a half-bow and sweeping his left arm out over the hall in a 'your audience awaits' kind of gesture. An embedded sense of civility made Arthur thank The Caller even as his proximity caused him to cringe. All those eyes on him, expectant and annoyed above the scowling mouths. Young faces, one and all. Here was his chance, his chance to speak out about respect for tradition and the sagacity of age; his chance to speak out for all the old ones such as Ethel and himself, lost and terrified but seeking to maintain some dignity in a world changing too much and too fast. There was a power in him, at long last a power had returned to him. And Ethel was at his side, his old friend Ethel. He could stop the rot, now, here; or at least could, until the day he died, at least say he *tried*, by God, at least he did that. Life was too short to waste. If age had taught him one thing, it was that a man's time on the earth was too, too short. You've got to seize your opportunities when you can. Tabby was up there, now, he could sense her, smiling down at him. Blessing him for what he was about to do.

—I first came to this hall, he croaked. Someone in the audience sniggered and he coughed to clear his throat and Ethel encouragingly squeezed his arm and he tried again in a stronger voice: —I had my first game of bingo in this very hall in the late nineteen forties, just after the war. I'd—

The Caller's karate chop to the back of his neck instantly shattered his old and brittle spinal column and killed him in three seconds. As Ethel turned The Caller drove the base of his palm with all the strength in his meaty shoulder up into her nose, smashing the bone and shooting sharp splinters of it up into her brain. She was dead before she hit the floor, or rather landed on Arthur's twitching body.

The cheering was sudden and explosive, and very, very loud. The applause sounded like scores of machine guns being fired at once. As Security removed the corpses from the hall The Caller took the adulation, smiling and bowing, but he took it humbly because all he'd done was his job, as outlined in Head Office's *Guidelines for Callers* booklet, in the 'Troubleshooting' section. He was pleased to see that his martial arts classes had paid off, however.

—Thankyou, thankyou…just doing my job, lazengenmen… sorry for the interruption but I'm sure we can safely say it won't be happening again…

Laughter.

—Let's get on with the game, shall we? Eyes down.

He felt his chest expand with pride. Security were giving him approving nods and smiles. He felt certain of being nominated for The Golden Caller Award when word got out about tonight's events.

—All settled?

Murmuring.

—And we'll continue. Number of Brits, as of this year, that local hero Robbie Williams has won…fifteen!

A lone cry from the crowd:

—HOUSE MUSIC! I'VE WON!

Industrial Estate

Matthew David Scott

Summer. Fucking mad hot summer that year; sweat like a bastard whatever you was doing – walking down the street, doing your shopping, straining for a shit – next thing you know you were sweating cobs. During the day, everyone was outside the pubs: lads with their tops off, showing off their tattoos and folding their arms to make them look bigger; birds in bikini tops and little skirts stashing buggies full of babies under beer-garden parasols. Yeah, a few lagers in the afternoon, home, food, kip, then on the piss all night with red raw shoulders. Class. Then there was me. Stuck in a dirty big warehouse on the Heywood Industrial Estate. Sweating to fuck.

Me mam was sick of seeing me round the house, poncing and shit. To be honest, I was sick of it meself. It probably *was* time to get a job. I was twenty-six, fit, healthy. No qualifications but a quick learner. That's all I had to tell them at the agency. And Peoplepower Employment looked proper. Nice plants, water cooler. All the staff sat behind computers, a few tasty-looking birds and a few queer-looking blokes with them Madonna headphone things wrapped round their swedes. I was taking sips of water from a little plastic cup the receptionist Monica had sorted me out with when I arrived. Yeah. Could see meself having a bit of this, I thought. Swanning round in a suit, drinking coffee-to-go, Hi, Monica, no more calls today, and Mon, babes, are you busy after work? That would do me a treat. I was already looking the part. I had on the suit I wore for me school leavers' do. Nice suit like, got it from Slaters in town. Didn't have a tie on, never liked them, but I looked smart, you know? First impressions and all that.

When Monica came back, I was sipping away, trying to earwig what they were talking about on their headphones.

'Paul Campbell?'

'Yeah?'

'Mr Campbell, could you follow me please?'

''Course.'

I checked her arse out the door and all the way up the stairs. Quality. Big round belter in one of those tight knee-length skirts. Proper tasty. I had to concentrate 'cause I could feel a bit of a Semi Ballesteros swinging in me duds. Oh, she was a darling. Some gelled-up twat in here is probably banging the shite out of that, I thought.

'If you could take a seat here Mr Campbell and fill in a few details.'

'No problem, Monica.'

She give me a clipboard with a form on it and a little cheapo Peoplepower pen. I filled in all me personal details, name, address, date of birth and all that bollocks and then me education and skills. When it came to the previous convictions bit I thought I'd better be honest, but not too honest.

There were two other lads there filling in forms. I knew one called Edwin who I used to go school with. Good lad like. Then on the other side of the room there was just this…fucking freak. He sat there, dribbling, no word of a lie, fucking dribbling and twitching like some schizo cunt. Me and Edwin kept giving each other looks and had to stop ourselves laughing at the poor fucker. He was some kind of mong or something, a bit dolly. Shame really, I thought. Anyway, I finished my form well before the other two and cruised over to Monica's desk again.

'Here you go love. Finished.'

She looked up at me pure shocked. Obviously finished in record time or whatever and she just says,

'Thank you Mr...Campbell. We'll just process this and be with you in the next few days.'

I told her: twenty-six, fit, healthy. No qualifications but a quick learner.

'Thank you Mr Campbell. We have all your details here and we'll be in touch.'

It had been about a month since the interview at Peoplepower and at first I wasn't really up for warehouse work but this one was different – I was going to be a Palletisation Engineer.

The first morning, I got up at six. I felt good. Me mam had made me a proper worker's breakfast with eggs, sausage, bacon, the lot. No beans though – hanging beans are. I'd never seen her so happy, even when I got out. Fair enough her being depressed all this time though, after what happened to our John when we were inside. But there's been enough written about that to last a lifetime and I don't really like thinking about it.

I wolfed me breakfast, took me JD Sports bag with me flask and foil-wrapped butties from the side, and kissed the old girl goodbye. It was a beautiful morning. Not being soft or anything but it was one of them mornings you dream about waking up under. It was quiet enough to hear the birds. The sky looked like a City shirt and all the blossom was out on the trees on the way into town. I was buzzing, cruising down to get the 163 to Heywood. I even stopped for a paper on the way so I could roll it up and stick it in me back pocket.

When I got on the bus I bought one of them Megarider tickets. One of them weekly ones, you know. Seeing as I was going to be doing this twice a day during the week it made sense to get one. Reminded me of when I was a kid, when people who worked in town could get on the bus, flash their pass at the driver, and just walk on. Thought that was mint, like some fucking secret agent or something. The driver give me the ticket and this little bit of cardboard with like a sticky cellophane front. I put the ticket on the cardboard and smoothed the cellophane over it dead careful so there'd be no shitty-looking creases or whatever and stuck it in the inside pocket of me jacket. The free papers you get on the buses were all in a neat stack where you keep bags and stuff. Not like later in the day when they'd be all over the bus, ripped up and dirty big footprints all over them. I picked one up to have a read but thought best not today, best just make sure I get off at the right stop. The bus was pretty empty really.

After giving the driver a nod and getting off the bus where I was told, I pulled out the directions I'd written down when Peoplepower rang me. Work was left at the top of this road and then about 500 yards on the right. Couldn't miss it. I started trotting down, me JD Sports bag bouncing up and down and the foil around me butties giving a little crunch every time they hit me back. I turned left, and up on the right hand side of the road I saw it – Heywood Industrial Estate. It looked like an army base or something, like Area 51 where they keep them aliens and that. Feller inside told me all about that – bit of a weirdo like but reckon he was on to something there.

A little road went straight up through the middle of the estate and past a security kiosk before branching off to reach the different warehouses dotted about the place. They all had numbers on the side of them so I checked me directions again and mine was D4. Adrenalin started up in me as I walked through. Big lorries and forklift trucks were waiting. A few cars were parked around the place. Probably people on night shifts, I thought. Approaching the kiosk, I got out me National Insurance card in case they were going to ask for ID but there was no security there so I just carried on walking towards D4.

When I reached the warehouse I had a quick scope around the place looking for reception but I couldn't find it. Round the back was a big loading bay and a couple of older-looking fellers in overalls were having a fag. Never have meself – filthy habit. I cruised over to them.

'Morning lads.'

They just carried on smoking, looked miserable as fuck.

'You couldn't tell me where the manager is could you?'

At last, one of them, skinhead with massive ears, answered me.

'What you here for?'

I told him, Palletisation Engineer. He nearly spat out his cig, and him and his mate started pissing themselves. When they'd calmed down, Big Ears spoke.

'Son, in here, you're either a FLT driver like me and Jimmy here, or you're a Box Monkey. Now looking at the cut of you, I'd say you're a bit partial to a banana or two, so what you here for again?'

I refused to answer. I just stared at them. I'd met plenty of this sort before and knew exactly the look to use. In the end, Big Ears' mate buckled.

'Go straight through storage, take a left, up the stairs to the mezz and there's a little office on the end. Ask for Sandra. Fucking Palletisation Engineer.'

Yeah, I thought. Fucking cunt.

Sandra's office was just this little box on what they called the mezz. The mezz was like a half a floor stuck on one side of the warehouse wall with some steel stairs going up either side. There were boxes of shit everywhere. I sat there in the office (nothing like Peoplepower's: scruffy desk, nasty old phone, lists all over the shop), and Sandra was sat there, feet on the table. Looked like a dyke.

'Right, Paul. Says here you've done time?'

'Well, yeah. Youth stuff, you know. I was a kid.'

'What were you in for?'

I lied.

'T. W. O. C. Bit of thieving.'

'Well before we start, if someone even accuses you of nicking in here, that's your arse through the door. Understand?'

I nodded.

'Good. Now, you'll be down in storage with the rest of the agency lot. This is what you'll be doing. Follow me.'

Sandra got up and I followed her out on to the mezz. She took me to a stack of boxes at the far end and then gave me a printout with loads of numbers on it.

'See them numbers there? Each one of them numbers corresponds to a box – see the numbers on the side of the box? Right. What you've got to do now is find the right boxes to match the numbers on that sheet and stack them on this pallet here. You've got two minutes starting now.'

Sandra pressed a stopwatch she had hanging around her neck. How fucking embarrassing was this? I started finding the boxes on the sheet and stacking them. It was a piece of piss and I finished well before the two minutes were up. She actually checked the stopwatch.

'One thirty-six. Good. Now what you've got to do is wrap them. If you just leave them like this, they'll fall off when the FLT drivers take the pallet. Now, I'll get Wizard to show you how.'

She shouted Wizard from the top of the mezz stairs and you could hear heavy boots running across the concrete floor below. The stairs started to shake as this feller ran up them, head down, all hunched up. When he reached us he straightened up. I couldn't believe it. It was that mong from the Peoplepower interview.

'Yeth Thandra?'

He spoke with a lisp and still twitched as he did before. He wasn't dribbling though.

'Wizard, this is Paul. He's starting today. I want you to show him how to wrap a pallet.'

With that, Wizard grabbed what looked like a massive roll of clingfilm from the floor and stretched a section out. He dipped this section under one side of the pallet, tied it off, and then shot off running around the stacked boxes, the shrink-wrap spinning like mad as he wrapped the boxes. Once he'd finished the sides, he stretched three separate sections of wrap across the top of the boxes so they were fixed as one huge brown cube, and then stood back to admire his work. Sandra looked at me.

'Now they've got to be wrapped airtight. Air. Tight. Reckon you could do that?'

I was a bit pissed off she asked. Some dolly fucker like Wizard could do it, 'course I could.

'Good. Once you've stacked and wrapped your pallet, you put it on one of these pump-trucks here…'

Sandra put one of her big hands on the handle of a trolley.

'…and then out to the FLT drivers who'll stick it on the wagon that's waiting for it. Got that?'

I nodded again.

'Right. That's your training done. Now, Wizard, take Paul down to the drivers' canteen to collect his orders for the day.'

'OK Thandra. Thith way Paul.'

Fucksake, I thought.

After two month I could do the job backward and forward, eyes closed, upside down. All of us Palletisation Engineers were agency, and most of them were students doing temp work so they came and went before you could really get to know any of them. As for the FLT drivers, they all thought they were fucking brain surgeons or something compared to us – all because they could drive a fucking forklift truck about. They wouldn't even let us eat in the same canteen as them but seeing as it was such a hot summer, I didn't mind sitting outside around the side of the warehouse where no one could bug me. Apart from Wizard. He was the only other Box Monkey who seemed to be permanent so he mithered the fuck out of me.

For a while, I was nice like, humoured him, but after a while he started to get on my tits like he did with everyone else. He used to lie all the time, daft shit. One day his kid was dying of some tropical disease, next day he was experimented on by the government when he was in his early twenties and couldn't have kids. Said he was waiting for a multi-million-pound pay-out. Get me a Ferrari when he got it like. Every day it was something different: I jogged to work today – twenty K – but I wath in the Eth A Eth tho it wath nothing. Fucking did my head in. But that's not why I did it.

It was a Friday. I was round the side of the warehouse as usual, eating me butties, and Wizard was chatting the usual bollocks. Out of the blue though he asks me what I'm doing this weekend.

'Probably out with the boys tonight Wizard. Finish off in the Ash like.'

'Yeah, I'd love to Paul. Thankth.'

'What?'

'I'll meet you at about half-ten.'

He took off before I could react. The fucker had just invited himself out with me. But he was full of shit. No way he'd turn up. He couldn't. I'd told the boys I was a Palletisation Engineer.

I sat in the Ash, about six or seven pints in, looking good, a bit a ching in my nose, but all I was doing was checking my watch every five minutes. The boys were taking the piss,

'Fucking hell, you waiting for a bird or something Paul?'

'That charlie's wired you to fuck Paul.'

'Nah, he's waiting for his boyfriend, innit Paul?'

I ignored them. Apart from the odd grin and snort, I was watching that fucking door. He can't. He won't. Nah, no chance. Poor bastard's probably in one of them halfway house things where they let them out for work and that's it. Care in the community thing. And then he walked in. Shit. He was wearing a black suit that was about four sizes too small for him, cream granddad shirt and this mad paisley waistcoat like something John Virgo might wear on *Big Break*. Pissing with sweat, he headed straight over to me, twitching as he spoke,

'Hiya Paul, you having a drink?'

The boys just started pissing themselves.

'Who let fucking Bilbo Baggins in?'

'Is this your boyfriend Paul?'

I snapped back,

'Fuck off boys. This is Wizard. I work with him.'

I wanted to twat him. Kick his little hobbit arse all over the pub but he just looked so pleased to be out.

'Nah, you're all right Wizard. I'm in a round.'

From that point on the boys had their teeth into him. They sat him down with us, invited girls over to meet him, sorted him out a bit of sniff and had him tell us all of his bullshit stories. Poor fucker didn't even realise they were laughing at him. They asked him about what he did at the warehouse and he reeled off exactly how to wrap up a pallet like it was some mad experiment that only top scientists could pull off. One of the boys pretended to be interested.

'That's amazing Wizard.'

'Yeah, ith hard at firtht but onth you get uthed to it…I can wrap a pallet in about…thirty-two seconds now.'

'Thirty-two! You hear that boys, he can wrap a pallet in thirty-two seconds. What's your record Paul?'

I ignored him. Twat. For the record it was forty-six and I was much quicker than Wizard.

'Tell you what Wizard, you reckon you could show us?'

'What?'

'You know, your old wrapping thing.'

'No problem ladth. Come up Monday and—'

'Nah, it's got to be tonight, Wizard. You've got us all excited hasn't he boys?'

The boys all nodded and yeahed and laughed. I just sat there, grill like fucking thunder. Wizard frowned in deep thought.

'Let me thee…yeah. I reckon there might be a way. Follow me.'

We got a minibus up to the warehouse on the Heywood Industrial Estate. Having no security it was easy to get in and even though the nightshift were on in D4 it was a skeleton staff like, hardly anyone about.

Wizard went in and grabbed an unwrapped pallet on his pump-truck. Really carefully, he dragged the pallet of wobbling boxes round the side of the warehouse where we used to eat at dinnertime. He smiled at the lads. I sat and watched them.

First of all they pushed him into the boxes. Shit flew everywhere, and Wizard just wondered what was going on. He didn't say nothing, didn't even struggle as they grabbed the roll of wrap he'd brought out with him and began to stick him to the pallet. All the time he looked at me. No hate in his eyes. Just confusion. I turned away. All I could hear was them laughing and snapping their fingers.

When the fuss died down, I turned around. The pallet was leaned against the side of the warehouse, Wizard shrink-wrapped up to his neck against it, feet not touching the floor. Most times I might have laughed – it does seem pretty funny. But there was no laughing in me.

He still hadn't said anything. Didn't ask me to free him, didn't even ask why they had done this to him. If anything, that confused look had disappeared and he looked like he understood. There was a mad connection between us and I knew that he knew exactly why they'd done this to him. It was the kind of look you learn when you're inside, the kind of look that makes everything all right 'cos it just says, Yeah – I don't like it but I understand.

I could hear the boys shouting me, telling me to hurry up and that they were going to bell a taxi back to the Ash. It was warm; he'd be all right overnight. Someone would find him in the morning. I shouted back that I was coming, and then walked over to Wizard. He looked straight at me, same eyes. Emotions that I've only ever felt once before in my life...It was like hate, and fear, and sorrow, and...you can't describe it, it's impossible but you can't get rid of it until it's done.

I picked up the shrink-wrap, pulled a section loose as if I was going to tie off the bottom of a pallet, and slowly wrapped Wizard airtight. Air. Tight.

A New Face in Hell

Jeff VanderMeer

What do I know about Terry Tidwell? I know we watched him for over three years. No real suspicions, just general surveillance. 'Secrets and scandals of deceitful type proportions', as they say. But there wasn't much to find out, and we've since stopped watching him, for reasons that will become clear. And for one other reason: I was following him so much that I began to think like him, to become him. This could be termed an occupational hazard. My superiors were not pleased.

So, Tidwell. He is a builder, a bookworm and a beer drinker. He likes to frequent bars. He has been divorced for several years. The rest of the bland facts can be found in his file. There is a perfect simplicity to his existence – or was, to a certain point.

One night, out with friends (I was there as a supposed friend of a friend), he bumped into a homeless man. (This man was not one of our operatives. The event was not planned; this alone sent a shiver down my back.) A miasma of sweat, funk and mustiness blew over Tidwell as he held the man in his arms, in one of those moments that permeate every life, one that to an observer might even look like a reunion of old friends.

The man's face, hidden by salt-and-pepper whiskers, imploded in an unmistakable grimace as he flailed to get free and as Tidwell held on long enough to make sure the man would not gain his freedom by falling.

Released, the man stumbled to the kerb as cars passed behind him and glared at Tidwell.

'Watch yourself,' he growled.

As he took a step back, Tidwell and I noticed something peculiar about the man's left eye. It was completely black, without a hint of white, and, when the man blinked, Tidwell swore he could see ridges in his eyelid, as if the object lodged in the orbit was not an eye at all, but something entirely more mechanical.

'Sorry,' Tidwell said, taking another step back, his friends waiting for him up ahead.

He turned to go, a shiver of fear making him hurry, but the man came up behind him and caught him by the arm. His grip was as strong and implacable as that of a robot arm.

'Vaucanson had a duck you know,' the man hissed in Tidwell's ear. 'He had a duck, and it broke. But it wasn't my fault. You'd think they'd know that by now. Vaucanson. Vaucanson has a lot to answer for.'

The man released Tidwell.

Tidwell whirled around, stared at the man, opened his mouth to speak, but found he had nothing to say. He simply wanted to get away from the man as quickly as possible.

I had walked back to help Tidwell and now said, 'Do you want me to call the police?'

Tidwell stared at the man with the impossible eye and the man with the impossible eye stared back.

'No,' Tidwell said, 'but let's get the hell out of here.'

'Vaucanson's duck. Find it,' the man said, 'and you'll find a whole lot more. My time is done. I've nothing left to find it with.' A look of unexpected sympathy on the man's face. 'Good luck,' he said softly – and then, as Tidwell and his friend looked on with bewilderment, the man ran down the sidewalk with almost preternatural speed and into the night.

Much later, when he got home, he could still feel the man's grip on his arm. That grip had left two uniform welts that took a fortnight to heal.

As might be expected, Tidwell could not forget his encounter with the homeless man. He played it over and over in his mind. For one thing, as he said to one of his friends, the more he thought about the man, the more the man seemed familiar to him, as if he had once known him, but no matter how long or hard he tried to penetrate the fog surrounding that particular mystery, it remained a mystery for quite some time.

So, instead, in his free time, Tidwell decided to find out about the duck and about Vaucanson, if either had ever truly existed. He would have liked to have forgotten about both the duck and Vaucanson, but since he dreamed every night of a magical duck and a shadowy man with a V monogrammed on his shirt, this was impossible.

'You going out with us tonight?' one of his friends would say and Tidwell would reply, 'I'm not feeling too good tonight. I think I'll just stay in.' And then he would go down to the local library to research 'Vaucanson'.

It didn't take long to realise that such a duck and such a man, Vaucanson, had existed – in France in the eighteenth century. In a mouldy old book of facts, water-damaged and coffee-stained, he found the following entry:

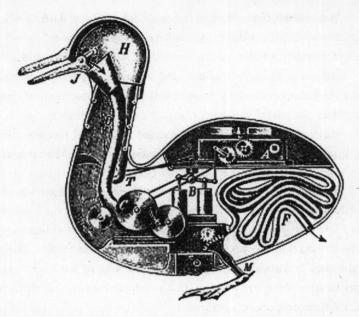

One of the most famous automata was built by a French engineer named Jacques de Vaucanson in the 1730s. His ingenious mechanical duck moved like a duck, ate like a duck, and digested fish like a duck. The duck had a weight inside connected to over a thousand moving parts. Vaucanson, by trial and error, made these parts move together to make the duck move and give it the illusion of life. It even had a rubber tube for its digestive tract. The duck and other automata made Vaucanson famous, and he travelled for many years exhibiting his duck and other machines around Europe. Although he collected honours for his work, he also collected scorn from those who believed he had employed infernal means to create his duck. After a time, he fell out of favour and took a position managing silk-mills in the countryside. Most of his creations were destroyed in a fire a year after Vaucanson died, but the

miraculous duck was spotted in 1805 by the famed poet Goethe in the collection of an Austrian antiques enthusiast. Shortly thereafter, the Austrian died and the collection was auctioned off to pay his debts. The duck has not been seen since. Even in 1805, Goethe had reported that the duck looked mangy and had 'digestive problems'. Strange sounds came from inside the automaton, and it is likely it ceased to function shortly after 1806, when it was sold to an anonymous buyer. Vaucanson's relatives have often claimed that the duck was Vaucanson's most prized possession and that he believed it held the key to solving several scientific mysteries.

It would be wearisome to relate how Tidwell came to acquire the duck – the money he had to save, the journeys he had to make to various European countries, the bribes given to this curator to look up records from centuries past and that old grandmother who claimed to remember seeing it in her youth, or even to convey the sheer ferocity of desire it took for Tidwell to continue on his course.

That I was with him, shadowing him in my various disguises, will surprise no one. I can still remember the exact hint of purple and yellow in the crease of sunrise from a balcony in Florence, the exact nuance of the green-gold scent of hanging vines at a winery near Marseilles, the unmistakable clip-clop of a donkey pulling a cart in a tiny village outside Berlin as I hid around the corner from the house in which Tidwell made his enquiries. I have such a memory of those years. I almost became quite fond of Tidwell, in his earnest, reckless pursuit. (I did wonder, however, when my superiors might recognise that his quest and ours had no points in common.)

Suffice it to say that in due course he did acquire the duck, even though he committed more than one crime to do so. All seemed forgivable to me, if only the duck came into his possession.

One rainy spring day, Tidwell came back from his final journey, holding a box. He wearily opened the door to his home, threw the box on the couch and went to fix himself a drink. It had taken over five years to find the duck, and several times he was certain he would fail in his quest, dead end leading to dead end. But, finally, a wizened old man in a beret, sitting in a café in the wine country outside Marseilles, had given him the lead that had led to the clue that had resulted in a box containing Vaucanson's duck.

Tidwell wondered idly whether his family and friends would ever forgive him for his obsession. Probably not, but the damage was already done. He could not undo it. Nor, he thought as he drank down his whisky, did he think he would have wanted to. He was not the same person he had been before. He had picked up a dozen new skills in his journeys, discovered in dangerous situations that he responded firmly and well. The world had, no matter what came next, opened up for him in a different way to how it had opened up for him in his previous life. (At least, this is what I, from my hiding place, supposed.)

Thus far he had glimpsed the duck only briefly – winced at its crumbled condition, one wing inoperable, the beak chipped, one foot half sawed through, the feathers that had once coated its metal surface weathered or gone, so that Vaucanson's duck looked as though it were half-plucked. A smell had risen from it, too. The smell of rotting oil, of metal parts corroding.

Could it ever be restored? Tidwell didn't know. But he lovingly took it from its box and set it out on the kitchen table. At some point, one of the duck's many owners had tried to restore the duck to its former glory, with mixed results. Now one eye appeared to consist of faux emeralds, while the neck had a pattern engraved on it more common to paper doilies. The one intact leg had a similar design inflicted upon it. The duck should have been self-winding, but even the emergency wind-up mechanism, twisted and torn, couldn't get the duck to work. Vaucanson's creation had survived the centuries, but only as a corpse.

Something wistful welled up in both myself and Tidwell as he sat at the table with his whisky and the mechanical bird. Something sorrowful.

He remembered the words of the man who had started him on this path to either ruin or enlightenment. He wondered now why he had taken them so to heart, why it had seemed at the time like a directive or a plea he could not ignore.

Well, it was too late now for regrets – for either of us. He sighed and went to get a screwdriver and some other tools. Almost from the start, he had decided to perform an autopsy on the duck should he ever get his hands on it. Between the homeless man's comments and the remarks of the people he had encountered on his quest – including the descendants of Vaucanson – it had increasingly struck him that there might be something inside the duck even more important than its worth as an automaton.

It took some effort to pry the matching halves apart and he was breathing heavily by the time he had finished. A flicker of deep excitement energised him, though, and it was with triumph rather than exhaustion that he finally peered into the mysteries of the duck's innards.

At first, he saw nothing of interest. Just gears and levers and rusted chains, the remains of a rubber tube that had served as the duck's intestinal tract. But when he looked closer, he found, nestled deep in the bird, a compartment in which sat a round, grooved black globe the size of a human eye, and a corresponding empty space beside it.

All the tension draining out of Tidwell, he sat back in his chair, arms behind his head, and began to laugh. This, this was what the homeless man had led him to. His journey had just begun, while mine had ended. Caught. Afraid. Curious.

After a while, he began to weep, and then to reach out with a trembling hand for the black globe buried in the guts of Vaucanson's duck, and then to pull back, as if from a flame. Reach out, pull back, reach out.

For all I know, Tidwell is sitting there still.

Totally Wired

Mick Jackson

Someone spiked me – spiked me something rotten. I'd gone to talk to a couple of lads who I was meant to be working with on the Tuesday and we chatted. I'd had maybe two or three but was nowhere near pissed. Twenty minutes later and it's a whole other story. Like someone's set about me with a two-be-four.

I remember when I sat back down thinking how my pint tasted sort of funny – sort of *chemically*. But it wasn't until the whole thing was over that I put the two things together and thought some fucker must've slipped me something. Although why anyone would want to do that is still beyond me and is, frankly, the kind of thing that can keep a man awake at nights.

I was talking to Denny. Then Denny went and I must've talked to someone else. I can't remember who. All I remember is beginning to feel profoundly weird. So I got up and went to the door of the pub – maybe thinking that I'd just get some fresh air inside me or maybe I'd already decided I'd had enough and was going to go home. Anyway, a few minutes later and I find myself walking but instead of going down the hill for some reason I decide to cut through the old school. And as I'm creeping past the old science block the smell of the chemistry labs comes back to me – the smell of gas or chloroform and how sick that used to make me feel on a Monday morning. And then not just remembering the smell, but really feeling it deep inside me. And then starting to worry about it. Like a splitting headache, when you start to wonder if you're going to be able to endure it for however many awful hours it's going to be.

So I walk right through the old school and come out at the park on the other side, where we used to slip into the bushes to smoke a Number 6 or B & H. And I head straight in, with my head still full of the smell of gas. And I decide that what I need to do right now is hide away, deep among the trees.

I plough straight through the bushes and keep on moving. Then I'm in the dark. Proper, can't-see-your-hand-out-in-front-of-you darkness. As if the whole world's shut down – and it's just me and the dark. So I start a-creeping. I decide that if I'm going to survive I need to creep, like a wild animal. And I have this idea of myself among all the insects and the other animals. And how I'm gonna have to creep about among them to survive.

As I'm writing this down I'm trying to establish some sense of some overall picture. But for that whole seven or eight hours that I must've been prowling around the place, I can honestly say that there was no beginning, middle and end. There was just me in the park and the relentless weight of time pressing down on me. At no point did I think – someone's been fucking with me. Or – I must be off my fucking face. All I thought was that things are different now and highly dangerous and that I need to do everything in my power to avoid being dragged down.

It's maybe worth pointing out here that the Corporation Park is not just some patch of grass with a couple of benches in it and a few paths that cross in the middle. It's a serious bit of land, which stretches for miles in every direction, with all sorts of lakes and aviaries and conservatories going to rack and ruin, tucked away among about a zillion trees. But I swear I must've covered every square yard of it. The brain just switched off and instinct took over. I mean, I'm not usually the outdoors type. I like my kip. I like my telly. I like lying in the bath. And yet here I am, suddenly, moving, like an old-style hunter-gatherer. One second I'm up on my toes, just like a meerkat. The next minute I'm scooting about the place like a wolf…like a fucking dog. What I'm saying is that whatever it was wasn't exactly in my *nature*. And even if it had been, buried deep in some ancestral cave, right at the back of my being, I can't honestly say that I enjoyed the experience or that I have any plans of going back there any time soon.

Very early on I became kind of resigned to the fact that there was to be no leaving. I found myself at the gates at the bottom of the park and once or twice later on could've quite easily skipped over a wall. But I just knew that if I stepped outside the park there'd be nothing and that would be the end of me. I'd either freak out and have to retreat to the park, if I was able. Or I would simply cease to exist. So on the few occasions when I came up against a wall or found the railings I just turned right around and headed back into the undergrowth. That was the deal and there was simply no fucking with it. I just turned around and went back to sneaking through the trees.

At some point I found myself up near all that long grass, where me and a mate once saw some couple dry-fucking. Way back, when we were about twelve or thirteen. Just a young lad and a girl who were probably no more than two or three years older than we were and wearing their school uniform who'd probably met up in their lunch break, but, man, they were fairly going at it and me and my mate (I can't even remember who it was now) snuck up and watched them for a while.

I lie there watching them, with the grass all wet around me. Watch them pumping and grinding. Do I remember being turned on by what I saw? Not really. I was too utterly fried to comprehend. Their mouths were locked together and their hands were up each other's shirts and down each other's trousers. But I might as well have been set some mathematical equation. I just lay there and watched them. Or remembered watching them all those years before. And when I wasn't sure whether I was actually watching or just remembering I crept away.

Like I say, the whole night's events had no real sense of chronology or cohesion. When they come back to me now each moment comes flapping straight out of the dark, like snatches of a dream. I get a little flash of something – maybe something sensory and I think, Oh yeah. I remember crawling around in the gravel. Or, I remember shimmying up that tree.

I certainly climbed some rocks. And again, we're talking a serious bit of rock here – like a single slab of maybe forty or fifty foot, that we used to mess around on when we were in the first or second year – the kind of thing that lads of a certain age like to climb up to show how hard they are and occasionally fall off of and have to be carted away in an ambulance. I remember the grit of the stone in the palm of my hand and under my fingers. The smell of the moss right up against my face. I got maybe two-thirds of the way up and just sort of hung there. I might've been there five minutes or a couple of hours with the stars slowly shifting above me. But long enough for me to think that given enough time I'd just sort of disappear into the rock-face, like a chameleon.

A good deal of it is completely lost to me now. Throughout that night there was any amount of slithering and sliding. I definitely took a couple of falls – had the cuts and bruises the following day to testify to it. But what still looms large – and gives me the willies whenever I think about it – was when I was holed up in the bushes and just sort of monitoring the situation and staring out at the world and some bloke went sneaking down one of the paths. He had his hood up and just sort of went sweeping past me. And, man, he was big – a huge big fella. And I remember thinking to myself – if he works out that I'm here and manages to locate me, then either I'm going to have to do away with him or that big fucker is gonna do away with me.

I remember the ground feeling cold and wet under my feet when I was watching Big Fella, so I must've lost my shoes prior to that. I think I still had my socks on, but not my shoes. I also feel reasonably confident in saying that it was the latter part of the night that I spent down by the lake. I just hopped over the low fence and crawled in among the ducks. The same ducks that those mates of mine got suspended from school for shooting up the arse with an air pistol. Or presumably those ducks' great-great-grandchildren.

Anyway, maybe they'd been warned, down the generations, to be wary of having anything to do with humans. Whatever the reason, those ducks were certainly not too chuffed to have me creeping among them. They made a big fuss, with plenty of flapping and honking, but I badly needed to get horizontal. And eventually they just sort of gave me the evil eye and waddled off.

The ground was pretty slimy and there was the powerful smell of duckshit all around me. But that didn't particularly bother me and I decided to lie there for a while. I think I must've sensed something safe about this neck of the woods. So I just crawled forward on my stomach and looked out over the water and kept an eye on things. I could feel the mud in between my fingers and seeping through my shirt. Then I watched the model boats – the little yachts and cruisers – that were sailing on the lake.

It was only after the event that this seemed so peculiar. Like the groping couple up in the long grass, I can't quite believe that they were actually there and at it in such uncomfortable conditions. But neither can I believe that those boats were nothing but my imagination taking itself out for a bit of a spin. I have to say that I've still not come to any firm conclusions. Those boats were much too real and too particular, with their little linen sails and their fancy paintwork, for me to have just dreamt them up.

So I watched the boats. I don't remember any children in attendance. These were like ghost boats, just out on their own. Doing their make-believe hops across the Channel and their re-enactments of historic battles with no one watching but little old me.

Not long after I caught sight of the first set of promenaders. They were right across the lake. A couple with a big old pram and him in his suit and her with some big, fancy hat on her head. I believe those two were the first. Then suddenly there was no end of them. Hundreds of them, all dressed to the hilt, as if it was some summer afternoon, having a stroll and tipping their hats to one another, marching up and down the place.

Now I do remember thinking that this was sort of weird. I remember it being kind of unnerving. So I retreated back to where the ducks had been sitting. I stayed there for a while, with my face flat against the ground, just trying to keep everything nice and peaceful. Until I heard a whirring. I lifted my head and had a look about. And a couple of yards to my right I saw a small stack of bricks. I crawled over to them, pulled the bricks off and looked down into the hole.

Three or four feet down was some sort of contraption. I couldn't quite make it out but it was keeping itself pretty busy. It was like a little pump or some sort of generator, merrily rocking and rolling away. I found this pretty interesting. In fact, after I'd looked at it for a while, I began to think that this was the fucking business. I tried to reach down, to get a hand to it. I just wanted to touch it, to see what it was up to. And as I did so it slowly dawned on me that this little pump was what was keeping the whole park going. The boats… the Victorian promenaders…the teenage couple feeling each other up in the long grass – they were all on some sort of circuit. And all plugged into this little pump.

I reached down to it, but couldn't get anywhere near it. And the more frustrated I got the more convinced I was getting that this pump was the nerve centre, not just of the park but the whole town – maybe the whole of Lancashire – and that if I couldn't actually get a hold of it then the very least that I should be doing was keeping an eye on it, like a sort of sentry, to make sure that no one interfered with it.

When I next opened my eyes it was just about daylight but still pretty early. I crept out of the bushes and decided to walk down the path, which in itself was a bit of a change of tack. When I got to the gates I had a quick think about it – just to check – but sort of knew deep down that it was okay to go through them. I wasn't going to evaporate or implode, like I was convinced I would do earlier. I was free to go.

I still wasn't quite the full shilling but a good deal closer to straight than off my face. Certainly straight enough to feel a bit self-conscious when the people I passed had a good old gander at me. It seemed to take about a month for me to get home. When I finally made it I must've just gone straight to bed. The next thing I remember I was waking up again and it was teatime. While I ran the bath I looked at myself in the mirror. I was covered in mud and moss and duckshit – all bashed about, with bits of grass poking out of my hair.

Most of the clothes I'd been wearing were too traumatised by the whole experience and never recovered. I ate some cereal and watched the telly. Which is when it first occurred to me that it probably wasn't natural for a man to leave a pub and slip into the park for a whole night's creeping. Then I went back to bed for another eight hours straight and hardly moved an inch. The next time I came round I had the mother of all hangovers, like I'd just gone ten rounds with Tyson. A day like that can take a long, long time to get out of the way.

I'm still no closer to working out who might have spiked me – if that is indeed what happened. The alternative is too weird to contemplate. I now accept that whoever it was will probably remain a mystery. As long as the whole thing is never repeated I can just about live with that.

Curiously, I've never been tempted to go back and have a snoop about among the ducks to see if I can find that little pump. Which is kind of odd, since I've thought about it any number of times. My gut feeling is that it's actually there, but whether I'd still feel the same way about it is another thing. A part of me wants to believe that there really is something at the heart of everything – that there's someone or something that knows what's going on. I don't spend my whole day thinking about it. It would just be kind of reassuring, that's all.

City Hobgoblins

Carlton Mellick III

There's more of them today, infesting the streets.

With their rotten grape skin, wooden horns and hairspray eyes.

'Don't play so loud,' Lenny whispers at us from the door of the band room. 'They're going to hear you.'

We've got to practise for tonight's show, a gig over in the tower shops with some band called Slaughter Shoes. Only we're trying to keep quiet. Don't want to attract any of them, don't want them to know we're here, so we're playing without amps. I'm whispering my vocals and Ass Fort, our obese drummer, is smacking his legs with his sticks.

'We can't get any quieter,' I tell him.

'Your guitars are still too loud,' he says, aiming his pointy troll nose at me.

The guitar player, Stag, spits at him. 'Get the fuck out.'

'There's probably a dozen of them just outside,' Lenny whisper-whines. 'They can hear you. I swear they can hear you.'

Stag scratches his nuts at Lenny.

I put my bass down. 'We'll take a break until they leave.'

'Yeah, fuck it,' Ass Fort grunts, his shirt covered in sweat stains and mustard. 'Let's drink some beer.'

Lenny, with his black hoodie and old-lady glasses, is sitting at the window watching the creatures wandering the streets, playing with his slidey skin. Even though he's always been skinny, Lenny's flesh is baggy like he's just lost half his weight. He can move his baby elephant tattoo from his wrist to his elbow by sliding his loose sleeve of skin back and forth. It wouldn't be so gross if he didn't fidget with it so much, like he's jerking off.

Stag always tells him he needs to get his arms circumcised.

I used to know Lenny back in high school, back when people called him a band fag. A drummer in the marching band who took art classes with me. We sat at the same table. My brain was usually pretty fuzzy from smoking groo at lunch.

As I tried my best to imitate H. R. Geiger with embarrassing results, Lenny sat there quietly, staring at his blank sheet of paper. 'What're ya going to draw?' I'd ask, but he would never respond. He was in deep concentration, like he was drawing a masterpiece within his head, and just needed to figure out a way to set it free. In the last ten minutes of class, he would begin to twitch. The twitching would brew in his baggy muscles, building up like a volcano ready to rupture. After six or seven minutes of twitching and sweating and the entire class watching/giggling with anticipation, he would then put his pencil to the paper and an explosion of lines would pour out. He would draw faster and faster, as if trying to purge the image out of his mind before it faded away. His back arched, his face two inches away from the page, nostrils flared, biting down on his lip, holding his breath for the most intense three minutes of artwork the world will ever see.

Only, nobody ever saw his work. His face would cover up most of what he was doing and his hands would hide the rest. And once the bell rang, Lenny would leap from his seat and crumble up his work into a tight little ball and bury it deep inside his backpack, then charge out of the room, pushing people out of his way. The art teacher never got anything from him, didn't question him about it either.

The art teacher mostly just sat in the corner of the room staring at the chalkboard. Sometimes he'd crawl under his desk for a nap. Sometimes he'd shovel bagels between his flaky dry lips.

I guess that teacher's probably dead now.

The infestation is overwhelming on that side of town.

Eventually Lenny and I became friends. Once he stopped playing Dungeons & Dragons and joined my punk band. I was hesitant at first. At the time, that band was my life. I didn't know if I wanted to bring such a creepy weirdo into my life, but drummers were in high demand. He worked out OK and turned out to be a nice guy. Our band was together for a few years, but we mostly just played parties and a couple of empty bars.

After the band broke up, I started a new one with Stag and Ass Fort. Lenny joined some straight-edge-in-your-face-vegan-hardcore band, where he was happy. We stayed friends though. Even became roommates. Still are. But my other roommate, Stag, just hates the guy.

'There's not that many,' Stag says to Lenny, looking over his shoulder at the creatures outside. 'You're such a douche.'

Stag, which is short for Stagnant, calls the creatures *hobgoblins*.

There are many different species of hobgoblin. There are the crispy black demons, the octopus-limbed cat women, the white rubbery snail people. A new breed of them appears every day. They came out of a doorway called the *walm* in the centre of the city. That's what they say. Lenny's been dying to go out there and check the walm out, but it's all the way across town and the streets are becoming too dangerous. If you run into the wrong type of hobgoblin you're going to be ripped to shreds.

Stag takes off his crusty shirt and sits in a chewed wicker chair. The tattoo of his face on his face is mostly shadowed by his Irish-green anarchy cap.

'Oi!' he says to Ass Fort in the kitchen.

Ass Fort nods and throws him a beer.

'Are we gonna get paid for this shitty gig?' Ass Fort asks.

'Yeah,' I say. 'A little. Probably not enough to cover your bar tab though.'

'I don't think any amount of payment can cover my bar tab,' he says.

We sit in silence sipping our beers, staring at the television screen with a crack down the middle.

The television isn't on. It doesn't work. Ass Fort tried to use it as a chair a few months ago and his weight broke the insides. Still, we find our eyes glued to the screen. A natural habit maybe. Even when we speak to each other, we keep our eyes focused on the tube. Like we don't want to miss anything.

I pick up my sketch pad, wipe the groo residue off the cover, and begin to draw some sharks.

'You're thinking about her again, aren't you?' Stag asks me.

I shrug at him, curling one of my dreadlocks around my finger.

'You're not the only one who wants her back,' he says.

I break my pencil lead at him.

'I was the one she loved,' I say.

'She has no idea how to love,' he says.

Stag and Lenny have much more in common than they'd care to admit. For starters, they both played Dungeons & Dragons for years. They might have even played together in tournaments. My first guess was that Stag played as a fighter or a thief and that Lenny played as a wizard. But it was not that way at all. Lenny preferred to play as a thief and Stag played as a one-eyed gnome illusionist named Guko who had a white braided moustache growing out of his nostrils. He even DMed a campaign once.

You wouldn't think of Stag as the nerdy type these days. He's a big guy and mostly muscle. He punches the walls when he's angry. He breaks beer bottles over his head to impress the ladies. Yet, he has a Boba Fett poster on his wall and an Atari 2600 game system shaped like the Starship *Enterprise*.

He's also writing a book about vampires in space. It's about a thousand pages long and nowhere near completion. He won't let anyone read it. He'd rather burn it than let anyone read it.

After a few beers we get back to practising. There are still plenty of hobgoblins outside, perhaps a few more than before, but we have drowned our worries in alcohol.

'Too drunk to fear,' Stag says.

He says *too drunk to fear* all the time. That's his motto. He has it tattooed on his arse.

Lenny isn't too drunk to fear. His twitchy body sits in the corner of the band room to monitor our volume. Whenever we get too loud, he gives us an angry thumbs-down until we soften our voices and guitar strokes. Then he'll give us an OK sign and go back to sliding his arm skin back and forth.

Our hit song is called 'Glass Sandwiches'.

We tend to practise that one every other song because Ass Fort likes it so much. He likes anything having to do with sandwiches, and screams *'Glass Sandwiches!'* after every song in a drunken fury even if we just finished playing 'Glass Sandwiches'. Then he laughs and wheezes like he's completely baked and has no idea what he's doing, which is pretty much the truth. It is also our most requested song at shows, but I wouldn't say it's our best.

My favourite song is the one I wrote for *her*. I never told Stag the song was about her, but I'm sure he knows. It's kind of obvious. Sometimes I hate Stag for sleeping with her. Sometimes I hate him for not loving her like I do. But if it wasn't for him, I never would have been with her. I never would have fallen in love.

He says it's because it was my first time. You always love the one you give your virginity to.

There's a crash in the living room.

'I told you!' Lenny cries.

We take our guitars with us as weapons.

Stag sticks out his tongue like Gene Simmons at Ass Fort and whispers, 'Too drunk to fear.' Ass Fort raises his beer at him in cheers.

Outside the band room, there aren't any hobgoblins trying to get in. But the window is shattered all over the puke-stained couch. In the middle of the floor there is a small green ball with squirming tentacles.

'What is it?' I ask.

'It's alive and shit,' Stag blurts.

'It's a baby,' Lenny says. 'A hobgoblin baby.'

ME: What are we going to do with it?

STAG: Toss it back out the window.

LENNY: No, you can't do that. It's just a baby.

ME: We don't know what it is. It's something from the walm.
           It could be poisonous or diseased.

ASS FORT: Let me step on it.

LENNY: Don't you fucking dare.

ASS FORT: Pussy.

LENNY: It's a living thing!

ASS FORT: Pussy.

ME: It's squiggling at Lenny.

STAG: It's got a woody for him.

ASS FORT: It wants your balls.

LENNY: It knows I want to help it.

ASS FORT: It knows you want to put it in your underwear.

ME: I'm telling you, the thing's not safe.

LENNY: I'm not just going to toss it back out there.

STAG: What are you going to do? Be its mommy? Keep it for a
           pet?

LENNY: If I have to.

Lenny looks out of the window, searching for where the creature came from. There's nothing out there.

It's twilight. The streets are empty of hobgoblins. The city is most quiet at dawn and at dusk. The day creatures have all gone back to the sewer and there's still a couple hours before the nocturnal ones come out. Those tend to be the more dangerous hobgoblins. Luckily, we'll be at the club by then and off the streets.

'We better get the van loaded up,' I say.

'I'll take the drums apart,' Stag says.

Stag's always the one who takes the drums apart. Ass Fort might be the drummer, but he's usually too drunk to bother himself with the construction or deconstruction of a drum set. Actually, he's usually too drunk to bother himself with learning to play drums properly either. Luckily we're a punk band and don't give a fuck.

Lenny wraps the baby hobgoblin in a towel, places it gently in a box and brings it into his room.

I follow him.

His room looks more like storage than a bedroom. All of his possessions are in boxes stacked from floor to ceiling, boxes spilling out of his closet, boxes stacked on top of his dresser, boxes on his bed. He has no posters on the walls. No junk on the floor. It's like he just moved into this place yesterday, only he's lived here for a few years.

'You're not seriously going to keep that thing are you?' I ask.

'Of course,' he says. 'You know I'm pro-life.'

'Lenny,' I say, 'how many times do I have to tell you pro-life is a stance on abortion.'

'Yeah, well I'm pro-life when it comes to all issues. If there's anything in my power I can do to keep a living being alive I will do it. Even if it's something that came out of the walm. Even if it's dangerous.'

'You weren't like this before you joined that vegan hardcore band.'

'Pete,' he squints his eyes at me, 'shut the fuck up.'

Then he pushes me out of the room and closes the door.

I stumble back into Ass Fort's giant belly and he laughs.

'He really is going to have sex with it, isn't he?' Ass Fort says. 'I wonder if he'll let me watch...'

Ass Fort isn't just a fat lazy half-arsed drummer whose only passion in life is drinking beer. He also has a passion for fucking things. And by things, I mean *all* things. It doesn't matter what it is. It could be a dangerously obese woman, a crippled elderly man, a small mammal, a toaster, a corpse, a cheeseburger, a mail slot, a teddy bear, a cow brain. It doesn't really matter to him. If he can fuck it, he will.

We think it's pretty funny. He's this big fat hairy guy who's always drunk enough to fuck anything in sight. Sometimes I think he's that way just because he's trying to be funny. Like whenever we see a disturbingly deformed person hobbling down the sidewalk and laugh to ourselves, Ass Fort will step in and say, 'I'm gonna go fuck it.'

If Stag's motto is 'Too drunk to fear' then Ass Fort's motto is 'I'm gonna go fuck it.'

It's kind of funny now, but when he becomes an old man he's going to be the scariest pervert in the back of the porn shop.

Ass Fort's main hobby these days, besides drinking beer and pretending he knows how to play drums, is looking for hobgoblins to fuck. He's always telling these wild stories about all these weird creatures he's been having sex with. From hog people to frog girls to anus-shaped plants.

Stag thought he was nuts, at first, until he saw some of the women Ass Fort was sleeping with. Not all of them were grotesque beasts. Some looked mostly human. They might have antennae or purple skin, but they were still attractive. So Stag started going out with Ass Fort on what they called their *missions*. Most of the hobgoblin girls were desperate. Living in sewers, on the streets. They were easily persuaded into sex if given some food or a place to sleep.

I didn't like it. Stag would bring these strange women home with him and they would hide out in his bedroom until he was tired of them and threw them out. I hated the way he took advantage of them, hated how dangerous it was, hated how jealous it made me to hear moaning through the walls.

Then he started experimenting. The women would get stranger and stranger. Less and less human.

I drew the line when he brought home a shark woman.

'Get her out of here!' I told him.

She was more fish than human. The rubbery flesh of a shark, the fins of a shark, the teeth and eyes of a shark. But amphibious, with human limbs, human-shaped face, human belly button, human breasts. It was the most dangerous hobgoblin I've seen. If it was desperate enough to sleep with Stag for food and shelter, it was probably desperate enough to murder us in our sleep...to use us as food and claim our home for shelter.

'No, she actually wants *me*,' Stag told me. 'She seduced me into bringing her back here. She doesn't care about the food or shelter.'

That only worried me more.

'You've gone too far with this one,' I said. 'Take her somewhere else.'

'Come on, it's cold out there.'

'She leaves after you're through. I don't want her spending the night.'

'OK, fine.'

'And she's the last. From now on, you get a hotel or take them back to Ass Fort's place.'

'Whatever.'

Then he disappeared into his room with her.

I didn't sleep that night. I locked my door, pushed my desk in front of it. Waiting for Stag to run out of his room screaming, missing a limb or half his face. But nothing happened. The usual moaning came through the walls. Then quiet.

In the morning, the shark woman was still there, dipping her webbed fingers into a bowl of water and moistening her skin.

I took Stag aside, into the kitchen.

'What's she doing here?' I asked.

'Just hanging out,' he replied.

'You agreed to get rid of her before morning.'

'I tried,' he said.

'And?'

'And she wouldn't leave.'

'*Make* her leave.'

'*You* make her leave,' Stag said. 'She scares the hell out of me. I'm not going to piss her off.'

'She scares the hell out of you? *You* slept with her.'

'Yeah, it was scary as hell.'

The day passed. She was still there. She slept with Stag again. He drank as much beer as he could and told me 'Too drunk to fear' before crawling into bed with her. I could tell he was kidding himself by the twitter in his lip.

She still wouldn't leave the next morning. She ate all of my Cheerios and sandwich meat. Days passed and she became like a fourth roommate. Stag started to sleep out on the couch so that he wouldn't have to share a bed with her. We didn't know how to communicate but she seemed to act like she was one of us. She'd watch us practise, eat dinner with us, even drink with us.

One night, she crept into my bedroom. Slithered under my sheets and made love to me. I didn't fight it. It was beautiful. Her rubbery skin sliding against me, nipples like pacifiers, her black ball eyes glistening in the darkness at me.

She tasted like spicy liquorice. Not fishy as I imagined. She was sweet and filled with passion. I stroked the fin on the back of her head like it was hair, fell asleep in her tight strangling arms.

By the morning, I was in love. Stag said it was because I lost my virginity to her.

It's OK. I don't mind that I lost my virginity to a shark. I always told Stag that the only way I'd get a girlfriend would be if one jumped in my bed at night and started having sex with me. It's not that I'm an ugly guy, it's just that I can handle drenching my eyeballs in jalapeno juice better than I can handle rejection.

But things fell into place for me. I was in love. She was like my girlfriend.

I didn't really understand who she was or where she came from, but I could feel her energy when we were pressed against each other. Her emotions seeped into me through the pores on her skin.

She wrapped herself around me while I wrote songs on my bass. She licked my neck with her white liquorice tongue.

But I don't think she came from a monogamous culture. Though she slept with me, held me, loved me, she would sometimes slip into bed with Stag or Lenny after she was finished with me. I guess one man wasn't enough to satisfy her sexually. But I did know that I was the one she loved.

Then one day she left. In the middle of the night, she just took off and never came back. I don't know why she left. Maybe she needed to get back to her own kind. Maybe she knew it just couldn't work out with us for ever.

But I know for a fact that she didn't leave because she didn't love me any more. The day before she left her love for me was probably the strongest it had ever been. Maybe that's what drove her away. She was frightened of her feelings.

I keep thinking that one day she'll come back. She'll crawl into my bed and squeeze her firm grey flesh against me until I cry.

But Stag says that will never happen. He says she got bored with us and is never coming back.

The van is all packed up and ready to go.

'Who's going with who?' Stag asks.

'I'll drive the van,' I say.

'Then you'll be driving solo.'

'Why's that?'

'It's all packed up. Only room for a driver. I'll take Ass Fort in my car. Lenny can drive his truck or come with me.'

Ass Fort fills his Power Rangers backpack with cans of Pabst and heads out to Stag's car.

'I'll go with you, too,' Lenny says.

'Well, we gotta leave now. I promised Gin I'd give him a ride so I gotta go all the way across the river to pick him up.'

'A lot of hobgoblins over there,' I say.

'There's a lot of hobgoblins everywhere,' Stag says.

They take off and I'm all alone in the house. It's getting dark.

The nocturnal hobgoblins will be coming out soon.

I take a piss in the bathroom sink and look at myself in the mirror. I'm starting to get wrinkles. Only twenty-three, but I'm beginning to wrinkle. Must be from all the years of smoking and drug abuse. My body's going to hell. Just like this city. Ah, screw it.

If I had a motto like Stag and Ass Fort, mine would be: Ah, screw it.

I lift my shirt and examine the bumps on my chest. They have gotten bigger.

Stag warned me to use a condom when sleeping with the shark

woman, but his warning came far too late. I didn't have a condom the first time she crawled into bed with me and couldn't stop the woman from putting me inside of her without protection.

Once these red bumps started appearing on my skin, Stag laughed his arse off.

'Serves you right,' he said. 'Now you've got some kind of weird hobgoblin STD.'

The bumps are all over my torso like chicken pox. A couple dozen of them. They are very sensitive against my T-shirt, the fabric rubs them raw. I take some of Lenny's lotion out of his toiletry bag and rub it on the bumps.

They itch like hell when I put the lotion on them, but it's soothing once the skin absorbs it. I squeeze one of the bumps to stop the itchiness and a grey fluid squirts out.

'What the heck is that?' I ask my mirror image.

I wipe the fluid off my chest and smell it. It smells like her.

Like black liquorice.

I change my pants and eat the last stick of string cheese, then cut my foot on the broken glass on the living-room floor.

'Crap.' It's one of the small slivers that you can hardly see but hurts like hell.

What the heck was that thing that came flying through the window anyway?

Some kind of blobby tentacled creature.

I can't believe Lenny wants to keep that thing. I should get rid of it while he's out of the house.

Yeah, that's a great idea. He can't seriously take care of that creature. It's probably going to give us some alien virus or bite off Lenny's pointy nose.

Inside Lenny's room, the creature isn't in sight. He's packaged it away into one of his many boxes. Which one? They are all the same size and shape.

I open up his boxes one at a time. One contains neatly folded argyle socks. One contains He-Man cartoons on VHS. One contains a lunch box filled with Garbage Pail Kids trading cards and a chocolate brain.

And in one of them, there are hundreds of pieces of paper crumpled up into tight balls, piled up like a marble collection. I unfold one of them. It's a drawing. A drawing of a shark woman. *My* shark woman. It's very well drawn, the lines are jagged and scratchy but it looks just like her…only she's masturbating with a high-heeled shoe. I open his other drawings and there are pictures of his vegan friends. They are naked and they too are masturbating with high-heeled shoes, in their rectums. Near the bottom there are drawings of his art classmates from high school, naked and masturbating with high-heeled shoes. I'm sure there's a picture of me in here somewhere, but I don't uncrumple any more of them.

I find the creature in a box on the floor under his bed. He has put strips of newspaper down on the bottom of the box and has a measuring cup of water as well as a pickle jar lid filled with hamster food pellets. Why he has hamster food on hand, I have no idea. A puddle of grey ooze soaks through most of the newspaper and cardboard.

The creature's tentacles are squirming at me.

'You're getting dumped,' I tell it.

When I pick up the box, the bottom flaps fall open and the creature drops out. Its tentacles wrap around my leg.

I shriek, topple backwards and shake my leg to get the creature off me. It only tightens its grip.

I stand up and walk out of the room. The chitter of nocturnal hobgoblins outside the broken window. A needle pierces into me and I drop to the floor again. My mind is getting fuzzy. Poison. It's poisoned me. What the heck is this thing?

I feel nice. The poison turns my brain into a cool summer morning. My hands feel like cotton candy and my belly is like a purring kitten. This is wonderful. I pull up my shirt and rub myself, caressing my STDs and inhaling the sweet liquorice scent my love left behind.

This is the best high I've ever had. Better than groo. Better than slur corn. I've got to find more of these creatures. Bottle their poison and sell it at raves.

I think I'm in love.

The alien cracks open. Its back pops into pieces and a grey ooze empties over my shin.

A dozen small people crawl out of the ooze. As small as my smallest finger, but human-shaped. They are fully mature, with breasts and pubic hair. Some of them have fins on their heads instead of hair.

Shark people babies. They are half human and half shark person. Some look mostly like sharks, others look very human, but most are a combination of the two. One of the male human-shaped babies stares up at me. It is a small version of me, looks exactly like me. My son.

These are *my* babies. The shark woman's babies. All our nights of unprotected sex have given us a litter. Buttery caramel feelings as the miniature people crawl up my skin, leaving trails of goo, to the STD bumps on my chest. They each take a bump into their mouth and suckle them like nipples.

One of them goes to my collar bone. My eyes focus on her. She looks human but with a large Mohawk on her head like a fin. She drinks from a red bump. Grey ooze leaking down her neck and pooling at her bare breasts. She sees me watching her and stands up at me, wiping her mouth.

'Don't worry, Pete,' the miniature woman says. 'She does love you. I'm sure she will come back to you some day.'

I nod at her and she goes back to suckling.

A smile widens on my face. My eyes drift shut and I let my mind swim in thick grey fluids, wrapping my arms around my children to keep them warm.

Breathing in the spicy sweet scent of black liquorice.

Lie Dream of a Casino Soul

Nick Johnstone

1

Rachel wants to know how you weigh freedom. Is it impossibly heavy beyond our imaginations? she asks. Or light the way invisible things are light, like dreams memories sunshine? It's Tuesday evening, we're having dinner at a Lebanese place on Edgware Road. Conversation is rich, fluid. She's telling me about a political prisoner they're trying to set free. She works for a human rights organisation. She's assigned to Myanmar, former Burma. I say something about freedom being a child's dream of the world. Rachel eyes me intensely. My impressions of her are romantic, widescreen. Picture a drop of the ocean inside a shell – that's Rachel. When the bill comes, my credit card is declined. Rachel pays.

2

I got a letter yesterday by recorded delivery from the bank telling me I've got fourteen days to clear the arrears on my mortgage payments in full or they're going to repossess my flat. I sat on the sofa, MTV blasting The Strokes, volume set to 22, reading, re-reading that letter. At dinner, I didn't tell Rachel. We've only been going out a month. She doesn't even know about the shop. She thinks I worked for a firm of management consultants, that I was made redundant in October. It's January 12th now and London is cold. I did tell her that last week I saw Mick Jones on Ladbroke Grove and Paul Simon a day later on Aldridge Road Villas. Rachel thought I was making it up. Where she works, everyone was raised on The Clash. I had three estate agents out this morning. The second was the best. I'll be sad to leave here. But the thought of the bank taking my home. No, no, no. I've got thirteen days to secure a firm offer in writing or I lose my home. Rachel thinks I'm about to sell because I want a bigger place. She lives in a studio on Chesterton Road, four streets north of the Westway. Living over here, on Powis Gardens, deep in Notting Hill, she thinks I've got it made.

3

I couldn't sleep last night. So I sat on the sofa in the living room, a legal pad in my lap, a 2B pencil in hand, made a list of all my debts. Who I owe. How much. When I need to pay it back. Who I can borrow from. What's left to sell. Recently, I've sold almost everything. First to go were the antique hand-me-downs. My grandmother's eighteenth-century French bureau. My great-aunt's silverware. My great-uncle's Dutch marquetry chairs. My other grandmother's art deco lamp. Auction, eBay: all gone. The money came in, went out again. Urgent circles of cash. I just keep spinning them. Barely leaving fingerprints. I passed the whole night like that. Until, eventually, came the first glimmer of dim winter daylight. In my basement flat, windows criss-crossed with white security bars, it's never light, only dim, dingy, then dark.

4

Rachel is impressed that I've got a member of the royal family living next door. Tom Hawksley-Richards. The only son of the sister of our future monarch. Lives at number seven. His coke dealer comes and goes all day, every day. I know it's his coke dealer because I've scored from him myself. Everyone round here knows Phil. He deals out of a flat on Tavistock Road. Makes house calls to the needy and rich. I hear you run up a certain credit you can't pay back, he breaks a hand. Then the other. Next, your legs. And so on. Susan, my ex-girlfriend, her sister Sam said she knew of a concert cellist who got both his hands broken. He couldn't work for months. Went to rehab in the end. Rediscovered Bach. Left Notting Hill for Paris. A new life. Rachel keeps up on royal family gossip. Says it's like following a repressed elliptical soap opera – that there's always the possibility of getting a peek behind the mask. Since we started dating, she spends hours at the windows, wrapped in the curtains, saying, There he is. Third time today. How much is he putting up his nose for God's sake. She's never tried coke. Stayed up five days straight. Or had money problems. That's why I like her.

5

I had my own optician's business on Kensington Church Street. A small shop selling designer frames. Oliver Peoples. Jil Sander. Prada. Gucci. Miu Miu. Armani. LA Eyewear. I opened it a year after graduating from Oxford with a first in history. I drifted for six months, parties, pubs, clubs. Susan, who I met in my second year, had this incredible amount of money at her disposal. Her family was old money, she had a trust fund. I helped her dispose of it. One evening, her brother told me about a friend who'd opened a designer eyewear shop in Edinburgh, what a success it was, how he'd sold glasses to celebrities, aristocrats, dot-com millionaires.

Something clicked. Back in London, I did my homework, sized up the competition, trekked around shops taking notes. I borrowed the start-up costs from Susan (at the top of the list the other night: *still owe Susan £35,000*). She got her old school friend Tatiana Ranovich in to design the shop. I bought stock. Hired Daniel as optician. We opened. Word spread. We got write-ups in all the right places like the *Evening Standard* who did a big piece on the shop. Sales boomed and for six perfect years, everything went to plan. Money flowed, the business turned a profit, my salary rocketed. I drank champagne, did a little coke here, a little coke there. Then a lot of champagne, a lot of coke, everywhere. For Susan's thirtieth, we flew Concorde to New York. Stayed at the Paramount. Room service, clubs, more coke. I charged the whole trip – a cool £7,000 – to a credit card. Soon I was charging everything to a credit card. Food, a courier at the shop, take-out pizza, the mortgage. I started turning up to work mid-morning. Then around noon. Then I'd call Daniel, ask him to run the shop. For a day. Then two days. Then a week. I took out loans. Maxed out one credit card, applied for another. Maxed that, applied for another. Susan and I got bored with each other. She went to Australia last summer for a two-week holiday, stayed six months. Fell in love with the producer of a hit Australian reality TV show. And then, last autumn, a designer eyewear chain, Zara Levy Vision, expanding from the States, opened on Kensington Park Road and during the fanfare – six A-list Hollywood stars were at the opening – nobody bought any frames from us for a week. Then another week. By the third week, I threw a pre-Christmas sale. Still nothing. Panic set in. Daniel quit. Debt collectors started coming to the shop, then to my flat. I wrote cheques. The cheques bounced. I borrowed. Soon as I paid one lot off, another lot came banging on the door. Then came real trouble: court. They seized the shop. All the assets too. When Susan finally reappeared, she'd stopped using, said I looked like a scarecrow. She gave me a business card for a shrink. Bill Peterson.

6

Nine days to go and Rachel is by my side sleeping. It's half five in the morning. I'm lying in bed smoking. The windows are wet with condensation. A looming shadow through the window: the 'for sale' sign. It's on with an estate agent on Notting Hill Gate. They're slick, fast, professional. I told them my predicament. That we needed the hand with all the aces and yesterday. No problem, they said. Apparently it's on the market at a *beyond competitive* price. They've done seven viewings. No offers so far though. If my dad was still alive, he'd know what to do. My mother, last time I called, begging her to lend me another £500, she said: Don't call this number again until you straighten yourself out. That was four months ago. Since then, I've left message after message on her machine. But she never calls me back. When this is over, I'll go and see her. Explain everything. Rachel sleeps so peacefully. I could sit here watching her sleep for ever. Till they kick the door down. Take the keys. Throw me in the street. Cover me with leaves.

7

Matt, the estate agent doing the viewings, called this morning. He said he's bringing over a couple at eleven. Very keen buyers, their place is under offer. In a good position. Looking for a two-bed in Notting Hill. This put me in a great mood. I turned MTV up to 24, smoked cigarettes wearing my best grey suit, my black Armani shades. I jumped around the flat when they played the new White Stripes video. Around 9.30, I sent Rachel a text, telling her she's fun, I like her. She hasn't replied yet. It's 10.10 now. Fifty minutes until the viewing. They're going to make an offer. I can feel it. This is where everything changes, change begins. I'll use the equity to clear the debts, start a new business. Maybe go to Bali or something to clear my head. Surf. Sleep. Swim. Fall in love. Walk the beaches as the sun comes up.

8

Rachel wants to know why I'm not looking at places to buy. She says she'd like to come along. See places with me. We're at Raoul's, eating brunch. My eggs are the wrong side of runny. And her toast looks better than mine. She may be hinting that she wants us to move in together but I'm not sure. Yesterday she said living alone and having her own place is important to her. I pretended that I've been around the block with this selling and buying game, that I'm not going to look at any flats until my place is under offer. I made it sound like everyone does this. She said, Oh. Bit into the last corner of her superior-looking toast. When the bill came, I made a big theatre out of opening my wallet and acting surprised that I hadn't actually been to the cashpoint on the way to meet her, that subsequently I didn't have £40 cash on me as I thought. She wrote a cheque. She wrote the letter 'R' big and looping like a dragonfly's wings in flight or the infinity sign. Her hand caught the ink, smeared the date. The rest of the afternoon, she randomly stroked my sleepy head with a palm stained blue.

9

Seven days to go and Matt just called to say the couple found it too dingy. They're after a top-floor flat. Light, apparently, is top of their shopping list. I asked him why he brought them over. He said, you never know. I said, fine. Hung up. Paced the living room, furious. Shouting at him. Out loud. My voice bouncing off the walls, now bare except for my year-of-1992 Oxford portrait and the John Lennon print Susan bought me for my twenty-seventh. I called Matt back, told him he wasn't doing enough. That I wanted results and now. He suggested a major price drop. Let's price it to sell instantly, he said. I said, OK, do it. Soon as I got off the phone, someone was knocking at the door. I had learned never to answer, otherwise you're legally giving debt collectors carte blanche to walk in, seize whatever they want. I checked at the curtains. A courier. Motorcycle leathers. Clipboard. An envelope. To be safe, I opened the window. He said it was recorded. I signed. Sat on the sofa. A notice from the bank telling me I now had seven days to clear the arrears on my mortgage payments or they were going to commence proceedings to repossess. I snatched at the Dunhill packet. Empty. I threw it at John Lennon's face. Struck him on the nose. Outside, the low murmur of a dub record. Outside, the screech of children having fun. I dialled my mother's number. She answered. I said, It's me please don't hang up. She did.

10

Great coke. I sold my suit, the Oxford portrait and the Lennon print to three different dealers on Golborne Road. Went to Tavistock Road, saw Phil. I mentioned that I saw him next door all the time and he told me to 'mind my own fucking business'. I walked down Leamington Road Villas smiling. A gram in one pocket. Forty Dunhills in the other. I put MTV on, turned the volume to 27. Jay-Z. '99 Problems'. All at once: music, coke, cigarette. The world dissolved. There was no letter on the sofa from the bank. I was taking a day off. Tomorrow I'd be back at the shop, selling frames to beautiful people with weak eyes. Tomorrow I'd go out with Rachel, looking at flats. If the moment presented itself, I might ask her to move in with me. Everything would figure itself out. These obstacles will obliterate. This day is beautiful. I think I'm falling in love with Rachel.

11

Five days to go. Matt showed an investment banker round last night. He made an offer on the spot. But the offer was too low. It wouldn't even cover the outstanding mortgage loan. When I explained this, Matt sounded distracted, said he'd try and get the buyer to go up. Susan came by earlier, tried to persuade me to make an appointment to see Bill Peterson. I told her I didn't need a shrink, I needed money, heaps of money. She said she couldn't lend me any more, that I still owed her for the shop. I told her I didn't want her stupid money. She asked me if I was getting high. I told her no. I didn't do coke any more. She passed me the same business card she'd passed me six months ago, told me to call him. After she left, I made an inventory of everything in the flat. A sofa, a TV, a bed, a coffee machine, a shelf of books, a shelf of CDs, two suitcases and some basic cooking utensils. Matt called back. The buyer's offer was final. No other viewings were scheduled. I took a shower. Filled a Tesco bag with all the CDs and a Marks & Spencer bag with all the books, headed up to the Record & Tape Exchange on Notting Hill Gate. They gave me £38 cash for the CDs. Then I went to their used bookshop. They gave me £42 cash for the books. In the icy air, I felt positively rich. So I went to Phil's.

12

Three days to go and Rachel's at the window again, waiting for Phil to come out of next door. Can you imagine how much money you'd get if you called a tabloid with this story? I didn't quite register what she was saying at first. Then I thought about it. What kind of money would a person get for bringing a story like this to a tabloid? £10,000? £20,000? £50,000? I calculated everything I owed, based on the list of last week, into these sums. This would do it. I know, I said. Finally, Phil left and Rachel was thrilled. There he is, she said, whispering, breathless. Then she sat down next to me, asked if all my furniture was really in storage.

13

Forty-eight hours until the repossession process begins and I meet a man at Fresh & Wild on Westbourne Grove. He's a reporter with *The Globe*. He says his name is Jim. He buys me a take-out coffee, says let's go somewhere more private. We end up sitting on a bench off Colville Square. Tell me everything you know, he says. Then he goes fifteen paces away, out of earshot, calls people on his mobile. Comes back, says: This is how we're going to do it. We'll have one of our investigative reporters follow this Phil guy and buy some coke off him. I tell him the reporter can go to Phil's place with me. I'll broker the deal. Even better, he says. I ask him what my fee will be, outline my situation. He goes out of earshot again, makes a call. Comes back, says there's £50,000 in it for me, if I set it all up for tonight. They'll pay tomorrow, in cash, if they get the story. I assure him they'll get the story. Two hours later, two plumbers arrive at my flat. Once inside, they take their overalls off, open their toolboxes. Cameras, lenses, film. We wait at the windows. I start to panic that Phil's not coming. Then, at 8.15, finally, Phil shows up. The photographers snap away. I later find out that another two are hidden across the street, snapping Hawksley-Richards as he opens the door to Phil. Phil leaves. Jim calls, tells me to head over to Phil's. On the corner of Westbourne Park Road and Aldridge Road Villas, their undercover man will be waiting for me. He'll give the code 'crowning glory'. I hurry round the corner. There's a man waiting. But he looks like RZA from the Wu Tang Clan so I assume it's not him. Then he says, 'Crowning glory' and off we go to Phil's. Jim told me later there were photographers planted everywhere. The reporter was wearing a wire. Phil sold us ten grams. The reporter paid in cash. A hidden spy camera captured the whole thing. When I got home, Jim rang, said my £50,000 would be dropped off in cash at seven in the morning. I threw the suitcases on the bed. Packed. Sat in all the emptiness, waiting. In my hand, my passport. Yes, my passport.

14

It's now June and I'm sitting in an apartment in Paris. The way it went down in the end, the story was front page the same morning I got my money. The headline: *Coke Shame of Royal Son*. They left my name out of it, but to those who knew, it was pretty obvious. Phil was arrested around dawn. We seized a large quantity of cocaine, boasted Scotland Yard. I went straight to my bank, paid off the mortgage arrears. Stayed there over an hour, moving money here there and everywhere until all the pending court cases were put to rest. Then I went to Waterloo, took the first Eurostar train to Paris. Just inside France, I called Rachel. Told her there were things I needed to explain.

15

I want to know how you weigh freedom. Is it impossibly heavy beyond our imaginations? Or light the way invisible things are light, like dreams memories sunshine? It's Saturday evening, we're having dinner at a little bistro off Boulevard St-Germain. Conversation is honest, real. Rachel says something about freedom being a child's dream of the world. I eye her intensely. Her impressions of me are romantic, widescreen. Picture a drop of the ocean inside a shell – that's me. When the bill comes, my credit card is accepted. I pay.

An Older Lover Etc

John Williams

As I get older I'm less and less confident as to the accuracy of my memory. Things that happened to me are more and more confused with things that other people have told me about happening to them, with things I've read, with things I've seen in films and in dreams. So, if I tell you that what follows is the true story of my involvement with The Fall a quarter-century ago, you are at liberty at least to wonder. I've tried using the Internet to confirm or deny things but that just makes it worse. Was I at this gig or that one? I remember many of the venues well enough. I could persuade myself I was there, but can I be sure? Not really. So I apologise if this is not exactly a story, but I can assure you it's not the truth either. At least not as anyone else involved would recognise it.

I first heard The Fall, like 99.9 per cent of everyone else, on the John Peel show. I could check their first session, some time in 1978, or maybe the end of 1977, but like I say...Anyway, it was the session with 'yeah yeah industrial estate' on it. I'd been looking forward to it, because back then, in the first years of punk, there weren't that many bands, and you'd read the live reviews in the *NME* and hear that so-and-so was good, and you'd wait with a sense of excitement until so-and-so made a record or did a John Peel session and you could find out whether it was true. And the best bands tended to keep you waiting: The Banshees, The Slits, The Subway Sect. Same thing with The Fall: I'd been reading about them for at least a year before I finally heard them. I hadn't seen them live as I was locked up in a boys' boarding school in Bristol at the time.

In the summer of '78, however, I was released into the community, as one very alienated seventeen-year-old. The first thing I did, more or less, was to hitch around Britain, stalking the Patti Smith Group on their one and only tour of Britain. The support band were called The Pop Group, and they were from Bristol and I knew them slightly, so they let me hang around a bit and, after a gig in Edinburgh, they introduced me to a fanzine writer called Oliver Lowenstein, who offered to give me a lift to the next gig, in Manchester.

On the way Oliver told me he'd just finished working as a librarian in Camden, and that the job was easy to get and something of a doss. This was useful information that I would soon act upon. On our arrival in Manchester we had some time to kill, so he decided we should go and call on a band he'd recently interviewed, name of The Fall. They, or some of them at least, were in a standard-issue depressing seventies flat somewhere in north Manchester. I remember Mark and Kay being there, probably Marc Riley, mostly though I remember the keyboard player Yvonne Pawlett, and sitting next to her in the back of the car as they all piled in for a lift down to the gig. I was a month or so out of an all-boys school and I was utterly smitten. She was a girl, she was my age more or less, she was in a very cool band and she liked Nico. Naturally I did nothing but blush and stammer.

Three months later I finally got to see the band live, up at the Marquee in London. They were supported by Manicured Noise who were friends of Oliver's, and probably featured a young Jeff Noon. I don't really remember anything at all about either band, to be honest. By then I was working as a librarian in Camden.

Three more months and I was writing a fanzine of my own, entitled *After Hours*, with my mate Charles. We went along early to see The Fall at a gig at the Nashville in west London. I said hello to Yvonne and Marc and Mark and Kay and they introduced me to a guy called Rob who had hitched a lift down to London with them. Rob turned out to be the lead singer in a group called The Prefects who were even more of a cult thing than The Fall. No records, just one radical John Peel session.

Rob was in London to sell a guitar that may or may not have belonged to him. The show was great. Staff Nine, with Craig Scanlon and Steve Hanley, supported, and their singer wore flares. Punk rock was over. The Fall were mighty and afterwards I watched Kay Carroll, a small woman, face up to the large and heavy Irish publican who was trying to underpay the band. He had a team of bouncers, but she was fierce. He gave in.

Afterwards Rob Lloyd came back to crash at our flat near Clapham Junction. We sat up most of the night drinking and recording an interview. Almost everyone I knew lived through music back then. Rob Lloyd hinted at a big wide world out there. The interview was full of eye-opening stuff about the Birmingham pub bombings and prison and sex and Marlene Dietrich. Rob left in the morning and the tape was inaudible.

Another month or so and The Fall were back in town for what the music press was calling, for one week only, 'the gig of the century' – a show with The Mekons, Gang of Four and Stiff Little Fingers at the Lyceum Ballroom in London. According to our fanzine, which I've just dug up, The Fall had bottles thrown at them by the SLF fans. I have a feeling I wasn't at the show itself but I suspect we may have hung around beforehand. Either way, the following lunchtime me and Charles met the band in a pub in Notting Hill, just round the corner from the record label, Step Forward, in order to conduct an interview.

Yvonne showed up with her new boyfriend. None other than Rob Lloyd. She had moved herself well out of my league, no question about that. The drinking was relentless. Somewhere along the way we paused for an interview. Reading it now it's a bizarre Jesuitical wrangle over the finer points of not selling out. Set down verbatim in the fanzine it ends with Una Baines, The Fall's ex-keyboard player, there in her role as guitarist Martin Bramah's girlfriend, saying, 'All these young kids now have a really positive attitude. I think it's much better than it ever used to be, it's getting better.' To which I reply, 'Well, I don't know.' At seventeen, I had already lost faith in the younger generation.

The evening ends in a blur of drinking with Rob and Yvonne. Somewhere along the line we stop at the Virgin headquarters to demand money Rob reckons he's owed. We buy carry-outs from a supermarket to drink while we wait. Then it's up west. More drinking. My crush on Yvonne gets worse. Next day I have the flu and remember I have nowhere to live.

A couple of weeks later I check out of the library job and spend my earnings on taking the magic bus to Greece (seventy-two hours on a knackered coach for £30 – a bargain). The day I get back to London, having spent all night on the bus, I check the *NME* and discover The Fall are playing in Cambridge. An hour or so on a coach later, and I'm there. Craig and Steve from Staff Nine have joined The Fall by now, while founder member Martin has left. I go for a drink with Marc Riley, Yvonne, Craig and Steve. Yvonne was probably the only one of us legally old enough to drink, it strikes me now.

By the time the gig starts I am beyond tired. There's a slew of support bands: one, The Dolly Mixtures, are fantastic and I tell them so but they don't seem to believe me. Later on I fall asleep, my back to the wall of the Corn Exchange. Later still I try to negotiate a lift back to London with another support band, and then Marc Riley suggests I kip on the floor of their B&B.

So that's what I do, sneak into a suburban B&B already crammed with Marc and Craig and Steve and, oh yes, Yvonne. Yvonne's on the camp bed, I'm on the floor. In the morning Marc smuggles up pieces of toast from breakfast, and I make it outside without being spotted by the landlady. The van's heading north, but I decide it's time I went back home to Cardiff. Yvonne's going to Birmingham to see Rob. We both get dropped off at Spaghetti Junction, walk round endless ring roads, and have a cup of tea somewhere. Yvonne's in a hurry to see Rob. I make a half-hearted attempt to hitch, then get a coach back to Cardiff.

That was the last time I saw Yvonne. Not long afterwards I received a postcard from Rob saying he was getting a new band together with her, and she'd left The Fall. By then I was living back in Cardiff, in a grim shared flat and playing in a band of my own. We were called The Puritan Guitars and we sounded a bit like The Fall would have done if they really couldn't play their instruments.

I went up to London and saw The Fall a few times. Once I hitched up to Manchester to see The Fall and The Watersons on the same weekend. The Watersons, a traditional folk-singing family from Hull, were my new favourite band. By that time punk rock was well and truly over. The Puritan Guitars made a single and I couldn't bear to listen to it. We played a handful of gigs, culminating in a show in London, with Geoff Travis from Rough Trade and most of The Pop Group in attendance. We were useless, it seemed to me, the end of something that had had its day, and I split the band up that night.

The Fall, though, were still a part of my life. More so really since I'd moved back to Cardiff: the sense of outsiderdom that's at the heart of Mark's shtick resonated easily. 'Rowche Rumble' seemed to sum up the kind of grey, provincial, increasingly post-industrial cities we both lived in.

I used to write a lot of letters, back then. I must have written to Mark E. Smith because, somewhere, I have letters from him. When I was in Manchester to see The Watersons I'd visited Mark and Kay at their flat in Prestwich. They were both suffering from terrible speed comedowns, but I still felt oddly as though they were my parents. Was I aware that Kay was older than Mark? I'm not sure. I remember walking to the bus stop with Mark and he pointed out the pub where he would go drinking with his father. It had never occurred to me that people – especially people in the music business – went drinking with their fathers. To me it had seemed like we all had to stride off alone, leaving all that family stuff behind, that we had to be self-invented. No wonder I felt so adrift and in need of guidance.

Guidance came when I went up to London, to help master a single by my friends The Janet & Johns. We were in this office in Portland Place, where a man called Porky used to master almost every record that was made. We got there earlier and found The Fall mastering their live album, *Totale's Turns*. We sat in the corner and listened and a track called 'New Puritan' came on. At a certain point Mark's voice stopped even approximating singing and said the words 'There's more to life than your record collection, John'. (Actually, now I've checked I realise the words are actually 'I curse your preoccupation/With your record collection/New puritan has no time/It's only music, John'.) Were the words meant for me? God knows. Either way they hit home. I needed a life, a girlfriend, some fun, not to listen to the John Peel show every night.

I did my best. Over the next year, I moved flats, got a job in an anarchist printer's, met girls, went to the pub more often, missed the one time that John Peel played The Puritan Guitars single. I made a plan, bought a van, formed a nine-piece doo wop group. We would go to Paris and sing and dance and leave the greyness behind.

Our departure was set for the 1st of May. A week before that The Fall finally came to Cardiff. They were playing at the university. That afternoon we rehearsed the busking act for the second time. Around six o'clock I went over the university, and walked into Kay Carroll.

'Hey John,' she said, 'have you got a band?'

'Yes,' I said, 'of course.'

'Well,' she said, 'can you support us tonight?'

'Sure,' I said and drove round Cardiff desperately mopping up band members before they went out for the evening. In the end I think there were eight of us onstage, playing rolled-up newspapers and kazoos and singing Barbara Ann and Willie O'Winsbury. We went down a storm, got the first and last encore of my performing career. Afterwards we hung out in The Fall's dressing room till Kay got fed up with us and kicked us out.

A week later, as The Skeleteens, we went to Paris. Another month or so of singing and travelling and the remaining six of us, four boys and two girls, wound up in Amsterdam, went to check out a place called the Melkweg, a kind of arts centre with added dope-dealing operation. The Fall were standing in the courtyard; as it turned out, they were playing there that night.

'Hey John,' said Mark, catching sight of me with a four-week beard and clothes from a Paris flea market, 'you've turned into a beatnik.'

The Fall had made a new record called *Slates*, a ten-inch LP. There was a song called 'An Older Lover Etc' on it. The refrain went 'You'd better take an older lover', repeated again and again before the pay-off comes – 'You'll soon get tired of her'. Did I know Kay was older than Mark? I must have intuited it – there had been a story that went round the punk rock scene that Mark and Kay had met in some kind of mental institution. One of them was a patient and one was the nurse. Except no one was quite sure which. When it came to the band, though, Kay was matron all right.

That summer I shed my new puritanism, moved to London, got a job in a record shop, started taking speed, going to clubs, the usual. I stopped listening to the John Peel show. Accepted that the world wasn't changing, at least not the way I'd thought I wanted it to. I started to fit in – we all did.

Then I saw The Fall play a big London gig, an awful band called The Au Pairs supported, pulling Rolling Stones poses. It was all starting to feel like business as usual in the world of rock'n'roll. Next time The Fall were in London they were supported by something called Danse Society. I didn't go. At the record shop I moved from the indie department to the soul boy basement, started listening to Maze and Luther Vandross. Marc Riley left the Fall at the end of 1982. The following year, I went to college. I saw Marc's new band play their first London show at the end of 1983. He told me that Mark and Kay had split up halfway through an American tour.

That was the end for me. It's like when your friends split up and, despite all your best intentions, you end up being friends with one and not the other. Except it was more than that, it was like my parents splitting up. For me, The Fall had been like a mom-and-pop shop, and I wasn't really interested now it was just the pop shop.

A while later I met a woman six years older than me, with a child. We got together, and then she went on holiday. While she was away I met a Japanese woman, a singer in a band. We went for a walk in Hyde Park. She told me her favourite Fall song was 'An Older Lover Etc'. I left her in the Serpentine Gallery at the end of the afternoon. I waited for my older lover to come back. I've never seen The Fall since.

Papal Visit

Nick Stone

(For The Count)

Joel arrived for his interview forty minutes early. Part of it was down
to the train connections being better than usual, the remainder
because he was back-against-the-wall desperate. He didn't want to
blow it. He hadn't had a proper job in over eighteen months.

The company was on the eighth floor of an impressive glass-
and-metal tower called Sparrow's Perch. Directly in front of the
building was a small park surrounded by plum trees. There were
sprinklers on the freshly mown grass. Joel decided to wait there,
gather his thoughts, compose himself, go over his spiel again
– and pronounce his interviewer's name a few more times: Mr
Mieduniecki – Meed-Unnn-Esss-Key. Polish, the receptionist had
told him. Mr Meed-Unnn-Esss-Key? Pleased to meet you. Even
though he could say the name without hesitation, he'd still written
it out on a sheet of yellow legal paper and folded it in his pocket,
just in case, as a prompt, for luck.

He found a bench and sat down under a tree. He was the only
person in the park.

OK, so he hadn't even walked into the building, or met his interviewer, and he knew that it was wrong to think that way, but he began to give in to feelings of optimism. He imagined what he'd do if he got the job. Leave that wretched basement flat he lived in for a start. The place had flooded three weeks ago and now, with the heatwave they were having, the stench was unbearable. He'd never liked the place or the landlord or the area he'd moved to, but he'd been desperate then – desperate like he was now. He'd buy himself a new TV and stereo. He'd get new friends, proper ones, ones who didn't bail on you when you were chest deep in shit, ones who'd wade in and help you out. People were always impressed one way or another when you said you worked in finance. Women thought you were loaded and a good catch, men thought you were a wanker.

He neither saw nor heard it coming. A mild breeze blew through the trees and then something soft landed heavily on his right knee with a low-key splat. He jerked his leg back and looked down. At first he didn't understand what had just happened, what he was looking at. He thought he should have been in excruciating pain, on the floor, howling, crying for a doctor, an ambulance, help.

But when he stood up there was no pain. His knee and leg were fine. No one had shot him.

So, what was all that dark dripping wet red stuff in the middle of his right leg?

Then he saw the three ruptured plums near his shoe, the stones lying in the wet crimson pulp – all that was left of what had just fallen from the tree above him and splattered his knee.

He looked up. The branches were bent and straining with clumps of heavy fruit. How could he have been so utterly fucking stupid? And why hadn't he worn his black suit instead of his grey pinstriped one?

Right next to the tree stood a small green marble sign, shaped almost like a common gravestone, but wider and shorter, and engraved in gold lettering: 'May 30th 1982. This plum tree was planted to commemorate the visit of Pope John Paul II to Sparrow's Perch'.

Why had the Pope come here, of all places – he thought – and had he kissed the ground where they'd planted the tree?

He checked his watch. He had twenty-five minutes to go before his interview and two choices – either try to clean himself up or go in there and explain what had happened. He nixed the last alternative almost as it formed: all interviewers made their minds up about you within the first five minutes. Walking in looking like he did would shorten his lifespan to five seconds.

He remembered he'd passed a bar on his way there.

The bar's lavatory was clean and spacious, everything just so, in the right place, not a millimetre out, like walking into a showroom. Two rows of sinks were in the middle, facing each other, with a mirror dividing them. There were urinals to the left and right. The floor and walls were covered with spotless, sparkling white tiles, while all the fittings, from the urinals to the soap dispensers, were made of gleaming stainless steel. Everywhere he looked he could see himself, his own mass audience.

Hall and Oates's 'Out of Touch' was piping through the speakers as Joel took off his trousers and went to work on the stain over a sink at the far end of the bathroom. He rubbed at it with water and liquid soap, making a thick cloud of pink then red foam. Yet when he rinsed it off he saw that the plum splatter had barely shifted. If anything, it looked worse after the wash – darker, heavier, bloodier, the colour of fresh raw liver.

He checked his watch. He still had fifteen minutes left; or he *only* had fifteen minutes left. He scrubbed away at the trouser leg, but he felt that it was futile. He didn't panic or even worry. He was beyond the reach of that. Instead there was something he'd never felt before, a weariness coupled with a sense of certainty and resignation. The game was up. He was in a tailspin, going down fast. For the first time in his life he thought of giving up, calling it quits; abandoning the interview altogether and heading back home. He'd make himself a cup of tea and let fate throw whatever dose of bad shit it had lined up for him.

Then he looked up and saw a man standing at the urinal nearest the entrance. He had a full head of red hair and a thin sharp-edged face. Joel guessed that he'd come here during his lunch hour and was going back to work. He was dressed in a white shirt and black tie, his sleeves were rolled up and he was carrying a thick paperback pressed under his armpit. He was whistling the tune coming out of the speakers.

Joel recognised it, certainly the chorus. He'd heard it before – at those sponsored karaoke nights his old company used to run at the nearby pub.

It was a song called 'Kyrie', by two-hit American non-wonders Mr Mister: typical eighties MOR bombast designed to be played loud in stadiums and at the funerals of people who liked that kind of shit.

Then Joel noticed something about the man at the urinal, something that had failed to register when he'd first seen him.

The man was wearing exactly the same pair of trousers as the ones he was washing – same mid-grey, same thickness of pinstripe, same material, same design – right down to the pleat and the turn-up and the triangular flap over the left back pocket – they were an absolutely perfect match. The guy was maybe an inch or two wider than him at the waist, but they were about the same height, and height was all in the legs.

Joel waited until the man had finished pissing and had gone over to the sink before he spoke to him.

'Sorry about this,' he said with a smile, nodding at his trousers, bundled up at the side of the sink. 'I've had an accident.'

'It's OK,' the man said, rinsing his hands, giving him the briefest of glances. Of course, Joel could tell, the man didn't think it was OK at all, being spoken to by a stranger standing in a public toilet half dressed in a suit and boxer shorts. He could see him speeding up his actions.

'This'll sound strange, but—' Joel began, moving towards him, '—but I'm in a bad situation here.'

The man looked worried now. He shook his hands to dry them, but he did so under the running tap and splashed himself. Annoyance flashed across his face, but it merely highlighted his fear.

'I can't help you,' the man replied, stepping away from the sink.

'But you don't know what it's about,' Joel said. He was deliberately calm and non-threatening, trying to keep the pleading tone out of his voice.

The man's book fell on the floor and landed closer to Joel than to him. They both looked down at it at the same time. *The Count of Monte Cristo*. A paperback doorstopper, heavily bookmarked with small multicoloured Post-it notes. The man had his hands by his side. Water was dripping off his fingers on to the tiles. His white shirt was stuck to his chest in opaque pink fleshy patches where the water had gone too. He looked from the book to Joel, eyes calculating, assessing, sizing up. Joel could see what he was thinking, almost as clearly as he could see inside the man's head. He was thinking that if it came to blows, he'd lose and lose badly. People were always saying that about Joel, how he looked like he could handle himself. And he could. And he had.

'Look…I've got nothing against you…you…you people,' the man said, raising his hands up, palms out, moving a step forward. 'But men aren't my thing. OK?'

'I'm not gay,' Joel said, almost laughing. 'This isn't what this is about.'

'Well, what do you want then?'

'It's just that I…I…I need to borrow your trousers.'

'What?' The man screwed up his face so tightly his eyes disappeared behind pleats of skin.

'Your trousers. That you're wearing. I need to borrow them.'

'Is this a joke?' The man smiled bemusedly. 'One of those hidden camera things? Peekaboo. You've been framed. Ha, ha, ha?'

'No cameras here, no joke, no ha, ha, ha…' Joel said. 'I'm being serious. I need to borrow your trousers. It'll only be for an hour or so, then I'll meet you here and give them back.'

'Don't be ridiculous!' The man, suddenly bold, reached down for his book.

Joel grabbed him by the wrist and held it tight.

The man fought, pulled, tried to twist free. Joel was way stronger and had everything to lose.

'Listen to me,' Joel said, getting on his knees so he could look the stooped man in the eyes, holding on tighter, holding on the way someone dangling over an abyss holds on to a stray root. 'I'm in a really desperate place right now…'

And then he told him everything, just opened his mouth and poured his heart and mind and soul out to this complete stranger in the toilet of a City bar. He told him the whole story, from the where he was now to the where he'd started from and how he'd got all the way down here, sparing no detail. He was hesitant at first, spitting out his tale in disjointed chunks, but then he found his rhythm and it grew more and more cohesive, as Mr Mister's 'Kyrie', with its anthemic, gospel-choir-boosted chorus, helped him shade his tale with the right nuance of regret and repentance. Joel told him how he'd been fired from his last job for theft. He owned up to it all – not just the money he'd been caught stealing out of petty cash, but the money he'd stolen from his colleagues' pockets too, from their purses and wallets and handbags, to the loose change they left in their desk drawers for emergencies; and he'd stolen from all the office collections too – the leaving dos, the birthday presents, the wedding gifts, the new-baby gifts, the charity whip-rounds, the sponsored walks and swims and runs and cycle rides. He told the man how he hadn't been able to find work after that, that no matter how many lies he'd told and how much he'd altered his CV, no one wanted to give him a second chance any more, because his past had a way of coming out of the floorboards and stinking out his lies. He told him how he'd lost almost everything – first his girlfriend, then his friends, then his family – OK, he didn't blame them, because he'd stolen from all of them too – and how now he was having to sell most of his possessions to keep his head above water. He'd had to sell all his Fall CDs, something he'd sworn he'd never do. And now he was down to the last things he owned, the hardest to part with, the most precious, the golden dregs. After they were gone it was the street for him. He realised, as he spoke, that he hadn't once told anyone any of this, that he hadn't ever unburdened himself, that he hadn't even ever said sorry. And he was sorry, sorry that he'd got caught and sorry that he'd fucked his life up so badly that he was reduced to being on his knees in a public toilet, begging an honest man to lend him his trousers.

Meanwhile the man had managed to get hold of his book, but he couldn't get free of Joel. He'd kicked and punched and pushed and slapped him, but the more he'd been spilling his guts, the tighter Joel's grip had got until he'd cut off the circulation in the man's hand.

The man had shouted for help, but no one had heard him all the way upstairs in the bar, which was too far away for sound to carry through two sets of thick doors.

When Joel finished his racked monologue he realised his face was wet with tears. He hadn't cried since he couldn't remember. He wasn't the sort who did. He let go of the man's hand to dry his cheeks. The man, who, at that very moment, had been making one huge, last-ditch attempt to pull away from Joel's grip, suddenly and very violently jerked back, then he lost his balance and smacked the back of his head into the wall. He hit it so hard his head bounced off the tiles with a crack and then flew straight back and hit them again. He crumpled to the floor, coming to rest face bowed, in a seated position, legs folded to his side.

The trousers were uncomfortable and scratched the insides of Joel's legs as he walked across the eighth-floor lobby of Sparrow's Perch, where a receptionist sat at a long dark wooden desk flanked by two red vases of white lilies. Brown hair, smart business suit, cream blouse, mid-forties, diet-sad face, glasses, all professional; but there was also a hint of thwarted aspiration that had long curdled to bitterness about her too. Joel could smell failure on people, however slight.

Joel was dead on time. He introduced himself and asked for Mr Mieduniecki, pronouncing his name perfectly, which impressed her so much she told him so and asked him whether he'd been practising. No – he told the first of the thousand and one lies he'd rehearsed – he had a Polish grandmother.

She asked him to please be seated in a practised posh voice that no doubt hid a far humbler background, one spent envying richer folk, trying to be like them. On the wall behind her, close to the clock, was a picture of the Pope greeting a row of people standing in front of Sparrow's Perch. He had his hand on a young boy's head, as if he was blessing him. There was a ribbon across the top right-hand corner of the picture, white and red horizontal stripes, the colour of the Polish flag.

Joel went over to a black leather couch and sank into it. The material sighed under his weight. There was a stack of all the day's papers tiered out on the glass coffee table in front of him, masts and front headlines showing.

He picked up the *Financial Times* and opened it somewhere in the middle. It shielded his face, gave him a little privacy, let him collect his thoughts.

He hoped the man he'd left in the toilet was OK. He was fairly sure he was. He'd only hit his head. There'd been no blood and, at one point, while he was dragging him to the cubicles, he'd sworn he was about to come to because the man's fingers had grasped at his and, as he'd been dressing him in his own plum-stained trousers, he'd kicked out slightly. After swapping the contents of their pockets over, Joel had left him there, sitting on the bowl, trousers around his ankles, leaning back.

As he'd walked out into the street, he'd seen that the exchanged trousers weren't quite the perfect match he'd thought they were. They were at least a shade darker than his jacket, the pinstripes brighter and slightly thicker; not overtly noticeable differences, but noticeable if you looked hard enough or wanted to find them. They were also baggy around the knees, too wide at the waist and itchy as hell too, as if they were woven out of wire wool. He hoped the man didn't have some kind of skin condition or fleas or crabs.

Ten minutes passed. He was grateful for the delay. The cool air conditioning and his increased body temperature had made him sweat like a pig. Now he was settling down, getting acclimatised, drying off.

Behind the paper he heard the receptionist doing her thing,

answering the phones, fielding calls and, when she wasn't, she was making them, speaking to people in a low murmuring tone which didn't quite carry the words to his straining ears.

Then she addressed him.

'Excuse me, Mr Wilson?'

Joel lowered the paper.

'Mr Mieduniecki will be a little late back. He had a meeting with a key client at midday. It must have overrun. We're very sorry about this. He should be back soon. Are you all right to wait?'

'Yes, I am,' Joel said. 'Day off.' The CV he'd sent in said that he was employed, freelance. Easier to get a job when you say you're already in one than when you were on the shit-heap. That's what he'd told his last employer too, and the one before that. They'd never checked.

'Can I get you anything? Tea? Coffee? Water?'

'No, thank you.' Joel smiled. Then he realised that he needed a piss really badly. He asked her where the lavatory was. Behind him, she told him, first door on the right.

The bathroom here was covered in black tiles so polished they were mirrors.

He took a long loud piss and then washed his hands and threw water on his face.

When he opened the bathroom door he heard a man's voice coming from reception. His interviewer had arrived, he thought, late but all apologies. Mr Meed-Unnn-Esss-Key. Pleased to meet you.

He quickly stepped back inside, checked his tie and hair against the tiles, took a deep breath, pulled his face into a half-smile and walked out again.

He took one step forward, turned and stopped.

Two policemen were standing facing the reception, blocking off most of the desk with their wide, flak-jacket-covered backs. One was doing the talking. He was holding something dark in his hand. Static from their radios drowned out much of what was being said, but Joel thought he could hear crying, discreet, part-stifled snuffles, coming from behind the cops.

Then he saw what the talking cop had in his hand: a wallet, and, with it, the sheet of A4 yellow paper he'd spelled the name of his interviewer out on. His first thought was that the receptionist would know he'd lied about his grandmother being Polish, his second was that the piece of paper they were holding really meant nothing at all, unless they tied him to it, which they could by dusting it for prints and running the results through their computer. And if they did that they'd know who he was for sure. And that would be that. Back to prison – and not a white-collar one this time either. No jury would believe his version, which, for once, would be the truth.

Joel considered his options for a moment, weighing up the possibilities and likely outcomes. The cops hadn't seen him yet, and they probably didn't even know he was standing right behind them. He hadn't had a bad run, he reflected. Five years, two full-time jobs, two full-time identities. It had to close out some time, the way these things always did. But then again, did they? Who was to say it couldn't last a little longer? Why not? Cops were only human. They made mistakes all the time. People were always slipping through the net. There were more of him than them. And these two were old. Old and still PCs. You know what that meant.

He lost the remnants of his smile and walked forward.

Fortress/Deer Park

Michel Faber

'Did you bring morphine syrup?' said Victoria, almost as soon as I had entered through the great wrought-iron gates of Bloedel estate. 'Or pethidine linctus?'

'Uh…no,' I said, pulling my overnight bag – which the guards had just searched very thoroughly with their leather-gloved hands – back on to my shoulder. 'Should I have?'

'My dad loves presents,' said Victoria. In the bright sunlight of rural Bavaria, her face seemed less beautiful than I remembered it from the nocturnal London party where I'd first met her. 'All his guests bring presents.'

'I did bring a present,' I pleaded. 'A five-hundred-dollar bottle of wine.'

'He won't like that,' she said, wrinkling her perfectly sculpted nose. 'He likes morphine. And pethidine.'

'In syrup.'

'Yah. He has a sweet tooth.'

I realised as she spoke that there was one thing about her I'd failed to notice when we were fucking in the guest bedroom of her Brompton flat: she was loathsome. Not physically loathsome – she had all the usual attributes, including a flawless long neck, feathery blonde hair and big hazel eyes. But vile to the bone.

She was dressed for the hunt, even though it wasn't due to start for hours. Her boots were green leather lace-ups, elegant but sensible. Her suede trousers probably cost as much as a car. She wore a windcheater with tartan lining, but the Italian blouse underneath was casually unbuttoned to display her cleavage. She had a champagne glass swinging in her hand when I arrived through the gates, but immediately handed it to one of her minders.

'Quite a sight, isn't it?' She meant the Bloedel estate, fifty acres of unspoiled woodland and manicured meadows under a cloudless blue sky. It seemed to go on for ever. Gardeners or gamekeepers were dotted around in the distance, small as mice, doing whatever they were hired to do. The turf was spongy underfoot, like carpet. Bloedel Castle was flanked with oaks that must have taken centuries to grow to maturity; the stables were the size of a multiplex cinema. Swans and ibis swam in a giant pond strewn with lily pads. Blackbirds wheeled around the tops of the fir trees. Waiters in white tuxedos were ambling back and forth over the grounds, carrying silver trays loaded up with champagne glasses and hors d'oeuvres. Observing that another guest had arrived, one of them approached me. I took a warm breaded scallop from his tray, holding it by the toothpick on which it was speared. The scallop fell off the stick and landed between Victoria Bloedel's feet.

'Not to worry,' she said. 'Have another.'

'It's OK, I've changed my mind,' I said. 'Is there somewhere where I can freshen up before the hunt?'

'Of course,' she said. 'Your room.'

'Where am I staying?'

'With me, of course.'

'I'll need to be shown the way.'

'Not a problem.' She pulled a cellphone from her jacket pocket and keyed in a number with her extraordinarily long fingernails, which were lacquered pale green. 'Is that Bill? Oh, Frank, is it? What's become of Bill? Bill is dead? Oh, right. Well, be a darling, Frank, and meet me near the front gates. We've got another poor lost soul here. Yah.'

I nodded towards one of Victoria's minders, who'd wandered off to a discreet distance out of earshot and were leaning towards one another chatting, their burly arms folded across their chests.

'Couldn't one of these guys have shown me the way?' I said.

'Oh, I can't spare them, lover. Never know when I'll need them.' And she turned and waved at the nearest goon. His fat hand moved momentarily towards the opening in his donkey jacket, then relaxed. He nodded and grinned. Two of his teeth were silver.

'Don't fall asleep, lover,' said Victoria, as a chubby, fresh-faced young servant hurried across the rolling green to fetch me. 'The hunt waits for no one.'

Bloedel Castle had several dozen bedrooms and any number of couches, ottomans, armchairs and animal-skin rugs that could have been used for sleeping on. No wonder the place had been billeted during the Second World War to accommodate a whole division of soldiers. Today it was humming with activity of a different sort. Hunt enthusiasts from all over the world were here, loitering in the drawing rooms and corridors, admiring suits of armour and eighteenth-century paintings. I recognised several heads of state. That is, not in the paintings, but standing around, in the flesh. The president of an African country whose name I couldn't remember gave me a big yellow smile as I passed him in the entrance hall. He wore an orange-and-purple robe with a grey double-breasted suit jacket, unbuttoned, over it – a tasteless combination, I thought. He'd been in the news lately. Thousands of his country's citizens had been shot, or starved, or imprisoned, I forget the details. We exchanged courteous nods and he went back to peering at a medieval tapestry, his bulbous nose almost touching the ancient embroidery.

Victoria's bedroom, if indeed it was specifically her room and not one of many she laid claim to as the need arose, was surprisingly unfeminine. I don't know what I was expecting – high-heeled shoes or Gucci handbags strewn across the carpet, maybe, or a vase of flowers. The room was immaculately clean and had the ambience of a waiting room in a swanky private medical clinic. There was one painting, a Manhattan cityscape in shades of grey, deliberately blurred as though suffering from camera shake. I massaged my temples, freshly aware of the headache that had plagued me since take-off in Munich. I went to the en suite bathroom for a piss, and found a mirror laid out flat on the marble sink, with a thin line of cocaine on it, neat and unsniffed. Victoria's equivalent of complimentary chocolates or toiletries.

I had a shower, changed into my hunting gear, and sat on the bed for a while. There were some magazines laid out on a coffee table. *Country Life*, *Vanity Fair*, a German gossip glossy, an Italian edition of *Vogue*, a Japanese magazine featuring many photos of a blindfolded woman whose swollen little breasts were so tightly tourniqueted with bondage ropes that they looked as though they would surely go gangrenous and drop off. There was an awful lot of print in this magazine. I wondered what it could possibly add to the visuals.

At five o'clock, a gong rang. I left the bedroom and, as I made my way downstairs, joined a thickening procession of guests. The African dictator had changed into jodhpurs. I glimpsed members of the British aristocracy, chief executive officers of software companies and oil firms, anorexic pop musicians and movie stars, former advisers to American presidents, German athletes, all sorts of faces and bodies I vaguely recognised from TV or from pornography. Everyone was chatting animatedly in English, the universal icebreaker. Some of them had already had too much to drink. A New York authoress with spray-on glitter stuck to her breasts was repeatedly fiddling with her impractical bodice, tucking the nipples back in. 'Is there some way they can tie you to the horse so's you don't fall off?' she asked her partner as they descended the stairs. Seconds later she tripped and fell. Men of half a dozen nationalities scrambled to help her, but she'd smashed her nose on the carpeted marble and was unconscious. A doorman in livery raised a cellphone to his ear and called a doctor, or maybe a cleaner. We all filed out into the courtyard. I took a last look at where we'd come from: the pattern of blood on the stairs was in the shape of an octopus.

Outside, conditions had become rather dramatic. The sky was strafed with weird lines of cloud, so that for a moment I thought a fleet of skywriting planes had passed over, trailing their exhaust fumes in formation. The late-afternoon sun had reclined towards the forested horizon, glowering incandescent but no longer giving out as much heat. The weather was still brilliant, though. Mild with a balmy breeze, just perfect. Everyone was remarking on it admiringly, as though the temperature and the air were unique design features of the Bloedel estate. The trees looked so lustrously green you were tempted to suspect they'd been touched up with paint specially for the occasion. Horses were emerging from the stables in a seemingly endless line across the fields, led by grooms in red jackets. There was a convivial hubbub as the grooms matched up the horses with riders, helping guests of all shapes and sizes into the saddle. Some of the guests had clearly been hunting since they were children, and ascended into the saddle with the ease of people falling into bed; others giggled and huffed, all buttocks and flushed cheeks, as the staff heave-ho'd them into place.

Victoria was in the thick of her family and staff, too many people for me to push through. She was already mounted, and looked magnificent. The sunshine gave her blonde hair a halo of dazzling gold. All her lipstick had been rubbed off, leaving her lips ivory pale, and she had fragments of new-mown grass on the damp knees of her trousers. Her father, also mounted, was older, uglier and smaller than I'd imagined – a fat little gargoyle in a red velvet jacket and check trousers. Various brothers, sisters and stepmothers were milling about, their horses rubbing flanks and snorting. I was shown to my own horse, a dark brown one with the number 137 affixed to her bridle. A friendly flunkey helped me into the saddle and handed me a cudgel.

The cudgel was an exquisite object: carved out of wood, yet hard and dense as titanium, as though an entire tree trunk had been compacted into this metre-long implement. It weighed about as much as my usual five-iron golf club, but was more satisfying to hold, smooth as ivory, lustrous and dark as an antique. Surely not all the cudgels were as handsome as mine? But they were. I peered into the crowd and found the servant who'd supplied me. He had a big leather bag strapped to his back, like a quiver but the size of a golf caddy, and it was bulging with hand-crafted wooden clubs. He was handing them out to any rider who didn't have one yet. Other flunkeys were doing the same. There must have been a hundred guests in the saddle by now. It was almost dusk, and there was a communal sense – a sort of buzz of tension passing through us all – that we should stop faffing about and get moving.

Now that it was time to perform I wished I'd taken the cocaine after all. Jet lag was dragging me down to earth, as if my sagging body might pass right through the saddle, through the dark innards of the horse, to drop on to the turf below. Bugles started blowing. 'What's the lay of the land?' said a Scandinavian-sounding voice to my left. 'Last chance to turn around, darling,' said a man with chinos so tight I could see the shape of the condom foil in his back pocket. 'Don't call me darling,' was the withering reply.

I wondered, for the first time, if I should be there at all. It had cost a great deal of money and involved a lot of travel. The chances of Count Bloedel having an intimate dinner with me, at which he admiringly drank the $500 bottle of wine and offered to bankroll the project I was keen to discuss with him, seemed slim. Victoria would never be my trophy wife; the most I could hope for was to be her befuddled hanger-on for a month or two, while she scouted around for fresh talent.

'They're releasing the deer now' – a Texan drawl from somewhere behind me.

'Where?'

'There.'

In the distance, about a quarter of a mile away at least, a posse of Land Rovers was shepherding the animals into place. My horse flexed and shivered beneath me; I could feel her anticipation coming through my thighs. Count Bloedel raised his horn to his purple lips. One toot and we were off.

The horses were slower than the deer, but the deer were amazingly tame. They'd been bred specially for the hunt. They would run for a while, then become aware that they were getting scattered, so they would slow down and regroup. It was the easiest thing in the world for us to catch up with them.

Even when the first of the deer was felled by Count Bloedel's cudgel, and its shocked carcass lay kicking its spastic limbs on the ground, other deer stood drinking at a nearby stream, apparently unconcerned. The Bloedel family started picking off the closest, and the air was noisy with horse breath, grunts of human effort and the thwock of cudgel against downy grey skull.

Within moments, everyone was doing it. I swung my cudgel at a frightened deer that was backing off from another rider. She, he or it hopped backwards into my reach, hindquarters trembling. I didn't even have to see its eyes. I swung the cudgel as hard as I could, and was relieved not to miss, in case Victoria was watching me. The impact was intensely satisfying, like hitting a tennis ball at high speed. The side of the deer's face changed shape and an arc of blood narrowly missed my horse. Another deer come bounding up so I hit that one too; everyone around me was doing likewise. The jerking, flailing motions the deer made when they were under our horses' hoofs were truly spectacular, like frenzied dancing. Their spindly legs made even better targets than the heads; your cudgel could snap them in two, like rotten tree branches, with a single blow.

In no time, you could hardly see the ground for dead deer. Hundreds and hundreds of them, sprawled all over each other, some still panting, others gashed to pieces, and us still lunging at them with our cudgels, our eyes half blinded with blood. I was using both hands, I was almost falling off my perch, my arms were just about jolted out of their shoulder sockets every time I smashed a skull.

The rest is hazy in my memory. I don't recall us deciding when it was all over, or getting off our horses; I only remember the slippery, slimy grass underfoot, and stumbling around, knee deep in deer flesh. We piled the carcasses in a huge mound. Twilight was coming down on us and we wanted to get the job done by dark, so we worked like madmen. I was labouring side by side with some of the richest and most important people in the universe. What can

I say? It was tremendously liberating, the biggest thrill. I would grab the ankle of a dead deer, and a tribal chieftain from some developing country would grab another ankle, and a gorgeous young woman would grab another ankle, and we'd sing 'One, two, three' together, swing together, and toss our burden through the air. It was the most powerfully communal thing; we were all one; it's so hard to describe to people like you.

Then we set fire to the fucking lot. Yes, oh yes.

Iceland

Nicholas Royle

Why do we long to wend forth through the length and breadth of a land,
Dreadful with grinding of ice, and record of scarce hidden fire,
But that there 'mid the grey grassy dales sore
scarred by the ruining streams
Lives the tale of the Northland of old and the undying glory of dreams?
William Morris, from 'Iceland First Seen'

Tony had been banned from driving and he didn't know whether public transport ventured to such places, but just the thought of taking a bus to Runcorn was enough to upset the balance of his medication. So he thought he'd walk. Runcorn couldn't be that far. He remembered it had been yoked to Warrington at some point in the 1980s. A failed attempt to big it up. Come to Warrington-Runcorn. Ring Eileen Bilton on…Some people still thought Eileen Bilton was a little old lady sitting by her phone.

So he thought if he set out early enough he'd make it in a day. Steve lived in Warrington, so Tony must have walked home from there enough times. The way he was at the end of a session with Steve, walking was the only viable means of transport, given that the local cab firms now refused to pick up from Steve's address.

Staying at Steve's had always been out of the question. His was the only house he'd ever visited that could possibly make Tony's look like the 'after' picture in a makeover feature. Runcorn couldn't be that much farther and he didn't have a lot to carry. Just a plastic shopping bag, a frozen cottage pie and an Evian bottle filled with vodka. Lightening the load wouldn't be difficult. It was a beautiful late January day with a clear blue sky.

Just before setting out, he checked the address. Turned out it wasn't Runcorn at all, as he'd read in the paper. Instead, it was 'near Runcorn'. Actually he'd be heading for Deeside Industrial Estate, Flintshire. He wondered at Flintshire for a moment, wondered what it meant. And then he realised. It was in bloody Wales.

So he took a tram to Altrincham. Tony remembered a local gig in which the audience had been invited to create acronyms from the names of nearby towns. Some smart-arse had gone for Altrincham, which got him marks for ambition alone, but then he scored highly with his acronym, A Long Tram Ride Into Nasty Cheshire, Hateful And Moneyed. When Tony got to Altrincham, he stuck out his thumb. Trudging dejectedly towards the A556, as hope dwindled that anyone would stop, he took out the cottage pie and read the box for the hundredth time. 'BIGGER PACK BETTER VALUE £1'. A pound! Was it worth it? Deeside was forty miles away and assuming a speed of five miles an hour (an optimistic forecast) it was going to take him a day, so there was little chance of getting there before nightfall. This realisation prompted a short break for liquid refreshment.

An enormous lorry shuddered to a halt fifty yards ahead. Half suspecting a practical joke – he wouldn't put it past Billy or Steve or one of the other lads from the band to go the trouble of hiring an HGV just to let him think he was getting a lift and then pull away when he came alongside – Tony hauled his sorry arse into a reluctant trot. He drew level with the cab, which bore an address in Mold.

The driver mumbled in an impenetrable accent that was rendered even more unintelligible by the thick red beard and moustache that covered the lower half of his face. Lip-reading was out, then.

'Iceland,' said Tony, and climbed aboard without waiting for a response.

The driver mumbled again, his eyes flashing, and it occurred to Tony that maybe he spoke only Welsh. He tried to smile, momentarily forgetting the gap left by the front tooth sitting in the zip-up compartment of his wallet, but the driver seemed appeased and pulled out into the traffic.

After a few miles, the driver started talking again, looking across at Tony from under his shaggy blond fringe, his great meaty forearms resting on the wheel.

A response was required. Tony took a gamble.

'Jazz musician. I play the bass saxophone.'

Mumble mumble mumble mumble mumble mumble. With a hand gesture, like swatting a fly.

Tony thought hard.

'Jazz-punk. Not really jazz at all. I hate jazz.'

The driver's response was no less incomprehensible and even contained a mild threat of violence, so that Tony shrank back and took refuge in reading the motorway signs, becoming worried that he'd suffered a blackout when he failed to spot an exit between junctions 12 and 14.

Shortly after the end of the motorway, the driver pulled over and stood on the brakes. He delivered a final tirade of unfathomable abuse followed by a cheeky smile and a friendly wave. Tony climbed down from the cab and ran as fast as his trembling legs could carry him right across the top of the roundabout and into the industrial estate.

What the industrial estate needed was a great big map at its entrance with an arrow marked YOU ARE HERE and another labelled THIS IS WHERE YOU WANT TO GO, but, strangely, there wasn't one. Nor was there anyone around for Tony to ask. He sought comfort from the Evian bottle and pressed on, eventually stumbling across Second Avenue. It was not even lunchtime. Bingo. Flicking his tongue in and out of the gap in his top set, he marched towards the long brown building on the right. He read the sign: 'ICELAND. CO.UK FOOD YOU CAN TRUST'.

The main entrance was an alienating construction of bronzed glass. It contained a revolving door, which was locked. Tony hammered on the glass, but no one came.

'Open up, yer bastards. Check this out,' he shouted, pointing at his missing tooth.

No one showed.

Tony drained the Evian bottle and started swaying and whirling the shopping bag containing the cottage pie around his head like Leatherface with his chainsaw. The still-frozen lump of minced beef and puréed potatoes caught him on the back of the head and he went down, hitting the tarmac with a resounding crack. Briefly his eyes fluttered open, allowing a glimpse of the blue heavens, across which a tiny white cruciform insect crawled north, excreting a thin trail of fluffy mash and appearing to Tony, as he slipped into merciful unconsciousness, like something from a dream.

The trouble started at check-in. Approaching the desk in his Acoustic Ladyland T-shirt and camouflage trousers and with a plastic carrier bag for his hand luggage, Tony leaned forward to request an upgrade but made the mistake of breathing into the check-in girl's face. She recoiled and could be seen making a discreet phone call as Tony headed off towards the gate. The look on her face said if she could have downgraded him, she would have done.

'Fuck her,' Tony said with a gap-toothed grin to Steve as they boarded together. 'She can't spoil my day. America here we come.'

The band had been invited to play the Knitting Factory in New York. This was a big break for Steve, Billy, Arthur and Tony, and they'd started getting in the mood at one of the airport bars. On the plane they wanted to sit together, but their seats were scattered about the cabin.

'Look, love,' Tony said, his hand on the stewardess's forearm, 'we'd like to sit together.'

'I'm afraid you have to sit in your allotted seats. The flight is very busy.'

'Fuck's sake.' Tony scowled and reached inside his carrier bag for his Evian bottle, which he had refilled that morning.

Glances were exchanged between the crew, who decided to let the matter drop in the hope that the situation wouldn't get out of hand. Unfortunately, it did, but not until after take-off. Tony got out of his seat to go to the toilet while the plane was still climbing. He made hard work of the sloping aisle, ignoring requests to regain his seat.

'You must sit down, sir.'

'No, love. I *must* take a piss,' he countered, unzipping the flies of his camo kecks and revealing that he was travelling commando.

A male steward grabbed him from behind.

'Want some, mate?' Tony asked. 'Must be true what they say.'

Tony was marched back to his seat, where he sat playing games on his mobile phone until the seat belt sign went off and he immediately got up again. Bypassing the toilet, he went to the galley and demanded a drink, as he wanted a break from vodka. When it was refused, he undid his flies again and took action that somewhat restricted the choice of hot meals for passengers flying economy.

When the plane landed, after what seemed to Tony like a remarkably short transatlantic flight, four uniformed officers boarded. They had to drag Tony from his seat. He wondered why the rest of the passengers weren't getting up to disembark. He saw Steve arguing with one of the stewards, who folded his arms and shook his head. The officers marched Tony off the plane and into the terminal building and put him in a featureless room, where he produced his passport from out of his plastic carrier bag and was questioned by another copper with a heavy accent. They took the passport but let him keep the Evian bottle. It was as he was being led out of the airport to a patrol car that the penny started to drop. He'd never been to JFK, but this wasn't how he'd imagined it. The rear door of the squad car was opened from the inside and Tony was shoved into the back seat. They didn't even do that thing with the hand on the head that they do on cop shows, so that he hit his head on the door frame as he got in and was still rubbing it as they drove out of the airport on to the main road.

'So where are you taking me, you miserable Canadian bastards?' Tony asked, looking out into the darkness and having a swig from his Evian bottle. 'Shouldn't you be on horseback, anyway? I assume this godforsaken wasteland is Canada.'

The driver turned to the officer alongside him and smirked.

'Reykjavik,' said the driver.

After further questioning at a police station in the Icelandic capital, Tony was allowed to leave. The officers at the desk laughed as they handed him his passport.

'I don't know what you're laughing about, fucking Viking cunts,' joshed Tony. 'If I'd wanted to come to Iceland, I'd have booked a ticket. *As if.*'

'Maybe you should have waited until New York to have a drink,' one of them said, heartily. 'Happy Thorrablót!' they chorused as he exited the building and walked straight into an enormous pitch-black open-air freezer.

Tony's warm clothes, along with his saxophone, were presumably still in the hold of the plane that must now be well on its way to America. At least he could feel the shape of his mobile in his trouser pocket. He took it out only to discover that the battery was dead. He reached for his wallet, which contained ten US dollars. His credit card had been stopped a while back and he hadn't got round to getting a new one. His carrier bag was lighter than it had been: the vodka was all gone. In short, he was fucked.

In similar situations at home, he would call Steve or Billy or even Arthur, although as Arthur was the drummer he was pretty much a last resort. Or he would fall back on the legendary kindness of Mancunians.

He started walking. At the end of the street, teeth chattering so violently he worried that those he had left would shatter, he turned the corner and within a couple of minutes found himself surrounded by young people dressed in jumpers, fleecy tops and woolly hats. As they swapped remarks, their breath froze in the air like ghostly speech bubbles. The sound of music drew Tony towards a bar with red and blue neon tubes in the window. Inside he was enveloped in a steamy fug. He waited at the bar, jostled by revellers, elbowed in the ribs, without much of a plan.

It was his T-shirt that broke the ice.

Within half an hour Tony had a glass of caraway schnapps (his fifth), food in his belly and a new friend.

'Thanks for the olives, Stig,' he said as the giant passed him another bowl.

'Sten – and they're not olives.'

'Whatever.'

They were the size and consistency of olives and, after five glasses of caraway schnapps, Tony's taste buds had packed up. He tucked in.

'You have to play the saxophone for me,' said Sten, leaning close to Tony, his pupils dilating.

'I've told you, my saxophone is on a plane going to New York, while I'm stranded here with no money in the most expensive city on the planet.'

'Second-most expensive, after Oslo,' said Sten, looking serious for a moment. 'I am economist.'

'Well, you know what? I'm glad I'm not in fucking Oslo, because if I was I'd have run out of money and I would never have met you and you would never have so kindly bought me all that lovely barbecued chicken.'

'It's not barbecued chicken. It's blackened sheep's heads and putrefied shark,' shouted Sten over the din as he grabbed Tony's leg. 'It's Thorrablót, the festival of traditional food. *Skál!*' They touched glasses and knocked back their contents, then Sten leaned in again and put his arm around Tony and spoke into his ear. 'You really play like Acoustic Ladyland? That jazz-punk thing? How did you lose your tooth?'

Tony laughed.

'I had a dream that I bit into a frozen cottage pie. I thought it said microwave for one minute but it said stand for one minute. I thought that meant stand and wait for one minute, but it turns out you were meant to cook it for fifteen minutes and let it stand for one.'

'You are crazy!'

'It was a dream. I did buy one, though. You know what it says on the box? "If you are not happy with this product we will cheerfully replace it or refund your money and that's a promise!" I love that "cheerfully". I didn't dream that. And do you know what, Stig, do you know where I bought it?'

A hurt look crossed Sten's great big round ruddy face.

'Sten. Where?'

'Iceland.'

'NO!' Sten roared. 'We don't make cottage pie. We make blackened sheep's heads and putrefied shark. Thorrablót! *Skál*!'

'Iceland, the frozen food store in the UK.' Tony looked at his empty glass, then suddenly remembered his almost empty carrier bag.

Sten's brow furrowed, then suddenly cleared and he beamed at Tony.

'Let's go,' he said, rising to his feet, oblivious to Tony's protests as he forged a way through the crowd to the door, dragging Tony behind him.

In the street, Tony felt strange. All the available data told him it was worryingly, possibly dangerously, cold, yet he couldn't feel anything. His bare arms were prickled with goosepimples, but it didn't translate into sensation. He felt then he knew what it must be like to be a Geordie out on the town. Trotting, he tried to catch up with Sten. Glancing back, he thought he could see two men following them, something glowing in their hands, but couldn't be sure. When he stopped and stared into the darkness, they disappeared, but as soon as he was moving again, it was as if they had a shadow. They seemed to have been walking for hours, but it may only have been minutes. What few lights there were slid past in a sickly blur, as if the director of the nightmare movie this evening was turning into had smeared vaseline on the lens. Tony felt like a glasses-wearer who's lost his glasses. A swimmer who's forgotten how to swim. He knew he mustn't lose Stig – Sten.

'This street is Túngötu,' said Sten. 'It's just down here.' He stopped outside a building and pointed.

'What?' Tony panted.

'Baugur,' boomed Sten. 'Baugur is very big Icelandic company. They bought your Iceland in 2005. This is their headquarters.' He brought his great ham of a fist down on the door again and again. 'Come out, cowards. See what your cottage pie did to my friend's smile. He has lovely smile and plays saxophone like Acoustic Ladyland. I will make them come out,' he added, looming over Tony, as he swayed.

'But Stig,' Tony reminded him in a weak voice, 'it was just a dream.'

Sten stood still for a moment and looked at him, then he sat down next to him on the pavement, draping his great log of an arm around Tony's neck. Pawing gently at Tony's face and nuzzling into his ear, he whispered, 'Then how did you lose your tooth?'

'I don't know. I'd had a couple of drinks. I walked into a door or something. And can I just make something clear, in case it's not? I'm not gay.'

'We are very tolerant of gays here in Iceland. There is nothing to worry about. Well, maybe the Lutheran Evangelists are a little resistant.'

Tony lifted his head up, trying to disengage from Sten's clumsy embrace, and his eyes opened wide.

'What the fuck?'

'What is it?' asked Sten, looking sideways on at Tony.

'Strange lights in the sky.'

'Aurora borealis.'

'I don't think so. I think it might be Lutheran Evangelists.'

The lights moved closer. They were two glowing cigarette ends held between the sausage-like fingers of two musclemen who made Sten look like the 'before' picture in a bodybuilding article. Suddenly a heavy boot shot out of the darkness, striking Tony in the chest and causing him to fall back and hit his head on the pavement.

When Tony came round, he was relieved to find that he was in bed, but then dismayed by the realisation that it was a hospital bed. Hooked up to various devices, he let out a feeble groan that grew in volume until a nurse appeared by his side.

'Where the fuck am I?'

'Warrington Hospital, love. You gave us a bit of a fright.'

'How did I get here?'

The back of his head had started to throb.

'A man walking his dog found you on the marshes and called the ambulance.'

He became aware of a different kind of pain in his gut.

'We had to give you a stomach-pump.'

'Olives.'

'No...' The nurse hooked the end of her tongue over her front teeth. She seemed to be enjoying this. 'Sheep's testicles. Dozens of them. The police want a word, when you're well enough. Apparently a farmer has lodged a complaint.'

Tony groaned again.

'Give us something for the pain.'

'We'll see about that.' The swing-doors opened at the end of the ward and a small party entered.

'Visiting time? Is it the lads?' Tony asked, brightening up.

'No. As you may know, Warrington is twinned with Lake County, Illinois, and these two gentlemen—' she paused to allow two huge men in dark blue suits with short haircuts to approach the bed '—are visiting from the Evangelical Lutheran Church there.'

The two men stared at Tony and Tony stared back at them.

'One more thing before I go,' the nurse said. 'You're no longer nil by mouth, so will you be wanting dinner?'

'What is there?' Tony asked, not taking his saucer eyes off the two men.

'Cottage pie.'

The Man Whose Head Expanded

Steve Aylett

Brank Osmen's head parted the city in slow surging waves, immense clouds of powdered glass and concrete getting in his eyes. Not too shabby, but more than he bargained for. As his forehead barged twenty blocks of offices and hotels into the river, he knew the truth makes no exceptions.

Headgloves had become popular when plastic surgery was found to be insufficient. Twitches of human expression would sometimes disarrange and disturb the desired blandness – headgloves avoided this problem by being entirely artificial, a whole-head mask. These became thicker over the years, incorporating embedded nano servo-motors to replicate certain select expressions. People could buy celebrity heads, the deader the eyes the higher the price. The real head of a headglove wearer had to be surgically shrunken to roughly the size of a potato. People wore the headglove their whole lives, their real head shrivelled and forgotten. Some, rich only in money, had their actual head dwindled to the size of a maggot.

The Contraflow Revolutionary Army fought alone, without any lies to help them. Their enemy seemed a weak one, a people who were helpless without disguise and feared honesty like fire.

Contraflow favoured girls who exploded out of nowhere with huge tiger smiles, faces of a thousand muscles and two-handled gullwing sedan guns with a retro Gatling drum the size of a turnstile. The media's misinterpretation prerogative named them the Nobhead Liberation Army and Brank liked this so much he changed the name officially, laughing the big laugh.

You could tell who was under a mask – smiles didn't reach the eyes, the eyes were false anyway and rain bounced off. Dr Buck's compound, administered by intravenous dart, reversed the head-shrinkage process and the public got their first view of this when a chat-show host's outer head spatted suddenly like a snipered melon, crumbling open to make way for a swelling grey abomination. His real head, which hadn't seen the light of day for forty years, squalled like a child against a dark caul of mould and steaming slime, several cockroaches darting to escape the sudden exposure. Overnight the Nobhead Liberation Army became oppression excuse number one. The authorities asserted that the assaults on headgloves were not activated by a desire to dispose of headgloves: why would anyone? Knowing that a crime investigation was doomed if the motive was so strenuously denied, Brank felt safe.

The Army's headquarters was upstairs from an old chapel fronted by relay monks who dispensed ominous looks to entrants and clasped precaution razors between their prayhands. The night of his weekly broadcast, Brank made the sign of the Errorverse and entered. Not for him an imprecise, amateur apocalypse open to interpretation. Upstairs he passed a rack of carbines and the modified Jacuzzi in which several gallons of Dr Buck's incendiary antidote swirled, enough for a city.

Brank loved how much people hated his adolescent doorframe sermonising, and so did a lot of other people. A thriving trade had begun in the sound files. He sat at the broadcast desk now and gathered his thoughts, feeling as useless as a hen on a garbage island. Usually he couldn't wait to finish one insult to the populace before beginning the next. He looked up at the skylight roof, and the striplamp swaying on its chain like a bit of sky come loose. Man was he one fried monkey.

Opening the mike, he began. 'This is the Nobhead Liberation Army. You've heard me say that part of enlightenment is knowing when you're being ripped off. Regret is a rope at the other end of which is a younger version of you, all full of beans and acting like a moron. It's not rebellion if they just sold it to you. The opposite of revolution is a script. But when the time comes to realise this, you continue replacing hours with the same hours. You select only from those options presented you by other people and so occupy a lifelong abyss of misdirection. You've been shafted, so what the hell are you grinning at?

'If people truly don't return from the dead, then humanity is constantly passing out of the world, something is being lost – yet there are still bodies and bodies and bodies, moving and talking. Does this explain the increasing blandness, the diminishing thought, the dead eyes? What is passing out of the world, and not returning, is spirit. At what point did street bribes stop paying cops to leave off criminals and begin paying cops to leave off victims? Such trickling transitions are silent as sap. Non-totalitarian governments exist because some populaces are naturally servile or distractible enough not to require a totalitarian one. Disappear there or here, you choose, that's democracy. This one has taken misdirection to intergalactic extremes. Yesterday's clown is tomorrow's mayor and the next day's clown. Even our tyrants are mostly ornamental. And the headglove is a godsend to this evasion, a mask incapable of anger, doubt, appetite or intelligent scorn, nor the freedom of being an ugly, honest cunt. The new flesh, bright zombie, going one younger. Moods without weather. And the utter sadness of generations not knowing what they've betrayed. Born into this artificiality with no intervening stages, they walk through life as if they have an appointment with their own ghost, a blameless blank crippled by appearances, living a philosophy which has its sensations only in imitation. They're so timid of their own skin that they live like a spirit departing or never present, immaculately inauthentic. They're dead men merely held in reserve.

'But things are more interesting than that. Earlier today I trod on a spider and it made a sound like the pip of an automatic car unlock. Now tell me this world's not a weird one.

'If you tape the average man's mouth shut he'll lie through his nose. That's undisputed. But we have to ask, what will be the last words spoken on this planet? Concrete cannot complete the universe. The derelict society glitters, celebratory with weakness. Facts are acknowledged only when the events they relate to are far in the past and safely irrelevant. Rare outbreaks of common sense are stifled and ignored by the media, never heard of. Fatuous influences shrug off the brain for reasons of balance. Warnings of catastrophe are dismissed as mere "warnings of catastrophe" but soon the little patronised problems of chance will be lethal. I await the brave dismay of the honest. Love has the innards of grief.

'Careful: a uniform is a dice. The Nobhead Liberation Army is slandered but who among you has witnessed a more reasonable frenzy than ours? Who has not experienced the desire to tear off his own face in the midst of society's bullshit? Don't decorate my name with importance. You can't name the saints of true atrophy – the label slips amid our rotting flesh. Irrational perspectives decide the angle of our wounds. We will crash your mind and serve a feast of discouragement. You can tame the loops out of my head when I'm fucking dead. We won't succeed, finally. But after all, what's the point of being doomed in a *variety* of ways?

'Riddle me this: who are you? It's hard to see a system of which you are part. It's hard to see your own eyes. You pay to make fools of yourselves. To hear your own veins drying up. Don't mistake intensity for hostility, mate – some people have things to do. You're a bloodless, clueless wanker and you think you're great – and that's why I get fundamentally disappointed.'

A blare of noise interrupted him, a helicopter above the skylight. 'Put it down, put it down!' came a cry through a loudhailer. 'Desist!'

'How are you spelling that?' Brank yelled, pulling a Daewoo only to sling it away at the end of the motion, all strength gone from his arm – the gun clattered into a corner. His shoulder was bleeding and skylight glass powdered the floor like sugar. There were booming shots from downstairs and as he reached for one of the gullwings a soldier entered. Brank swung and two rashers of uniform flew in different directions.

Then something slapped him in the head. The hot wind from it surprised him. Blood looped out behind him, hitting the wall. It was a graffito exclaiming 'O'. He'd known he'd end this enterprise utterly licked against a drystone wall, shot-up and bucking in dust, but now it was happening he felt as dumb as an adult in a teacup ride. To be insulted by these fascists was so degrading.

Blood hanging out of his face, he fell backward into Buck's vat.

Feeling squirly, he could still see cloud above the skylight roof. It seemed to be getting closer. Was he ascending like a cliché? Then the window frames were pressing against his face like a griddle. They burst outward and he continued to swell, his head tilting aside so he could see the neighbourhood getting smaller. His head was expanding like a slow bomb, his body a useless doll beneath it. The house began to crumple, dust exploding down the surrounding streets. He felt like hell and tried screaming the fact. Confronted with a massive head momentarily capable of opinion, the authorities were unprepared. Brank was dilating across districts, his head a confusion ball of white and pink fat arching through a spritzed halo of bloodcloud. Power lines spanged, fizzing out. Upheaval edges powdered to rubble. He was making good on his promise to replace glamour with swampy death, to the extent that he was now breaking through a bridge as a train shot up his nose. Of all the ways I expected to die, he thought, this seemed the least likely. The inhabitants of the train were having similar thoughts. Sonic booms shattered windows as tectonic skull plates changed position.

Beyond a certain reach he began losing integrity. Dilating blood vessels tore and brain canals broke. Veins whipped open, hosing the town and tangling with spires. An eye burst like a water-bomb. A tumbling onward wall of cortex was rolling through its own pink rain, proportions stretching, blasting through whole blocks before exploding finally and washing a cascade of wreckage through the tilted city. His last thought was, *To live past hope, like walking into thin air…*

A slow-motion shower of shredded brainweb like cotton candy floated down on the ruins. Nerve netting stretched between bridges and towers. Pink scum foamed the river. Seagulls picked at the tangle of disease-ridden flesh in yellow liquid. Streets were clogged with dark, hardened gore. The decade-long task began of clearing the slurried headflesh and dismantling the titanic skull which, rested on its side, was almost a mile tall from cheekbone to cheekbone.

Even dismantled it was inconvenient. As in any conflict, false motives had to be set in place. But with this strange episode, invention failed. Humanity had to use time to evade it, a desperate measure. So, inevitably, Brank was canonised. Once an idea has become universally accepted, it's easily ignored.

God-Box

Stav Sherez

There's this Jew that's been after me. A woman.

How she finds me, I don't know. She leaves voicemail messages at every hotel I pass through. It's always her on the white courtesy phone at the airport, minutes before my flight boards. When I come home from a lecture tour, it's her voice which fills the ribbon of tape in my answering machine. Her handwriting on the plain brown envelopes that stack up on the other side of my letter box. The whorl of her fingerprints marbling the photos within, over the faces of the dead, the headless, the tortured; smudging the broken bodies and telling me she knows.

But not this week. This week she's been quiet. I can only hope she died in a freak accident or clutching her failing heart on the floor of a rented flat, reaching for the phone, not making it. But I know she is alive. I know she will call me or text me as surely as I know she is my burden to bear for this path I've chosen.

'And so, to conclude tonight's lecture, we must remember the fight we are facing. This continuing struggle against their fictions and the wars they propagate. It is our duty to open the box of lies they created and tell it for what it is: a box within a box in which they have hidden the truth. We must take guidance from our hearts, our honour, and from the great past that sleeps behind us like a phoenix.'

A cascading roar ripples through the crowd as it always does on these occasions, followed by a chorus of *Sieg Heil*s and raised salutes as I walk offstage. I light a cigarette and stand in the wings, in the total darkness between the stage and the world, listening to their applause, wondering how much longer this can last.

'Dr Hume?'

A pimple-smeared skinhead is staring at me like a doting schoolgirl.

'Your work, Doctor—'

I cut him short, tell him I have to prepare myself for the press. He *Sieg Heil*s me and marches off towards the crowd.

I can see others coming, young men in faded jeans, shaved heads and beaten-down faces; adorned like primitives with tribal tattoos, carrying copies of my book, the seventeenth paperback edition.

I can't bear it. I turn and make my way towards the toilet they've given me as a dressing room. People claw and grab as I walk past. I manage to filter out their buzz and chatter. It's easier to do that after a lecture. You get so out there sometimes, following the line of your thoughts, watching the rapt audience lapping it up, and then it's just you and the sound of the words coming out of your mouth and nothing else matters, nothing else exists but those words.

I drink two large brandies from a warm bottle someone left me, enclosed in gilded swastika wrapping paper; how pretty. Smoke two cigarettes and think about outside: the press; the supporters; the police; the Jews.

I wonder if she will be there. If I will recognise her, if she will be crying. I button up my shirt, check my hair, put on my newspaper face and walk out.

Flashbulbs are popping, people are screaming and, for a moment, I feel like a celebrity caught with his pants down and a pipe in his mouth. Then, suddenly, it all subsides, the volume diminishes and I can breathe again.

The reporters are pushing their way forward. Their faces look like angry dogs. I turn and face them. It always pays to talk to the press.

'Dr Hume. Is it true that in your new book you claim that Auschwitz was manufactured by the Allies? That the site *itself* was false?'

She looked like she was with the BBC. Strict Catholic glasses and long red hair. Perfect.

'Of course it's true.' This gives me a chance to smile.

She looks momentarily distracted. 'But…but, your evidence has been discredited, how can you…'

'Absence of proof is not proof of absence.'

'Dr Hume,' someone screams, 'we will see you in hell, Herr Doctor.'

I recognise the accent, can always recognise it. The way the words come out mangled as if spoken by a mouth chewing on cheap meat. That thick *Mitteleuropa* accent that has staunchly remained even when those speaking it were now thinned and dispersed.

'*Sieg Heil! Sieg HEIL! Sieg HEIL!*'

A group of my supporters march through, snapping their arms out in time with their footsteps like all good soldiers should. The redhead looks away from me and starts shouting at her cameraman to *film it, film it for fuck's sake, this is exactly what we want.*

I watch the boys do their choreography, practised in a thousand small rooms with no partitions, bare walls and shared facilities. An army of the disenchanted, disillusioned and disenfranchised.

I watch them and I smile as the camera gracefully pans over their triumphal exit, smile at the knowledge of the good they were doing the Cause and of how this smile will look on the evening news.

'Dr Hume, have you any comments to make on the president's visit to Israel?'

I look at the bespectacled young man who's asked the question. I put myself in the frame of his camera and say, 'The president's been making plenty of visits to Palestine, not all of them reported. If you don't see that he's just a stooge for United World Jewry then you're in the wrong business.'

'What's United World Jewry? A dairy company?' the smart-arse comes back at me with.

I give him one of my special smiles, the ones I practised from old photographs. The way Himmler smiles when he's watching a train full of human cargo disappear over the horizon. 'The Jews have always tricked us over money, from the time of Jesus on, and they always will. You think it's a coincidence that Judas is called *Jew*-das? You think that wasn't intentional? A record of the first con? The first stab in the back? Jews are everywhere; human cockroaches scuttling and bumbling along, spreading virulence and ruining good stock. Your viewers need to be informed of the danger.'

He cuts me off, making frantic movements to his cameraman, but that's OK. I got to say what I wanted on the live broadcast, so I was pleased. A good day's work all round.

I ignore the other questions and follow my bodyguards, who have finally decided to turn up, out of the building and into my old Mercedes, the very one Himmler drove.

The Internet is truly a wonderful thing. If you're into Naziana or any of a hundred other forbidden pastimes, that is. If you have the money, time and, of course, the desire to, you could buy virtually the whole of Nazi Germany over the Internet, bit by bit. Like the story of the man whose proclaimed goal it was to recover every single, dispersed piece of the Berlin Wall and recreate it in the middle of the Utah desert, I spend my days in the folly of trying to accumulate as much from the period 1933–45 as I can possibly afford.

These days, with my books being international bestsellers, I get a lot of money from unsigned parties, postmarked from the Gulf states, the Mississippi Delta and the estates of south Leeds.

Some include little letters, usually badly written, telling me what an important historian I am and how they should be teaching my books at school and not that Jew-written crap which had got it all wrong.

Sometimes the letters come from men of obvious refinement and position, not to say wealth and passion. They tell me what an important thing it is I'm doing for *our* people and how in the future I will be accepted as the great visionary I am; but whether the letters come from somewhere in the White House or from a council estate in Blackpool, they always say the same things, encouraging me in my work.

I put all the cheques into a separate bank account which I use to fund my purchases. The cheques are always in the name of a company or corporation and signed by some ghost director. I pay them in and I have no problems, not even with the Inland Revenue. I guess someone up there must be a fan of mine too.

I have four rooms in my house filled with Nazi memorabilia. Half the basement and most of the attic too. I have boxes of yellow stars, Iron Crosses and Hitler coins. I have toilet paper from Berchtesgaden and reels of film depicting the medical experiments at Auschwitz. There are flags and china pots, various autographed editions of *Mein Kampf*, a signed love letter from Adolf to Geli, supposedly marked with the Führer's semen; though, after close inspection, I cannot vouch for that, but I guess time takes its toll on all things.

There are filing cabinets filled with official correspondence, letters of repossession, transit passes and postcards from the work camps. In the attic there are Lugers and daggers with *blood and honour* carved into their metal spines, souvenirs from the Eastern Front, necklaces and belts made of soft body tissue.

I collect everything. Some people only collect Hitler stuff, they're interested in 'specialising'. I even have a contact in Norway who won't touch a thing unless it's directly related to Goebbels, but for me anything and everything is fair game.

It's what I have to look forward to after a long lecture tour.

But when I get home, it's her voice which greets me. Like a phantom wife, she welcomes me back from my trip, her voice a thin metallic strip of reverb crackling from my answering machine.

'Dr Hume, I beg you...' she says, and then starts crying until finally the machine decides it's had enough and cuts her off.

She does this often.

I get perhaps twelve to fifteen messages from her every week. Mostly she cries. Long, bone-shaking sobs that sound twice as eerie coming from my little speaker. Deep, dry sighs rendered almost silent with grief and loss. Sometimes she tells me that I will burn in hell, that there are special places reserved for people like me.

She quotes Dante and Pasolini and I know that I am in love with her.

The next morning I am lecturing again. Behind me is a projection of the so-called death camp photos. I take out my laser pointer and guide the audience to where the seams are, where the hoaxes are at their thinnest. The spaces between what is and what should be. The audience is particularly rowdy this morning, breaking off into *Heil Hitlers* and *Sieg Heils* every time I mention a German name. I guess we are in the South now and things are different here.

For the finale I take a photo out of a small box that I keep with me wherever I go. I place it gently under the white shower of light from the overhead projector. It's this photo which always brings about the best reaction in my audience. It is a camp photo like any other on first inspection. A line of living skeletons in those familiar stripes, pressed against barbed wire, staring out at nothing.

But there is something about these faces which always brings an audience to its knees with hate and righteous fury. There is something *so* Jewish about the faces of the men and children behind the wire – frozen in this one instant of time, almost caricatures to these skinheads and blond, suited financiers – that it drives them into a rage that shudders the whole auditorium until I am finished.

In particular, there is a tall, needless to say thin, man who towers above the rest in the centre of the photograph. His shaven head and numb look are filled with black-and-white despair. If you look closely you can see he's clutching the cause of that torment – his son, about four months old, almost hidden in the warm embrace of his father, both newly arrived at the camp. There is a wrinkle in the man's nose which tells you he has caught the peculiar smell as the wind changes direction.

It is at this juncture that I usually point to the wristwatches that someone has carefully rendered on to the surface of the photo, on the hand of a man at the edge of the frame or on the little girl at the bottom. Anachronisms seem to convince the audience much more than the list of facts, and it makes them feel good to have 'worked out' how the Jews perpetrated their massive, six-million-strong fraud.

I go through my talk and, as usual, at some point, I fade out and only the words remain. I can vaguely hear the applause but it is far away now, like music from another room.

When it's over I take the photo and place it carefully back into the box.

An old man knocked sternly on my dressing-room door after the lecture. He took his time sitting down and greeted me in German with a strong Black Forest lilt.

He sat there, slowly taking an unfiltered cigarette out of a silver case. His thin, manicured fingers delicately put the cigarette to his lips and he smiled at me.

'Your devotion to the Führer is touching, Dr Hume. He needed a man like you when he was in his prime.'

I nodded, politely, used to this kind of flattery, but certainly intrigued by the man's accent and age, which, at my rough calculation, would have placed him right at the heart of things.

He spat out some loose strands of tobacco and snared me with his eyes again.

'But, Dr Hume, I have to say that *mein Führer* would have been astonished at these claims you are making, at how you have spent your whole career in refuting his greatest achievements. *Our* greatest achievement.'

I tried to say something but he waved me off so dismissively that I didn't even get a word out.

'You young people, I do not understand you. You talk about how you want to wipe the Jews off the face of the earth. You say it is our most pressing priority, you arm yourselves and tell everyone that the day of liberation is imminent and yet you waste your time and career in trying to deny that we very nearly succeeded in doing just that back in 1945.'

'I understand, but how can the Cause gain sympathy when people are bombarded by those images everywhere they look?'

'We are not after sympathy, my dear doctor. We are after loyalty and honour. People do not need to have sympathy with us. They know about the cancerous growth of Zionism and their attempts to control the world. People are no fools. They just need to be shown where the path is. The rest is up to them.'

It took me all afternoon to get over the meeting with the old man. The hate that served him well fifty years ago had only matured like the best wine. I caught a taxi back to the room. Drained several drinks and spent half an hour browsing auction sites, eventually buying several items relating to the Anschluss.

I was just beginning to ease into my evening when she called.

I don't know why I answered the phone. I hardly ever do any more. But there was something about the conversation with the old man, something which had unsettled me.

'Dr Hume?'

'Yes, speaking.'

'I was beginning to think you were just a tape message, nothing more than the words you publish.'

It was strange to hear her voice stripped of the mechanical reverb that always covered it like a cheap fur coat. Unadorned, she sounded like a careless girl. 'You're not crying this time.'

'No, you're right, I'm not.'

'Well, that's good.' I waited but she didn't rush to fill the silence as I thought she would. 'Will you tell me your name?'

'Hannah.'

'It's nice to finally talk to you, Hannah. I've been listening to your messages for nearly a year now. I never thought to pick up.'

'You should have done.' There was no judgement or reproach in her voice, just a statement of fact.

'Why are you talking to me now?'

'Because you picked up. Because it's time.' Her voice turned back in on itself and I thought I heard her suppressing a cry.

'Time for what?'

But, by then, she'd already hung up.

I finally spoke to my ghost and it left me with nothing but the sound of her unaltered voice and the way breath hissed through her lips before each sentence. I hadn't asked her any of the questions I'd rehearsed for this day. I hadn't learnt anything.

The phone woke me. It was 3 a.m. She cried for five minutes, then hung up. I put the phone down and made sure I'd got her on tape.

I'd been recording her messages for the past six months. At first it was on the advice of a friend, *for future evidence against her*, but later…

When the first cassette was full, I started on a second, and it was about halfway through when I realised I was hearing the tapes in a different way. I'd listen to them more and more, in some vague pretence of checking to see whether they were all right, closing my eyes at night and listening to her cry.

It provided a certain balance, a measure of relief, and I found that after hearing her voice, I always slept much better. I began listening to her in the car or on a Walkman, flying between conference destinations. I bought special headphones that pressed her voice right into my ear and I burned the tapes on to CDs.

I listened to what I'd recorded again. I became lost in the grain of her voice as it fell like snowflakes on to the magnetic strip of tape and the way it stayed there, captured in its own plastic box.

I couldn't sleep. I could hear her whispering in the creaking of floorboards and sighing in the wind-stroked curtains. I reached over for the phone and speed-dialled.

'Good evening?'

I gave the woman my password and account number.

'What is it you desire tonight, sir?'

Already I felt better. Sometimes it can be as simple as that.

'Not over five foot five. Black hair. Not thin, not fat. Olive-coloured skin. That's crucial. I want someone with dark shtetl eyes, a sad expression and a black dress. I want her to look like she's just stepped out of a Second World War coffee-table book.'

'She'll be with you in half an hour.'

As with everything else, the more you pay, the more specific you can be.

She was everything I'd hoped for. She looked like a victim waiting for a disaster. The way she slouched in her dress, her shoulders turning themselves in as if from a blow, made me take her hand and lead her inside. I don't let them in if they don't fit. Experience has taught me that it's better to be upfront than face trouble later on. I made her a White Russian. She said she was surprised I kept Kahlua. I told her someone had once left it behind after a party.

There was small talk and silence. There always is for the first twenty minutes. We played the game as we both knew it. Then I asked her.

'I don't do that,' she said, turning away, her hair a black waterfall spilling over her face.

'Money's no object.'

'It's not a matter of money.'

They never want to do it. Which is strange, because you'd think that tying up a client would give them the ultimate power balance and safety assurance. But they just think you're bad news if you suggest it. Trouble. Get out of here now, their radars flash. Luckily, money makes the most deeply held beliefs disappear like snow figures in the rain.

I only felt it as she was tying up my hands. I gave her the fine silk scarves I kept for this purpose. She had the dexterity of a piano player. I thought it was the anticipation which was making me woozy. The rush of blood to the head when I lay down. But when I looked at my glass of Scotch I could see the powdery, white residue that clung to the bottom.

When I came to, she was bending over me. Her hair fell like dark tears on my face. I was naked and the silk scarves I used for their tearability had been replaced by plastic ties. Blood trickled from my wrists and the hair on my chest had been shaved.

'I've been waiting for you,' I said. 'I always wondered how you knew just where to find me.'

She allowed herself a smile, thinking I hadn't seen it. 'As you know very well, Dr Hume, if you make something your life's work, it's amazing what can be accomplished.'

'Yes,' I replied, wondering just how much she understood.

'I am a Jew.'

'That, I know.'

'I have come to kill you.'

'That, too.'

The White Russian stayed in her left hand, steady as a sermon. The smile stayed on her face. 'If you shout, Dr Hume, it will only be worse for you.'

'I assure you, I have no intention of doing that.'

'Good, but don't think that by being compliant you can get out of this.'

'That, I do not. But how, may I ask, are you going to get out of this? I *will* scream. This is a big and busy hotel.'

'That is irrelevant. Only your death matters.'

'If you kill me you can only make me greater. My death will be taken as a call to arms, a validation of my work. Have you even considered that?'

'I have and there are a couple of things I need you to do first.'

She looked at me, cold and steady – so at odds with the languid way in which she moved across the room, the click of her heels on the bathroom tiles, the delicate taper of her ankles.

'These things. Why should I do them? If you've already said you're going to kill me, no matter what?'

'A bullet is much faster than a pair of nail scissors, I think you'll agree, Dr Hume. You really think people will be reading your books, even taking them seriously, in ten, twenty years?' Her mouth looked like something you'd throw away.

'Why not? My books are the truth. People will see that. The old syllabus will be chucked out. It's happened before.'

'Where, in Rwanda? Kosovo?' Sarcasm turned her lip into an upside-down question mark.

'No. But it's happening right now in South Africa. They don't teach history at school any more. There's nothing left to teach. The old syllabus, the books and articles and legends, are chronicles of white settler history. They can't teach that to the children and black history is still too fragmented. A new history is being written, at this very moment – until then, though, history has been suspended. It's as if we've been looking into the wrong box all this time.'

'It's a shame you did not use your intelligence for something more interesting, Doctor.'

'You think I've wasted my talent?'

She nodded and I laughed, laughed so hard I thought the plastic ties were going to split.

'Have you seen the papers recently?'

'What?' she said, the word snapping out like the black tongue of a whip.

'All the coverage of this...' and since I couldn't point, I turned my head towards a table stacked with newly reprinted and freshly signed copies, '...my book?'

'Yes.'

'Aren't you happy?'

'Happy?'

'That it's in the press, in people's minds. Have you seen how many Holocaust documentaries have been on television this last year, since all this controversy broke out? How it's become a subject of debate again?'

There was something in her eyes for just a second, swiftly disappearing as she decided to ignore me and pour herself another drink.

'Have you noticed how suddenly the British press is pro-Jewish? How the Holocaust is a front-page story? And what about the press I get? You think that amounts to much when it comes to recruiting for the master race? Ask yourself, who makes the Nazis? A polarised society is a safer society. Racism has to show its head for it to be effectively cut off.'

'I don't understand you.'

'Yes, you do.' And I knew she did. I could see it in the fervent fire that had led her to this room, and I thought back to what the old German man had said about how it was just a matter of being shown the right path.

'You capitalise on and exploit people's fear and anger. You give them simple solutions for things that cannot be simplified.'

'Yes. Very well put. That is what I do, capitalise on people's anger and fear. I should print that up as a bumper sticker, don't you think? Let me ask you, who made the bigger sacrifice, Jesus or Judas? To die on the cross and be resurrected as the son of God or to be vilified, hated and outcast for century upon century by the very people who would not exist were it not for you having set the narrative of history into motion?

'Of course, I'm not making a comparison here. Don't think me so presumptuous. I was just elucidating a certain point. Imagine, for instance, a young man, a child of the camps who saw his parents die. Imagine he makes a vow that he will forever keep this atrocity in the public mind. Then, imagine he begins to tour, to tell his stories and the stories of the others who survived. He fills out small halls and theatres and the audiences love him. But they are all Jews. Soon enough he realises this. They already believe. His whole act is pointless. His mission was not to keep it in front of the eyes of Jews, who already have it tattooed in their hearts, but in the eyes of Gentiles, and he doesn't see many of them coming to his lectures. And that's when he realises what he has to do.'

'I hate you.'

I thought she was about to cry again but she stood still, her face pulsing with black fire.

'I hate you. *You* turned me into a Nazi.'

'Me?' I was astounded by her remark.

'Yes. You put me in this room and I'm going to kill you, don't have any doubts about that, and I'm going to kill you because I disagree with what you believe, what you write. I never thought I would be brought down to this level and it's for this, more than anything else, that I hate you, Doctor.'

She began to cry.

She took my hand in hers. It felt small and soft like a gift. 'Imagine God as a box to which there is no outside and whose centre is everywhere,' I whispered. 'Then imagine that inside this box is another box with exactly the same dimensions. Say we call this box language. The universe is a box within a box and our solar system a box within a box within a box. We ourselves are boxes within boxes waiting to fall into our final box. If this is so, then we must accept that God too is a box within a box within a box within a box...'

'How can that be?'

'You're asking the wrong questions.'

'Tell me a story. Tell me something I can believe.'

And so I tell her about the man who gave his lover a box of rain and said to her that it contained all the tears that she would now never need to cry. And about the lost Amazon tribe who had captured God and kept him in a box so that when anyone expressed disbelief they could open it up and show them proof. And, as I told her, I saw understanding tremble through her, the clenching of small fists against the shaking tide and the realisation that she fought so gallantly to deny.

It's ten years later and I'm lying in a bed in a cancer clinic in the middle of the Mojave desert, just west of Palm Springs. They like to keep us away from that promise of everlasting youth and vitality, but I think we're all past caring.

The sun shines every day here. They say it is good for you but I long only for the memory of her heat.

She cried for me for five years and then, one day, she disappeared, leaving me no note or clue. We lived together in my house during that time and collected more artefacts which she organised and catalogued while I went on lecture tours around the American South, Germany and eastern Europe. The fire that had driven her to find me served us well in our task.

When she left, I knew it was all over and the house and its contents burned down to the ground one night, sending fine traces of history up into the welcoming air.

Not all the stuff was destroyed, however. The Holocaust museums in Jerusalem and Washington received large, anonymous donations of documents, films, diaries and other matters of evidential importance.

I still listen to the CDs I made of her crying. I listen to them all the time. I have them neatly stacked so the nurses can easily find the ones I ask for. I've filed them in chronological order, from her first whispered death threats and stuttering tears to the full symphony of her grief and then, as we came to live together, to the dry, choking sounds that she made every night as I lay awake in bed beside her.

I long for her more than for the tatters of life I have left. I want her to devour me, to take me away from this disease and this body.

The sun shines all day here. The CD plays all the way through and then starts again. I always hold one of her tapes under my pillow along with the photo, that photo of the man and his four-month-old baby which, for years, burned my hands so badly that I had to keep it in a box of its own.

The only surviving photo I still have of my father, of my childhood.

I think I kept his promise. The one I discovered many years later in a book of diaries published from the camps. I just don't know whether I was right or wrong.

The CDs shine every way you look at them. I'm almost invisible. That's good. That's almost as it should be.

Cruiser's Creek

Peter Wild

what really went on there?
we only have this excerpt

'…Come on,' he says, whining like a surly dog on heat.

'No,' she says firmly. '*No.*'

But she's smiling.

'Definitely not,' she says. Smiling.

Now he's smiling, too. 'Come on.'

He crouches ever so slightly alongside her. His thumb and index finger lightly rest upon the back of her neck.

'Just come look. Just come look-see.'

She says 'no' again, with greater emphasis than previously, but – all the same – she stands and lets him take her hand (the four fingers of his right hand gently brushing her wedding band, aphrodisiac).

He leads her slowly across the office to the row of steel filing cabinets. She knows from experience that each filing cabinet contains drawer after drawer of client information, claim after claim after claim paper-clipped alongside personal data and follow-up evaluations and photographs and…all manner of words and images, each of which is as dry as trapped gas from a thousand-year-old corpse.

He stops and turns to her with that look on his face, the old cat-that-slurps-the-cream look.

She places a hand upon her hip in a way that she understands is both slutty and alluring, and she says, 'What?'

His eyes flick upwards, feigning mild exasperation, as if it was obvious. A file on the top of the nearest cabinet is pushed to one side as he pats it gently.

'The filing cabinets,' he says.

'You don't—' she looks from his face to his hand and back again '—you don't expect me to climb up there, do you?'

He's grinning.

'You've…got to be kidding. We're in an office. Anybody could walk in. I'm not—'

She laughs and shakes her head at the…fucking idiocy of the boy.

'You really don't expect me to have sex with you on top of a filing cabinet in the middle of the morning in the middle of the office. Do you?'

'Not on top,' he says. 'No.'

'Then where?' she says, the humour giving way to…an edge. 'Aw listen,' she says, without giving him the chance to answer. 'I haven't got time. Bewers wants the—'

She gestures towards her workspace, looks at her PC and her chair, which is turned out and facing the doorway.

'—the preliminary evaluations compiled by lunchtime and—'

'Sssssssh,' he says.

'Connie,' he says.

'Con.'

'Look.'

'Look where?' she says, edge inflamed.

He indicates the space at the back of the filing cabinets, a ten-inch gap between the filing cabinets and the wall.

She shakes her head, looks between his face and the gap twice. 'What?' she says. 'You want to have sex back there?'

He nods, that same idiotic leer beaming back at her.

'You've got to be out of your fucking *gourd*,' she says.

He takes each of her hands and draws her a step towards him (but there's still space, enough space, to...excite, enough space to...*tantalise*, and she...feels it, all of her better, prouder instincts in revolt, but still – she feels – the sense of him, the possibility – in the air that fills the space between them).

He says: 'I crave sex behind steel cabinets.'

And the word crave is all it takes. She can feel him in her knees. He *craves* her. She thinks, briefly, of her forty-something husband (his socks, mainly, and how he balls them once used and flings them across the room to rest upon the floor in the kitchen by the washing machine, another steel cabinet), and then, again also briefly, of the young man before her (specifically his cock, his lovely young eager bobbing cock, his cock and his lovely balls, she wants his cock right now, this instant, inside her, rules be damned) and then she dips, looking to unclasp the ankle strap and remove her shoes.

'No,' he says, cupping her elbow. 'Keep your shoes on. Keep everything on until we're back there.'

Lucifer over Lancashire

Nicholas Blincoe

It seemed to me I was getting better looking and my cock was getting longer. It's good to start the week on an optimistic note, especially a grey Monday in the offices of Bolton Works Department, though I knew there were other ways to interpret my gaunt, tanned face and surprisingly weighty penis. I'd just returned from a fortnight in India and where I saw signs of health, others might have seen symptoms of the sickness that kept me glued to my hotel bathroom for six days. Also, an effect of ageing is that skin begins to lose its elasticity, which was why my slack dick seemed a touch longer. The extra length doesn't reflect a change in the size of my erection; perhaps it says nothing but that, one day, my erections may become less frequent.

I'm going back a week, now. I was ten minutes late for the meeting at the Bolton council offices, but kept everyone waiting while I visited the Gents. As I stood at the stalls, holding my cock in a loose three fingers, I caught sight of myself in the mirror and smiled: I looked good and felt fine. Then I remembered that Greg would be in the meeting and felt bad for feeling so cheerful. No one who had known Greg for as long as me would call him an optimist.

I was in Bolton to negotiate a paint contract. The council had asked for tenders and I was offering to supply at a fixed price, over five years. These days, all the councils are run by MBAs who earned their degrees at the local university. The councils are given a discount if they put their staff through the course. After four years of evening classes, essays and away-days, the managers have digested enough theory to know they want paint only when it's needed, because warehouse space costs money. To me, it's a joke: they're the council, all they've got is warehouse space. I'm talking about the northern councils: Rochdale, Oldham, Bury, Blackburn, Preston. If they could persuade anyone to take property off their hands, they would; as it is, they've got spare capacity out of their ears. You have to see the negotiations as pointless, even depressing. I'm not going to get excited about carving up a local works depot, not when I'm doing it on behalf of a multinational and I still have to pay my council tax.

The deal was already set; I was only there for the final negotiations. The head of sales spoke to my secretary, she set my diary. I read through the deal memo on the Thursday of the week before, and thought nothing of it. But there was one point that needed clarification, so I asked Sandy to get hold of a number. I told her, better make sure it's the top guy or we'll be at it all day. She got a Greg Heaton on the line and we talked through the potential problem. At the end of the conversation, I said, 'I used to know a Greg Heaton.'

'It's me, David. Greg Heaton.'

I was taken aback. 'You knew it was me, Greg? Why didn't you let on?' We had just spent forty minutes in conversation. But I was thrown by the tone of voice as much as the fact that he had waited till I spoke up. You couldn't even say that he was cold. He flat-out didn't care: a David he knew, a David he didn't know, either way it was the same.

I met Greg Heaton when he lived in one of the fireman's cottages behind Rochdale fire station. His grandfather had been a fireman. His grandma was still alive, a woman in a nylon housecoat who could do housework sixteen hours a day, as long as she had a mug of tea in her hands. There were three of them in the one house: Greg, his nan and his mum. Even as a ten-year-old, those cottages looked like Toytown to me, but the estate had a nice atmosphere. It was arranged like a racetrack, an outer ring of houses surrounding a paved ring that the kids used as a playground, and finally a core of houses at the centre. That inner ring was great. It had no obvious purpose, except for hanging washing, and most of the women made do with their tiny backyards. It was as smooth as a roller rink, perfect for playing speedway, which was the craze. The UK speedway champion was a local hero, with a house on Manchester Road that you could walk past, see his trophies on the mantelpiece. I always took my bike when I visited the fire station, but we also played footie and, in summer, cricket with spring-loaded stumps set on a metal plate: England vs Pakistan.

Greg was the most popular kid on that estate, no question. He had more energy and ideas than anyone else. The rest of the kids would just scuff around until he decided what they were doing, whether it was organising races or stunt jumps using planks of wood as ramps, or kicking a football into the crowd for mass football matches with all of us piling in. Greg was a bony kid with large, dark eyes and a wonky smile. He was a little smaller than me and looked like his mother, whose made-up eyes were even bigger than his, and whose smile was just as wide but, somehow, kind of helpless. The way she dressed was kind of old fashioned: minidresses and macs, her hair back-combed and lacquered. She always wore false eyelashes. This was the mid-seventies and yet she seemed to be caught in a sixties timewarp. Looking back, it seems all the stranger, because she could only have been twenty-seven: I'm judging by my own mother, who would have been thirty yet seemed so much older than Mrs Heaton. Greg's mum had never been married: I am sure of that, why else were there two Mrs Heatons in the same house? But I don't know what she did for a living except that she took the train to Manchester early in the morning and arrived back, often quite late, in the evenings. I'm guessing that she had a low-level office job. Maybe she was seeing an older man who liked her to look a little glam, a young girl teetering under a beehive.

The fire station and the train station stood on two sides of a flash roundabout with an ornamental lamp-post at its centre, a tapering concrete pillar with a blue-green steel saucer at its crown. On the opposite side of the roundabout to the fire station, there was the Catholic church with its big plaster dome and, next door, St John's RC Primary School. That could have been Greg's whole world, right there, around the roundabout, but he was too adventurous. That's why the two of us got on. In most ways, we were very different to each other; I couldn't keep a football under control, I couldn't bowl or catch to save my life. But I got around. Why else would I have found his estate? I was passing the fire station one day, when all the trucks were out and the station's front and back doors were open wide. As I looked through, I saw the kids playing speedway, so I strolled across the empty, echoing garage space and, leaning on the low wall, asked for a lend of a bike. Greg offered his and soon we were pals, going all over the place together. We cycled across to Heywood, to the foggy overgrown park with the rickety slide, or to Springfield Park where we played on the banana boat in summer and made slides on the frozen pond in winter. We took the bus to Whitworth to try the new plastic swimming pool, though we preferred the old Victorian baths in Castleton. We explored the half-demolished school at the top of Drake Street and broke into the new school they were building at Sparrow Hill. If we cut through the multi-storey by the council flats, eight times out of ten a gang of older lads would try and bang our heads against the tin doors. But we were both tough enough not to care, though Greg was so slight and I wore NHS Joe 90s. Anyway, eight times out of ten, we could outrun anyone who came for us.

What passed for banter, back then, was me calling him a *Provo* and him calling me a *Proddy dog*: as though I even knew what a Protestant was. I had proof that my parents had been to church, because I had seen their wedding photographs, but I doubt they had been inside one since. But that was one of the other differences between me and Greg: we would never go to the same schools. When we talked about older boys – the legends, the nut-jobs – I had never heard of his heroes and he had never heard of mine. The only times I went inside his primary school was Mondays for Cub night. Our Akela was an odd-looking woman who ran a fancy-goods stall on Rochdale market. Year round, she wore a wool army cap and a sheepskin waistcoat. She was an easy woman to joke about, wrinkled and ugly with a huge warty nose. We held back because she tried so hard, though she never delivered on the army manouevres and the knife games that Greg had promised me. I don't know why Greg stayed in the Cubs after I left. My problems began when Akela started taking us on Church Parade once a month. You can imagine, in a pack that contained Ahmeds, Mohammeds, Pavels and Declans, how many of the Cubs were available for Church Parade. It was just me and Akela, dressed in our uniforms, sitting in a pew on our own.

The other thing we could always do, along with every other fire station kid, was watch the firemen practise putting out chemical fires or scaling the fire station tower. There isn't a ten-year-old alive who doesn't like watching his father at work. I used to love going down to the family paint shop, coming through the back door from the yard and walking between the shelving racks of the warehouse to find my dad sitting with a grubby mug of tea, arguing with the reps or the local decorator crews. Watching him at work, I saw another side of him: his language worse and his jokes funnier, at least judging by the way the other men snorted. But still, my dad wasn't a fireman, he didn't wear a helmet or drive a fire truck. The fire station kids got to see their fathers transformed: like waterproof astronauts, testing their breathing equipment under the warm summer sun, shouldering heavy loops of hosepipe and struggling in three-man teams to bring the powerful jets under control. There were mad fires back when we still had cotton mills. When Marland Mill went up in flames, it lit the whole sky. I think everyone in Rochdale was standing in their gardens, staring at the heavens. Then there was the huge fire between Oldham and Manchester that took twenty crews to bring under control. It brought the evening news to a standstill, they just showed the fight live on television. I was in one of the fire station houses with Greg, crowded around the TV set and trying to spot the Rochdale Brigade.

It was Greg who said, 'That's Brian,' pointing to the man swaying at the top of a three-storey ladder.

We wanted to believe him. But how could he tell? Then the camera drew back and we recognised the Rochdale fire chief and, above him, on the back of the engine, the crew pushing the ladder deeper into the fire as Brian sailed above them, using the jet from his hose like a combination shield and sword as he jousted with the flames.

Brian was one of the youngest members of Rochdale Fire Brigade and he lodged with a family on the estate. He was unmarried and had no children, which left him free to be adopted by me and Greg. Brian took it in his stride. He was a big, lovely man who never got tired of us. When he wasn't working, he was happy to have us sitting on top of his motorbike as he fiddled with the exhaust or tuned the engine. We paid him back with constant mugs of tea, courtesy of Greg's nan.

One evening after Cubs, Greg and I were running across the roundabout when we saw Brian's motorbike outside the train station. It was enough to make us stop and turn to find out what he was doing. This is almost thirty years ago, when Rochdale still had the old Victorian station. The ticket hall was enclosed by heavy doors. On the inside, Brian was bouncing from foot to foot on the worn wooden floorboards, smoking a cigarette. Before we could pull open the doors and shout to him, we saw him throw the cigarette and trot to the foot of the stairs. Greg's mum was coming off the Manchester train. Brian was twice her size. I can see him now, smiling and shifting awkwardly. Greg's mum blinking her big, lashed eyes. Her teeth showing in her wide and helpless gawky smile.

When she nodded, Brian flushed pink. They crossed the echoing waiting room together and the doors that we could barely open were loose and light in Brian's hands. As they walked out, there we were: two round Cub caps, two little faces, smiling upwards.

'How's it going, lads?' Brian asked.

'All right. What're you up to?'

'Your mam said she'd like a ride on't bike.'

'Bags us next.'

'OK, lads. But not today, eh?'

Greg's mum put a hand on Greg's shoulder and squeezed. 'Won't be long, love.'

All I can remember thinking is, how's she going to get a helmet over her hair? It was lacquered bigger than any helmet.

It was a chaste courtship. Perhaps it had to be on such a small estate. Greg's mum would come back from Manchester earlier on Fridays and join the firemen and their wives in the Woolpack. Later, she and Brian would head up to the disco at the Grange. This went on for months and Greg never showed he had any problems. The opposite: he loved Brian. His life was becoming entwined with that of the most popular guy in the whole brigade. As Greg was the most popular kid, it all seemed to fit.

The change was sudden. Greg appeared at my door, early. His face was white and his eyes were red. I remember my mother asking if he was all right and he only nodded, when normally he was full of stories and plans. He just hung around the door until I had finished my cereal, refusing to sit down or take a cup of tea.

On the street, I asked him what he wanted to do. He didn't have his towel and trunks, so I hadn't brought mine. Maybe we could go playing in the car park above the shopping centre or climb the monkey rocks. He didn't jump at any of the choices, he only shrugged and sank deeper into his anorak.

We ended up walking to Springfield Park, which took us past Marland Mill. This was a half-formed plan in my mind. Greg and I had seen the burnt-out hulk since the fire, but we had never gone inside. Some of the lads at school had told me of a way in around the back. Mark Hall's cousin had been inside and broken his arm falling through the floorboards. I wanted to see where it had happened. But, as we reached Marland Mill, I slowed and Greg quickened. I had to shout for him to hold up. I touched the stone columns of the loading bay and felt the cracks opened by the heat of the flames. I stared up at the four storeys of boarded windows set into the blackened brickwork and remembered the photographs in the *Rochdale Observer* from the day after the fire, when the windows were hollow casements and through them all you could see were the stray branch of a leafless tree and the low grey sky. I remembered the lines to the school song, the school song of every school I have ever been to: *Among these dark satanic mills*.

Greg said, 'Are we going to the park or what?'

'There's a way in at the back. Let's have a look.'

'No. I don't want to.'

I knew he had something on his mind, but I didn't want to pass up a chance to explore. 'Come on, Greg. I'm going.'

We had to circle the block and drop down a gulley behind a row of terraced houses. The gulley was overgrown with brambles but if we crossed it we could easily get inside. No one had bothered boarding the back of the mill. I led the way. Greg was still holding back.

I found a piece of wood from a fence and beat a path through the gulley. When I hoisted myself through a window, I paused. Greg had followed, but slowly. Now he was stopped five yards from me. I was beginning to feel his reluctance drag on me, but as a frustration more than anything. I couldn't imagine there was anything wrong. So I waved Greg on, and slipped over the other side of the casement.

I was inside the stairwell, looking up through the storeys of the mill to the sky above, framed by the ragged beams of the roof. The floor beneath my trainers was strewn with broken glass, dotted with globs of melted plastic bobbins, kicked or thrown by the kids who had entered the mill before me. I wandered through to the loading bay, which was black with soot and sunless, because the front windows were boarded up. I splashed through a pool of water, left by the fire hoses or by rainstorms. I shouted out for Greg and, when I got no reply, worked my way back around the loading bay to the offices that overlooked the gulley. Greg was gone.

I found him in the stairwell, by the window, staring boss eyed at his feet.

'Let's go up,' I said.

'I don't want to.'

'Why not?'

'What's so great about a burnt-out building?'

It was a stupid question: what wasn't great about a burnt-out building? I said, 'Come on, we'll get up to the first floor where Brian said the fire started.'

'I hate Brian. He's a twat.'

We stood there, for what seemed like ages. A few spots of rain began falling through the open roof. Eventually, I asked Greg if he wanted to come though to the loading bay, where the roof was intact. We sat on the edge of a bobbin skip, with me waiting to hear about his fight with Brian. In the end, I had to nudge him. I asked what was the matter and, slowly, Greg answered that he saw him all the time.

'He lives opposite you,' I said. 'He's going out with your mam.'

'I see him in my head. I see him at night when I'm trying to get to sleep.'

I didn't know what to think. In all honesty, thirty years on, I can swear that I never thought Brian was abusing Greg. I doubt that I was clear on that stuff at the time: on the kinds of men we were warned would wait at street corners with bags of sweets. But I could never believe that Brian was funny in that way. He just wasn't. He wasn't that kind of man. So I asked Greg what he meant. 'You see him how?'

'With my mam.'

'Like...kissing.'

'All of it.'

'Sex?'

He nodded.

I knew something about sex: perhaps more than a Catholic kid. I had seen grainy black-and-white sex education films at school, of chicks and cows, mothers breastfeeding and cartoons of cross-section penises entering cross-section vaginas. The films made such an emphatic connection between the act of sex and the arrival of babies that I assumed my own parents had only done it three times in their lives: once for each of their three children.

'You've seen them having sex? Didn't they go in her bedroom or something?'

'Every time they do it, I see it in my head,' he said. Greg held his mouth so tight, his lips were drawn white, and the words came spitting out. 'Every night.'

'You picture them doing it?'

'I can feel them do it. I feel Brian sticking it in my mum.'

This came out so full of bitterness and pain and knowledge, I knew that Greg had gone somewhere that I never had. He had experienced something that I couldn't yet imagine. But because I couldn't imagine it, I wanted it explained, in detail.

'Like shagging for real? You feel like you're really putting it inside?'

He wouldn't say any more.

Greg never really went back to normal. The popular, lively lad was gone, leaving behind this morose kid with wide, haunted eyes. Once Brian and Mrs Heaton married, they moved away from the fire station. Greg carried on living with his grandma and, for a few years, he reverted to something like normal. He still hated Brian, but rarely saw him. This period lasted until we were about thirteen years old, when Greg withdrew completely, avoiding all his old friends and locking himself in the dark of his bedroom.

I heard this from the other fire station kids, whenever I happened to bump into one of the old crowd. I hadn't proved equal to being Greg's friend. I had moved to the big school, made new friends and lost interest in speedway. We all had, once the local champion broke every bone in his body and retired, soon to be forgotten.

But I knew about Greg. I knew he had gone mental. I would see him occasionally, a dark figure drifting on his own, riding buses or sitting under canal bridges with a fishing rod. We only ever exchanged a few words, both anxious to get away from the other. So that day with the Bolton Works Department was the first we had spent in each other's company in maybe twenty-eight years. And all we spoke about were management systems for paint supplies.

I felt I couldn't leave it like that. At the end of the meeting, I hung about and asked if he had time to get a pint.

When he asked if I was seeing anyone, it would have struck me as weird, if I hadn't already known that Greg was weird. He was a good-looking man, though quite short. He had black hair and piercing black eyes in the Scottish or Irish way, but it came with a kind of squat darkness, as though a heavy cloud had engulfed him.

I told him, 'Me? No, mate. Footloose and fancy free.'

I had broken up with my last girlfriend just before my trip to India and, though the end of most affairs leaves me depressed for months – in one case, a couple of years – this had been a relief. Karen, a name I really dislike, had been a nightmare: she had a fixed idea of what life with a multinational lawyer would be like, and spent her time imagining our detached villa on the Cheshire plain, right down to the outdoor swimming pool with a winter all-weather cover. When I was young, in my early twenties, I knew that I didn't like the girls of my age. So why was I dating twenty-somethings, now that I was on the cusp of middle age? It wasn't as though we had more in common, the older I got. I could only explain it as a kind of inertia, brought on by my return to the North. I had lost touch with my older friends, and the only people who were available for drinks and nights out were younger than me.

Greg nodded when he heard I was single and said he had an hour free. I expected him to suggest a quiet pub, away from the centre of town, but he led me to an Italian restaurant. It was early to eat, but he said he was hungry and, as I took a glass of wine in the empty restaurant, he ate a seafood salad followed by spaghetti vongole. Brain food, I joked: he was eating nothing but shellfish and squid. He shrugged, telling me the negotiations must have left him depleted.

I drove the conversation: it was clear that Greg was not going to, slowly eating his molluscs, his bivalves, his cephalopods. So I told him the story of how my father had conned me into returning home. This was four years ago, when I was feeling lost in London, on account of both my work at a commercial law firm and my love life: the break-up that had taken a full two years to get over. My father seized on my vulnerability and suggested I give the family firm a try: paint and gas wholesales. He told me that he wanted to retire. The truth was, he was negotiating to sell the firm, though I didn't find that out until I quit my job in London. My dad's target figure was a little under a million pounds, and he needed all of it. You know, a million quid provides an income of thirty thousand a year? He couldn't afford to eat into the capital and didn't see why he should pay for a decent lawyer when he'd spawned one. He needed me, and expected me to work for nothing.

I soon realised he had conned me, but I hardly cared. I hadn't come home because I wanted to run a family paint business, I had done it because I was fed up. So I set to work, drawing up the contracts and taking pleasure in a piece of brinkmanship that almost scared my father to death. I got him a million, which was more than the firm was worth, and I impressed the buyers so much that they offered me a job. The head office is close to Chester, where I went to law school. I was out of work, I knew the area, so I accepted. After two months in Chester, I was bored to death and bought an apartment in Manchester. Forget the car journey each morning; it was better than most London commutes. Manchester seemed like an exciting city. Or so I thought. I'd begun to change my mind after a string of wildly unsuitable girlfriends, no matter how dressy and sexy they had all been.

That was my news, and with digressions about my brother and my sister, and my parents' new life in Bournemouth, I brought Greg up to date. All I got from him was a sketched history of his career, the news that his grandmother had died ten years ago, and that his mother was still married but he saw her only two or three times a year. He didn't mention Brian.

I was startled when Sandy asked how I'd enjoyed my drink with Greg Heaton. It hadn't occurrred to me that she would notice as I waited behind to speak to him. It turned out that she had gone for a drink with the other members of the Bolton Works Department and the more they had spoken about Greg, the more intrigued she had become. She would have been interested anyway, watching this large-eyed dark man at the end of the table, punching away at the contract document and making everyone else look as though they were half asleep. Though Sandy was ten years younger than me, she had been married for ever and liked to know all the goss on the hunks, as she said.

'Greg's an old friend,' I said.

'Everyone is scared of him.'

'Because he makes them looks stupid?'

'Maybe because he's new. He's only been in the job a couple of months, and there are all kinds of rumours about why he left Bury Council, and Rochdale before it. Apparently, he's some kind of super ladies' man. Two different times, he was caught out with a colleague's wife and had to leave town.'

I didn't believe this. 'Greg Heaton? You're kidding.'

I was sure that she was wrong. I may have lost touch with Greg before we were thirteen years old, but that doesn't mean I knew nothing about him. There was one night, in my late teens, for instance, when I bumped into another of the fire station kids and we began talking about Greg's breakdown. The other guy, another David, claimed that Greg was seen by educational psychologists throughout his last few years at school, and that his grandmother had sent him separately to see the priests. The outline of his problem was clear, even to two nineteen-year-olds: he had flipped out when someone started sleeping with his mother, and he withdrew completely at puberty. Our diagnosis, two nineteen-year-old experts, was that Greg was queer. We weren't saying this in a sniggering or sneering way: you look around, and you see that someone has to be. According to the figures, one in ten people. We linked Greg's jealousy over his mother with his later troubles, when all his friends started bursting with testosterone and thinking about nothing but girls, and we put it together. Greg was homosexual, and the realisation, or its repression, caused a breakdown. The other David insisted this was the diagnosis of the educational psychologists, though there was no way that he could have seen Greg's file.

Once I saw Greg again, I still kind of thought he might be gay. Not because he asked if I was single. But I found the choice of a restaurant odd: two men, alone, in Bolton. And Greg had a confidence as he ordered: this was from a man who had never lived outside Lancashire. Though he was educated, he had gone through the system slowly, in night classes as he worked his way up through the council. I'm not saying my countrymen are backward, but there is a strong conservative streak in the North. Greg had none of it. This was evident in the meeting, before we even reached the restaurant. He wore a better suit than anyone else on his team, a lightweight grey that suggested the kind that a film star might have worn in the sixties: in some ways, he resembled a short version of Sean Connery. The other members of his team wore dark blue suits that hung off their shoulders like potato sacks. There are ways of explaining this relative sophistication, terms like 'metrosexual', but Greg looked as though he had been dressing that way for years.

I would have suggested to Sandy that Greg was gay, but without telling her Greg's story, I would have come across as a bigot. So I asked, 'What happened, then? Greg had to move because he broke up someone's marriage?'

'That's the story. The woman from Bury turned up at Greg's home in the middle of the night with a suitcase. He refused to let her inside, and she started screaming that he was with another woman. She ripped up half his garden and threw the plants at the windows, and then tried to post her clothes one by one through his letter box. When she wore herself out, she collapsed on his doorstep and started crying. Greg only came out then. He scooped her up and dumped her in a taxi.'

'That's your idea of a ladies' man?'

'Maybe he did have another woman with him. But the point is, when she went back to her husband, it turned out that the same thing had happened in Rochdale. Now the Bolton team are scared that he makes a habit of seducing his workmates' wives.'

An unexpected hitch turned up in the contract. I only saw it as I reviewed the deal with the other directors, and I was the only one to notice. They did wonder why I suddenly went quiet. Rather than come clean, I excused myself, explaining that I needed to double-check something. I felt their eyes on my back as I left the boardroom.

Greg's job, beyond negotiating contracts, is dealing with inventory for the whole of the council's Works Department. Like everyone else in his job, he was under pressure to reduce stocking levels. His aim was to keep warehouse costs down, but there is another side to the argument. It's a question of keeping a tidy ship: management studies suggest that reducing inventory improves effiency, reducing the amount of time taken to process stock. Greg's aim was to order paint only as it was needed, keeping his inventory flowing without bottlenecks or shortfalls. The way he had set up the contract, we had become his warehouse in an odd kind of way, while he had become a channel for everything the council Works Department might need. The hitch in the contract was that – somehow – his stock system had become the only measure of the process. Like a computer virus that takes over your operating system and imposes its own, there was no way of us checking if we were fulfilling our side of the contract. We would receive his demand, but there was no way of us verifying that it had been delivered until it moved out of Greg's hands.

This had a knock-on effect on the clauses detailing the compensation we would pay, if we failed to deliver. The usual safeguards were in place, but they had become meaningless. As long as we used his system, we had no way of proving we had delivered anything.

I couldn't explain how the contract had been rewritten, so I didn't try. I was embarrassed, but I was also genuinely perplexed. I needed to talk to Greg again, but first I called an old law school friend that I had met after moving to Manchester. We had once been close, though our relationship was barely even sexual. When we were at Chester, she was still seeing an old university boyfriend. We spent a few nights in the same bed, but only fooled around. It doesn't sound like much, but it was warmer, and left a longer-lasting warmth, than most of my other sexual experiences.

She was working at a law firm on Deansgate. When I called, her assistant recognised my voice and, laughing, asked if I was planning on giving Joanne another hangover. I was pleased she remembered me; it made me feel a part of Joanne's life. The reference to the hangover reflected the way our few meetings had gone: on the eve of my trip to India, before I finished with my last girlfriend, and the others after my return, a free man. Joanne and I had settled into an echo of our old student life: sitting up drinking and talking until all hours. Though neither had invited the other back home, it was clear that would change soon.

Joanne listened to the problem, and asked if there was any practical reason to use Bolton's management system to track inventory. I offered a fairly innocuous rationale: we were doing his paperwork, Greg had to see that as a benefit.

'But if you receive a demand, and process it using their system, what happens? Does it appear in their warehouses as stock received?'

'It's complicated. We're like the hopper feeding the grain supply. If they demand delivery and their warehouse is closed, then the stock is either with us or with them.'

'But it can't be anywhere in between? It's like that physics problem, what's it called?'

'Schrödinger's Cat. That's it. Until someone opens the warehouse no one can say if the stock is in or out.'

'Then you've got a problem. One way of looking at it is, they could demand delivery when the warehouse is closed for holidays and then claim compensation when you fail to deliver. But, if they take delivery and refuse to acknowledge receipt, you can't do anything. You can't produce your documentation because that's not recognised under the contract. You're dependent upon them, and if they steal it, you can't prove it's gone.'

'That would be crazy. This is Bolton Council. We're not dealing with the Gambinos.'

'How much is this deal worth?'

I told her, over five years, a few million. But we did the same deal all over the country: schools, police stations, council houses, anything that a council was responsible for, almost anywhere in the country, we supplied the paint. If Bolton's contract became the boilerplate, we could face compensation demands from all over the UK. Or we could see our entire output stolen.

'Is the deal signed?'

'Yes. I don't know how I missed it.'

'Maybe you have other things on your mind.'

I admitted that I had – and asked if she fancied a drink some time soon. Or we could go for a meal. I let her know I was free that night and, though she put me off for a couple of days, she was warm and flirtatious.

I called Greg later that day. He came on the phone, saying he'd been expecting my call.

'I don't know how this happened,' I said.

'We laid it out in the meeting.'

I had spent almost the entire afternoon going through Sandy's minutes: it took so long because they were so uninformative. She had noted the relevant clauses, while leaving the impression that we had skated over them without comment.

'It's going to give us a real headache, Greg. I can't see a way out, unless we welsh.'

'Fine. We'll sue.'

'OK, but what are our options? We can't honour this contract. It's either welsh or scrap the whole agreement and start again.'

'Which would suit you.'

'Absolutely. But who else would deliver at our price, on your schedule? If we go into dispute, you're just going to have find some other mug.'

'There are other mugs.' He sounded as though he was chewing something over. 'I tell you what, David. There might be another option. I have to come to Manchester tonight. Do you want to try and work something out?'

'When are you free?'

'I'm busy until seven-thirty. Could you meet for a meal? I won't have eaten.'

He suggested a restaurant in a narrow backstreet off Deansgate: another Italian. I had never noticed it before, perhaps because I avoided the older, family-run places with all the junk on the walls, the bottles caked in wax and the huge, lathe-turned pepper mills. My prejudices eased as I waited, sipping a glass of Aperol in the candle-lit warmth of a corner booth. Greg arrived, and the waiter took his dark mac and hung it on the bentwood hatstand. Beneath the mac, he was wearing another lightweight suit, a neat tie and a white shirt with a thick collar. As he sat, I noticed the collar had a lipstick mark.

I pointed it out.

He looked annoyed, casting his dark eyes down, though it was out of sight, under his chin. Then he brightened, and the lines faded from his forehead. 'You know, I can imagine the bitch did it on purpose.'

Outside of the lyrics of Snoop Dogg, I wasn't used to hearing girls described as bitches. I let it pass, but brought up Sandy's rumours, culled from his team at the Bolton Works Department. Greg shrugged at the words 'ladies' man'.

'I don't know about that.' He snapped his menu shut without reading it. 'You know the way rumours spread. I came to Bolton because it was a promotion, but they're convinced it was because my assistant at Bury found out I was seeing his wife.'

'A guy who worked for you? That must have been nasty.'

He nodded, but I could tell that he didn't think so. Something about his shrug reminded me of that toneless voice he used the first time we spoke. He had been caught shagging the office boy's wife. So what?

He ordered seafood again. As I picked at a lasagne, I tried to steer the conversation back to the contract and the missing clauses.

'Why do you care?' he asked.

'It's my job.'

'Yeah. But it's not going to cost you your job. And even if it did, you could find work anywhere.' He looked bitter. In a sense, it was true: I was law-school trained, he had an MBA from a northern polytechnic. But the bitterness disappeared as fast as the dark look when I pointed out the lipstick stain. As he scooped the flesh out of his clam shells, he said, 'Let's talk about the contract when we finish eating.'

I nodded agreement, but the suspicion was there: he knew he had pulled a fast one. Christ knows how he'd done it, but he had. I wondered if he was trying to punish me because he thought I had escaped, somehow. No matter how often he had moved towns over the past years, he'd remained stuck inside the same old Lancashire landscape.

I waited a while before speaking again. Finally, I asked, 'Do you ever think about the old days, when we used to cycle all over getting into trouble?'

'Probably more than you. That's the last time I had anything like a normal life.'

I hadn't thought it would be so easy to breach this subject. 'What happened to you, Greg? Was it like a breakdown?'

'I don't know what you'd call it, but it wasn't that. I thought it was a curse.'

Again, his voice came in a monotone, though I assumed he was trying to be wry, or perhaps putting a metaphysical spin on a problem that came when he was too young to understand it.

'Someone put a curse on you?'

'That's what I thought. I persuaded my gran to get the priest to perform an exorcism, but it didn't work. The bastard didn't believe I was possessed.'

'Possessed?'

'Cursed or possessed, I didn't know. The priest wanted to strike a deal. He would perform the exorcism if I spent a few weeks talking to him. He made it clear: he wanted to get to know me. I had to trust him first. But that only made things worse. Maybe if he wasn't screwing Mrs Hughes from the primary school, it would have worked out. But he was a priest and, as I got to know him, I spent nights seeing his pale flabby arse thrusting up and down between her legs.'

His account was so similar to the story he had told about his mother and Brian that I was drawn right back to that day in the burnt-out shell of Marland Mill. 'What do you mean, you saw him?' I must have sounded like a ten-year-old again. 'You saw the priest having sex with one of your teachers?'

'Anyone I've ever been close to, I see what they do in bed,' he said. 'Any man, at least.'

'You imagine them having sex?'

He shook his head. 'I don't have any imagination. I just see them do it. Whatever it is they do. And I've seen the lot. The queers, the masochists, the freaks dancing in their wives' tights. The average once-a-week guys who don't know how crap they are. The guys who think they're studs, acting out moves they've seen in porn videos. Everything, in every position, in every situation.'

I sat back in my chair, staring, not wanting to give any sign of what I was thinking. Because I didn't know what to think. Except the obvious: Greg was crazy.

'You don't believe me?' This came as a challenge. 'What's your explanation: a hysterical phantasm? Whatever theory you come up with, I've heard it before. But it's real. If I know a man well, I know what he does in bed. In fact, I know more than him, because I see it from the outside, and I've already seen so much. Why do you think I'm here, tonight? You're my oldest friend, and if you had any sex life at all, I'd have to make you hate me, so that I could hate you back. But I'm in luck, you're loveless and lonesome – and, as long at it lasts, I can stand to talk to you.'

'You set out to make people hate you?'

I tried to make sense of this. Who would go out of their way to be hated? I knew I was dealing with a sociopath, a man who had constructed an elaborate fantasy to justify living like a leper. But even this rationalisation didn't explain the change: how the friendliest kid you could ever meet, a kid who loved being in the thick of everything, could become this bitter and determined loner.

I asked him, 'Do you remember the first time this happened, when your mother started seeing Brian?'

'That's another favourite with the shrinks: a mother fixation. But you know what I thought about Brian. I wanted the guy to be my dad. I thought he was next in line to Jesus.'

It was true. Greg loved Brian and did everything he could to welcome him into his life, right up until the moment he flipped out.

'The next conclusion, right after they hear about Brian, is to suggest I might be queer. Believe me, if you'd seen as many cocksuckers as I have, you'd know if you were queer. Do you want me to describe your first sexual experience? How was your handjob off Quentin Gainly?'

I choked – so hard I almost inhaled a piece of lasagne. Greg was right, though the kid's real name was Stuart, not Quentin. As I struggled to catch my breath, I tried to figure out a rational explanation. I couldn't have been the only kid to get a handjob off Quent Gainly: maybe Greg had too. Maybe Quentin had told him.

'So, are you gay?' Greg asked.

'No.'

'No. With you, it was always Gary's older sister Sally. She let you squeeze her tits, gave you a tug and then never spoke to you again.'

No one had ever known about Sally Forsythe and me. At least, I thought that no one had known.

'You believe me, don't you?'

I didn't know what to think. It seemed easiest to just nod. 'So why did you want to meet me?' I asked.

'Because you're my friend.' The word 'friend' was spat out. It felt like a hard, dull slap. 'At least, you're the last friend I ever had. So this is what I'll do. I'll fix the paint contract, if you move away.'

'Move? Where?'

'Anywhere. Your love life's hopeless now, but it's only a dry patch. One day, you'll get your end away. I want you out of my life, far enough away so I never have to see it.'

'I can't move,' I told him. 'I'd lose my job.'

'Then give it up.'

'And go where? How far is far enough? What about Stoke or Leeds or Kendal?'

'As long as you never set foot within twenty miles of Lancashire, it'll be fine.'

There was an obvious question. 'Why don't you move?'

'It wouldn't matter. You know the play about the doctor who sells his soul to the devil? He says, 'This is Hell and I am in it.' That's the way it is: wherever I am, it's hell. If I stay in Lancashire, at least I'm on home ground.' He cast the last of his clam shells into the bowl set aside, already overflowing with tight brown nuggets. 'I wish I had struck a deal with the devil: I might have got some kind of compensation. I tell you, I'm a wizard with contracts and small print.'

He stood, beckoning the waiter to bring his mac. I looked up at him.

'When do you have to know?'

'Two days.'

He started for the door.

I caught up with him in the street. I had one last question and, although I knew the answer, I needed to hear him confirm it.

'How do you make people hate you?'

'I screw their wives. It works out: the guys end up loathing me, and I get a minimal, dysfunctional sex life. It's not like I'm a monk.'

'But why do you have to be so alone? If it's just a problem with blokes, can't you find one woman who'll love you and stick with her? Just the two of you?'

'And where are we supposed to live? Do you know any normal woman who would give up her friends and family and live alone with me? And what about our kids? How would it be, when my son grows up, and I see him fucking, every time I close my eyes? Could you stand that?'

He turned and stalked away.

Over the next two days, I kept returning to the contract. I still could not see how he had pushed through a rewrite without anyone noticing: but the clause was so slippery, and phrased so economically, I could only think that I had blinked and missed it. I showed Joanne the contract and she told me she had never seen anything like it. She was convinced that no one would introduce such a clause, unless they intended to rob a company blind.

And she took me back to her house.

It was a beauty, a large Victorian house that backed on to Prestwich golf course, the suburb where she was born. She kept it after her divorce and, though she claimed the mortgage was killing her, it was obvious that she would hate to live anywhere else. She admitted that the house had never felt like her husband's: it was hers alone, bought and decorated in the expectation of another life. She trailed off as she said this and I knew why. She meant another man, a new husband who she could build a family with.

I knew I was in love. I'd loved Joanne from way back, though I had tried to squash my feelings because she refused to cut her ties with her old boyfriend. But when she led me to her bedroom, even as we made love, I saw Greg Heaton's face. Not in the way he would claim to see mine: I just imagined him in the air and I dreaded him. But it had been two days since our meeting at the restaurant, just long enough for his story to have lost some of its vividness. And the warmth of Joanne's body helped to keep the fear at bay.

Over breakfast, I made a show of admiring her kitchen, with its sunny windows on the high trees above the golf course. She slurped at a big cup of black coffee, giggling as she squeezed my knee between her two legs.

'Are you sure you would never move?'

'I know when I'm lucky.' She smiled. 'I love my work and I get to live at home.'

'What about your parents?' I had met Howard and Ruth about

fifteen years ago, and found them intimidating, especially at the moments their bright cheerfulness subsided and they began to ponder among themselves.

'They've lightened up a lot since they realised Danny was such a twat.' She named her ex-husband. 'As long as you only see them once a week, Mum and Dad can be a lot of fun.' Then she grinned. 'Asking a lot of questions, aren't we?'

I blushed, then grinned back. Yet I could not stop thinking about Greg Heaton and Joanne picked up on it.

'What is your problem with that guy?'

I could not tell her the whole story, so I invented one, as close to the truth as I dared. 'We fell out at school, and he had some kind of nervous breakdown. Maybe he thinks I wasn't supportive enough, or maybe he thinks I know too much about his past for comfort. But he promised to scrap the contract if I moved away, so we would never have to see each other again.'

'That's crazy. Are you sure he's over his breakdown?'

'Maybe not.' I gritted my teeth: I was coming to the most difficult part. 'He may try and contact you.'

'Me? How does he know me?'

'He doesn't. But if he found out that I'm seeing someone, he might…you know…try it on.'

'He'll try to sleep with me to get back at you? How did you fall out? Did you steal one of his girlfriends?'

This seemed the best story, so I nodded. I did not want to get into any more lies.

I was late into work, partly because I did not want to leave Joanne's house, and partly because I lost my way on the road from Prestwich. Sandy had placed a Post-it note in the centre of my computer screen: 'Call Greg Heaton ASAP'.

I stared at the note for about five minutes and then set off to make coffee. The phone was ringing when I returned.

'Can I put Greg Heaton through?' Sandy asked when I picked up the phone.

'No. Tell him I'm out.'

'I just told him you were in.'

'Then say I'm in a meeting.' I slammed down the phone.

Two seconds later, Sandy was at my office door shouting, 'Never slam down the phone on me again.' Then she stormed out, slamming the door behind her.

This was school playtime and, though I knew I was aggravating the situation, I leaped across my office and rushed to her desk.

'What the hell's the matter with you?'

'What's the matter with me? What's the matter with you? Greg's trying to solve your problem and you're acting like a jerk.'

She glowered at me from the other side of her desk, that wide thick forest of family photos, souvenir coffee mugs bought on holiday and lumpen clay dinosaurs made by her kids. Her eyes were bright and fierce, her lips pursed into a mean little pout – the exact same shade as the lipstick mark I had seen on Greg's collar.

'Oh, bloody hell, Sandy. What have you done?'

'Me? Nothing.'

I let my arms fall to my side, dragging me down. As I turned, I said, 'When Greg calls, put him through.'

I watched as the clock at the bottom right of my computer counted through three minutes.

The phone rang.

'Smart move,' he said when I answered. 'You and your bouncy little Joanne. You couldn't wait just a few days, could you? What did you think, I'd give you a break? I wouldn't destroy a mate's life?'

'Greg. Give me a few more days, please.'

'Too late.'

He put the phone down. All I could hear was Sandy's shallow breathing as she eavesdropped on her extension line. I sat there, waiting for her to speak. It was a minute, at least, before I heard her little voice.

'What did he mean, David? Who's Joanne?'

I shook my head. A pointless gesture: she couldn't see me. 'Sorry,' I said. 'I'll speak to you later.'

There's a Ghost in My House

Clare Dudman

Good. Everything in order. The old ones caught in their high-winged chairs, silent, not moving, hands outstretched on the chintz that has been greased and then polished by their skin to shininess. Their thoughts come at me like waves. They want to know why I'm here, where I come from and why I haunt them now. *Quiet, old ones, enough.* When I let them talk they prattle on about ancient battlefields, a betrayed and murdered lover, and a young girl left to rot in a bricked-up room, but I am none of these things – and all of them. I just am. I wait, dwell, hover, lurk, and when I get bored entertain myself by reminding them of my presence.

I started with a slammed door: one and then another along a corridor, bang, bang, bang. *The wind*, they said, so I started on the corridor above. *Ah, a change in direction*, they said, *that's all*, but I could see it unsettled them. Now I have found out how to set off their alarms, which causes the fat attendant by the monitors to tut and prise herself from her snugly fitting chair and check a couple of the rooms near to her on the first floor. She doesn't bother with all of them. Then she presses another button which calls someone else; the thin long one with a worried expression and the smart uniform, or sometimes the small pretty one who has the same brown curls that used to warm my head (but no longer). The pretty one giggles as if it is a game and searches each room with a lamp. A bluish weak light. Florence Nightingale of the light-emitting diode. You see, I know the words. I keep up.

It's amazing what they can do these days – cupboards that go up and down on their own: a hum and then a breath as the doors open. And the old ones waiting outside totter forward, anxious that they will make it inside this time, get through the doors before they close, the great steel jaws brushing them with their whiskered edges, like a mouth I knew once. They shut and the cupboard moves off, three of them inside, up and up. But they meant to go down. They jab at the buttons on the side with twiggy fingers but nothing happens. The door stays shut. No one says a word. One of them jabs at the buttons again and the cupboard moves. How strange to travel in a cupboard. It is a cell lined with mirrors – in them they can see each other's frightened faces. Down: the floor gives way. They hold on to the sides and one gives a wheezy little cry. The doors open between floors and they peer out at a grey wall of broken ancient cobwebs lit up by the light from the cupboard's ceiling. I allow it to pause just long enough for them to move then make it fall to the bottom so quickly that they crumple against the side.

The fat assistant at the bottom wedges open the doors with a couple of plastic chairs and helps them out. The old woman is whimpering now and the old man is keeping up a wordless moan. The other old one has both bosom and beard and stares silently ahead, the feminine part of her swelling and then shrinking with each breath. When they reach their chairs their heads loll and the fat assistant talks into the small silver packet she keeps with her all the time. *It's the lift this time, it's spooked. Tell Evans to get over here, pronto.*

— 170 —

Time for me to go, but not far, I can be at many places at once but it is easier to be in just one, with just one of the minds, the last one, the most recent, letting her voice swamp the rest. In the dining room the tables are set, the plastic surfaces wiped down, the bottles of sauces arranged in neat clusters in the middle of each one. I pick a bottle up; when I squeeze the ketchup emerges too thick and red for blood but I write with it anyway – what I loved, what I want, my letters too untidy to be read, over the tables, the chairs and the floor. *Tony Blackwell. Tony Blackwell. Tony Blackwell. Bastard, bastard, bastard.* Before I hated you I loved you. I look and I can see you are here, a shadowy image, between the plastic chairs, as you were then, in this place, the music convulsing you, sending you into the air as if the sound is charged, one shot and then another, making you look strange and stiff then transforming you back into air. The chairs topple. Only I am allowed to perform tricks. Why am I still here and he is not? I take the legs of a table and pull. The *Tony Blackwell*s smear into the *bastard*s and before they can come running in at the noise I am gone, the room warm again, all trace of me vanished.

I have more subtle tricks which I save for the night. A ghost does not need to sleep for there is nothing for the mind to order. My memories are clear, surfacing one and then another, the older ones pale, the ancient ones faded to dark grey on grey, the modern ones bright as washed paintwork. All at once an image of new shoes in lime and orange – when I strapped them on my feet I was higher than I had ever been. But I do not need them now. I can go wherever I like: and tonight I choose to go into the rooms where the old ones sleep curled up in their beds like grubs. I prod them into that state between waking and sleeping and they rise. They know exactly how far to walk and when to stop: outside the lift, inside the lift, a few paces forward until they reach their place at the table.

The moon shines in through the windows of the dining room.

The fat attendant has not bothered to draw the curtains. It is an awkward thing to do. If the chairs are not shoved out of the way the closing mechanism breaks as it strains to force the curtains against them. Last time this happened the cost of mending it was deducted from her pay, so now the plump one thinks it safer to pretend to forget. But she is not on duty now. Tonight it is the turn of the thin worried one. She has three children and all of them are wild. At this moment her eldest child is breaking into a house while the youngest is being questioned by a uniformed officer. The middle child is wild only when she dreams and soon she will wake as she always wakes, screaming that she has been killed or is killing; and it is this child who worries the attendant the most. Every hour the worried thin one leaves the book she has been trying to read and with some relief realises it is time for her to inspect the residents. When she walks through the dining room she doesn't see them. She is wondering about the character in her book, whether she is too young for the man she is after and whether he will in the end marry her. Then she thinks about her middle child and thinks of what she might do to keep her safe. Then the old man who is sitting motionless by the window sneezes and at last she stops and notices what is around her. Each chair is occupied with a motionless upright form. Each pair of eyes reflects an image of the moon or a street lamp. Mr James is not wearing his glasses and Miss Roberts is not knitting but Mrs Dutton is still drooling. The attendant automatically wipes her mouth with a handkerchief from her pocket but the old one seems not to notice, then she walks around them examining their faces. Their eyes blink but they do not seem to follow her. She straightens up, hands on hips, her head shifting slightly to take in the scene around her. She has been in the business for over twenty years now but she has never heard of anything like this happening before. Maybe it is a protest; there have been so many problems recently, the lifts, the food and the lack of hot water. Yet they seem so peaceful – except for the open eyes they could all be sound asleep. She stands in front of Miss Roberts and waves her hand in front of her face but the woman doesn't flinch. She tries the same thing with Mr James, then with Mrs Dutton, but neither of them stirs. She stands again for a few moments and pulls her cardigan farther down over her shoulders. It is so cold in here, something must have gone wrong with the heating. She walks quickly over to the light switch and for a few seconds her hand hangs there, her finger on the switch. She shivers. Why is it so cold in here? The muscles in her finger tense then relax again. Maybe it is dangerous to wake them. She drops her hand to her side then reaches across to another button – a large red one proud of the wall – and punches it down with the palm of her hand, then after dragging the cardigan around her folds her arms and waits again. Her teeth are beginning to chatter – maybe it is the strangeness of it all which is making her cold, she thinks, a form of shock.

I do not wait around; she will know I am gone by the sudden warmth around her and the seed of the idea that I leave with her now will burst into growth, a single word sprouting sentences and then paragraphs: ghost.

A ghost is not one thing but many. The voices inside me clamour and clash, each death unsettled and unavenged: the Roundhead killed in battle by a sly blow to his head from a cousin; then before him the great-grandson of a Roman centurion killed by hemlock by a monk who should have known better; and in a time before that a Celt, the less favoured son, replacing his brother, who had been the one chosen for sacrifice – all are subdued and grey, their colour fading against the later ones, who stridently shine as if in a bright light: the small servant girl who was missed only by the jealous uncle who bricked her into a space in the wall as she slept, and then the most recent, the one with the glow-in-the-dark shoes: the one who waited and waits still.

The small attendant with the brown hair and the laugh is called Doris. When the thin one tells her about the ghost she presses her hand over her mouth and walks away with her mouth and mind pressed shut – and that night is the first time I am touched by someone else's spirit.

I am turning on taps in the women's bathroom when I feel it – turning them hard to the left so the water drains the tanks and the valves creak in the loft, and then back again to the right so that the drip, drip, drip makes the old women turn in their sleep with an unconscious annoyance. I am just fine-tuning them for maximum irritation when I know suddenly that something is there beside me, something too cowardly to show his full self and so at first he sends another in his place: an elderly rat with a diseased snout. It touches me and I wince backwards, I cannot help it. *Who are you*, it asks, *what do you want in this place?* Then I feel it reach out and touch me again: a cold hard claw with sharp nails trying to discover a shape, a substance, but of course there is none. I just am. I exist and there is nothing to me: a vapour, less substantial than a cloud, but cold, a coldness that sucks away all heat and makes even this rat eventually withdraw. *I shall come back*, it says, and it does, this time with another spirit – a bird – as featherless and bare as a plucked turkey.

How cowardly they are. They return night after night without letting on who they are and who they represent. Sometimes I hear Doris's name at the back of their thoughts, but she is distant, some part of a conduit that led them here. *Sorrow*, says the rat one time, *I can smell it souring the air*, and the bird agrees, *and a waiting*, she adds, *an impatience*, and then I know that they are close.

They come in the morning when I am busy with the pans and

the dishes in the kitchen – throwing them on the floor when the cooks are not looking, shorting out the fridges and freezers, turning up the gas while they stir, making sure that everything burns, or goes sour.

*We call upon the spirits from the north, the south, the west and the east...*sings a voice in the dining room. *We call upon the Archangel Michael to help us with our task.*

I go towards it. I cannot help myself. The pan I was tipping from its stand rights itself, and the lids settle into place. The cooks look around at the sudden quiet and burst of heat. It is as if something has caught me with a hook and is drawing me close. *Oh great spirit of the north, help us, oh great spirit of the south, hear our plea...*

There are two of them. A small man and a smaller woman standing where Tony Blackwell danced, kneeling beside something on the floor. Around them are the attendants – the fat one, the thin one and Doris, as well as the woman who sits behind the computer screen and swears when I make it freeze, and the one they call Evans – a large man with a desk and filing cabinet. There are two small red patches on his cheek – last night I emptied the contents of the top two drawers on to the floor and he has spent hours putting them back in order on his desk. The small man and woman rise from the ground. His hair is grey and yellow and swept back into a knot at the back of his head. Around his neck he wears a necklace of beads and the long curved tooth of a rodent. Beside him, sheltered by his arms, is a tiny silver-haired woman, hunched, her shoulders like those of an eagle. I know then who they are. The small man's nose sniffs at the air then twitches.

I go closer to inspect what they are hiding at their feet. There is a small silver tray and on it a purple crystal, next to it a feather, a lighted red candle and a small goblet of water. I laugh. What stupidity is this? But when I try to go closer, when I try to pick up the water or blow out the candle, nothing happens. Even the feather stays where it is. Next to the tray is a large drum with feathers decorating the side, three bells of different sizes, a fan made from more feathers and a long thick stick which smokes at one end.

It is here! I know that voice: the voice of the rat, but also of a man. *Your blessings, Archangel Michael,* he says, *guide us in what we are about to do,* and he picks up the drum, slings its string around his neck and soon the boom of his voice is matched by the boom of a drum.

I feel a warmth that cannot come from that small weak flame. They have attracted something to them. Something strong, powerful, good. The small fragile woman with the thin brittle bones of a bird knows it – her face holds the small smug mouth of the righteous.

The drum booms as the man walks and there is something in the sound that shakes me until I am broken into pieces. I shirk from it and from them. The tray covers the ground where I came from and the place to where I would now like to return; it is a weakness in the earth with fissures and long-abandoned spaces where I can go to hide. I look at the tray and will it to shift a little to the side but it does not. I look around me – I cannot stay and I cannot go. I am in every corner of this place, every space: between the threads of the closely woven blankets, entwined in the springs of the chairs and mattresses, and coiled around the spaces inside every television and radio. There is no space free of me. Everything that can absorb me has me but the drum is beating me out.

He uses the stairs, the woman hopping quickly behind him, arrives in the top corridor panting for breath then enters each room quickly, beating the drum into every corner until I am shaken free, into the smoke from the stick that she holds and fans from her so that I choke and wither. I have never known such relentless chasing; even the monks were less persistent. After the drums come the bells: a large bell to exhume me, a smaller one to sweep me into one place, and a small one with an unbearably high note to chase me out. I pass by them like a prediction of fresh snow and they gasp. The warmth that replaces me tells them I have gone and then they follow me down the corridor and into the dining room, my cold air mixing with the warm air to form a haze, and I know they will have me, that there is no place to hide.

There is a figure among the chairs when we get there: almost solid, almost real, strumming a guitar that isn't there, his head lowered, absorbed in the music only he can hear. His right hand plunges down and around with each beat, while his left hand works a complicated pattern on his imaginary fingerboard. *Tony Blackwell!* He looks up. *Bastard!* His mouth opens. *You didn't wait.* I am concentrated now, my essence swept into one place, the colour and smell of me back in the bottle from where I was once poured. *Bastard. You didn't come.* He can see me. I am as I used to be. My last incarnation. *I waited and waited. You didn't come.* I lay on the bed. I watched TV but I mainly watched the clock. The late film spooled through and I got cold and dressed. You didn't come. It was late and I needed you. I had things to say, plans that scared me. So I lined up the bottles I'd bought and drank yours too: two tequilas, two gins, two shots of rum, and then smoked your joint and mine then the two more I had kept back to surprise you. You didn't come. Then the world started moving and I couldn't make it stay still no matter how much I tried, and when I shut my eyes I was so alone I couldn't bear it so I ran and ran until something stopped me. Something too big for me. And so I waited again, my spirit dispersing, mixing in with the rest, becoming ghost. *Where were you?*

And the essence of Tony Blackwell looks down at his hands and sees that they are empty, listens for the music and knows that it is gone, that it never was. There is just him and me and all the others that have gone before me still unavenged.

Go, says the rat, trying to gnaw at my feet. *Leave*, says the bird, and hops to the tray, shoving it back, exposing the place where the ground is weak. So I reach out and grab Tony Blackwell's hand and it is there, as solid and as cold as mine. The drum beats louder and with it the bells. *We are strong together*, I tell him, and I pull him with me. Down and out of sight. Peace, silence, nothingness. The cold earth. A crystal lid.

Edinburgh Man

Kevin MacNeil

If he hadn't touched his whisky, well, at least he knew my work. When I was his age – seventeen or eighteen – I'd been, as far as I can recall, quite like him: skinny, nervous, brighter than average, and achingly, if vaguely, desperate. Moulded but hormonal – a typical islander. Excited and apprehensive about leaving the insular nest. He fidgeted constantly, kept his hooded eyes lowered most of the time.

I tried to see something of his mother in those gaunt features. No; his mother hadn't been birdlike, all jerky and pecky and insignificant the way he seemed to feel, writhing in the hopeless camera of *Leòdhasach* self-consciousness. She had been a vivacious, sultry young woman, whose family was rumoured to have been blemished – in islanders' terms – with Spanish or Portuguese blood. Ah, Alice! She'd understood her power over boys and men fine well and used it to her temporary and her lasting advantage…but what a stunner she was in those days. Had I—? No. Hardly. The thought almost made me smile. But that was probably the drink.

I glugged some more Lagavulin. Now that wasn't cheap, for someone who's about to cross the water from goldfish-bowl high school to the vast international sea-change of university.

'Are you sure I'm not disturbing you?' His words ran together in a quiet, embarrassed blurt. When he spoke his face turned a sharp crimson, as if his talk hurt other people. I watched him swish his glass.

'Disturbing me? With a bottle of Lagavulin? Which, by the way, you can't afford if you're going to be a student, so get the fuck out of that habit right away.' Between breakfast and now, early afternoon, I suppose I'd already had a half-bottle of piss whisky.

'Sorry, Mr MacEwan.'

'Don't apologise for bringing *me* whisky.'

'Sorry—'

'And knock off that grovelling attitude. It's the city you're going to now. Be a man. Be proud of where you're from. That's the problem with this place – all the people here do is kowtow to all the rest. No backbone. Have you a backbone?'

'I, uh, well, I mean…'

'Ah, fuck it. There's plenty valid reasons if you don't. Historical. Cultural. We're the invisible minority in this nation – unheard, unnoticed. Do you know what I mean, Innes?'

'Uh, Angus, sir.'

'How many people in this country can even pronounce the word Gaelic, let alone tell you anything about the language?'

'Um, I don't know.'

'No! And will they teach you that at university? 'Course they won't! Listen to me, man. You're not a bad person. I can see that. Your ole man's the dictionary definition of a fuckwit, but that's OK. You remind me of me when I was me – I mean, young. All right?'

'Uh…yes, sir.'

'Don't sir me! You'll do all your university learning outside of the university, you hear?'

'I'm not sure I—'

'Outside of it! In the real world! Get into the pubs. Get into the streets. What do you think the City of Edinburgh's made up of? Plush little offices for academics to seduce and/or belittle their students? Or streets with real people doing real things, thinking real thoughts in the real world?'

'Well, sir—'

'Hey!'

'Sorry—'

'Hey!'

'I mean…um…well, my mum just wanted me to come here for some advice. With you doing so well when you were at university.'

'Heh heh! Well, look, I did do well at university if it's first-class honours that count, that's the square truth, no boasting about it. Fine. And I can give you advice. Fine. But first you have to accept one thing.'

'Fine.'

I paused. And laughed. 'Good. Speak up for yourself. Also… don't go to university or anywhere else in life with expectations. What do you expect university life in Edinburgh will be like?'

'Well, I…don't have any?'

'You can lie as long as a dead dog lies, Innes, but not to yourself and not to me.'

'I expect it…to be…' He paused and looked down, inward, into the heart of a private galaxy. 'Lively. Full of colourful people. Big conversations. Uh, avuncular professors. Appreciation for learning. Happiness in books and words and exchanges of ideas.'

'You got some of the words, the big words, and you've got all of the expectations that will start to crush you and lead to your downfall.'

He gulped – actually gulped – and shot me a startled look.

'Tell me, Innes, are you scared about leaving the island?'

'Well, a bit apprehensive, yes…'

'I said *scared*.'

'Um…I suppose I am scared. I've never lived on the mainland. I mean, it's all new, I've only known the Lewis way of life.'

'Well, don't be scared, right? That's just like having expectations. Think about it. Just like shyness is a kind of arrogance too – you know, egotism. There's a good student expression for your essays – *different sides of the same coin*.'

He blushed. 'S-some people can't help it.'

I grunted. 'You'll learn to look at things in a different way.'

'Is that how you became an artist? Edinburgh made you look at things in a different way?'

My lips wreathed into an inadvertent smile. 'Now that is a good question. That's a malt whisky of a question.'

'I saw *Glaring Dream* at the Western Isles Arts Centre. I—I could hardly believe it. I loved it!'

Glaring Dream was a work I'd made late last year and had planned on destroying, but what the hell, they practically begged. I completed a 20,000-piece jigsaw – a Mondrian jigsaw I'd commissioned – then painted it all over glossy white. I told some people – because most people hadn't seen much of me for eighteen months – that doing this fiendish pure white jigsaw had occupied me for all that time. I told them that nowadays I dreamed in white, that my dreams had a purity they'd never previously had. Art critics love that kind of shit.

Meanwhile, my newest piece hung lonely upstairs like a sad perfume. It was a diptych. The left plate carried an upside-down map of Stornoway, its street names replaced with the words:

Greybrownblack moorland, hot strong decaff and a banana muffin, Donnchadh Bàn split open in front of you collecting crumbs, a pensive road-digger muscled and lean chinging spades in your head, drunken guts-open conversations at the young-once bar, crofters with no restlessness, no itchy questions, a granddaddy star winking between two ragged clouds, you filling shelf after shelf with packets and tins of youth and bliss, a brand-new sun pouring love into the room, the pearl necklace like a year of strung moons glowing round her neck, the token gesture of midnight bed and that semi-coma of sleepless image-mongering, the previous night's shenanigans coming slowly together like flotsam to the shore, the final Christmas tree glowing contentedly in the corner, its glinting baubles and mint and lavender and vanilla lights hanging like a constellation of childish perfume bottles.

The right-hand plate consisted of an upside-down map of Edinburgh, its street names replaced with the following:

Cabs streaming like fish in the drizzling night, schools swarming with gimmeorelses and fists, streets made of drink, mildly poisonous and finally depressing, Stanley knives glittering with history, dyslexic shopfronts, football scarves turning grown men cold, a dozen sisters with different fathers, rottweilers dragging their arseholes through the streets, notes flying from cobwebbed purses on state-sponsored horses at fourteen million to one, babies glinting with earrings and snot, teenage boys swaggering through malls with alcohol-heavy aftershaves sampling their cheeks, café striplights like cheap neon lighters thrumming your eyes, dry familiar rape, young

*bikes greenly entangled in traffic, all of a sudden glimpsing The
One as the lift doors close.*

Somehow the boy's coming to my house today made me
feel...*implicated.* I remembered Princes Street, Dalkeith Road,
Newington...all those glances that flashed like arrows...those
sexually luminous mainland and American and Continental girls.
And the drink. An old song: *How Edinburgh's grey brewery/made
a man of me, poisoned me slowly.* A vivid memory ran like an old
film through my mind: that autumnal night a tall Italian girl with
hair like raw black silk had taken me back to her flat, concerned
that I was in no condition to find my way home and, drunk
beyond all reticence, I whispered, 'I'm seriously needy right now,'
and she replied, 'That's OK, I'm seriously givey' and I didn't know
whether to be more astonished at her sheer human warmth or her
supernatural command of English. And I wept for the first time in
my adult life—

'Uh, are you all right?'

He looked concerned. He was a good person.

'Yeah, yeah. Just remembering Edinburgh. You'll – you'll go
there a teenager, not much more than a boy – but you'll come back
a man. How long's the course, four years?'

'Four years. But, I mean, I'll be back at Christmas.'

'You might start by coming home each chance you get. Holidays,
long weekends. But the city takes a hold of you. It gets a grip on a
boy from the islands. What are you studying anyway?'

'Ancient History, Latin and Spanish.'

'Well, take it from me, your best friend at university will be
the library. *Read the books you want to read, not the books they
prescribe.*'

'Uh, OK – the library.'

'A library is more than a library. It's a café full of gossiping authors, a cinema full of drama, a silent concert hall, a garage of greasy-engined books, a sports arena, a place of outdoor pursuit, an anytime ceilidh at which people do shut up when you want them to, it's a university that's more democratic and enlightening than the one you'll be enrolled at.'

My head was swimming now.

He looked at his twitching, lap-nested hands. 'OK, I'll spend a lot of time in the library.'

'Good. And study synchronicity.'

'Um…I'll try. Maybe I should be going home now.'

'Home? Home will soon take on a new meaning. Listen, son. Eighteen years ago I was made of starstuff, molecules transfixed by brilliance, the earth was at my feet, especially the Scotland part of it, especially the *Edinburgh* part of it. I went to Edinburgh despite and because – as we students used to say – despite and because of the fact that my friends weren't going there. Most of us from Lewis, male and female, went to Glasgow or Aberdeen. It was the done thing. I went to Edinburgh because the city in my mind and the girls in it seemed to me, ah…hyperactive with possibility.'

I stood up unsteadily. He made to stand up too, but I gestured him to sit down. With a slight sway, I crossed over to the dead fireplace.

'And listen. Don't think that you're dragging to Edinburgh by ferry, bus and train the same sorry person you'll always be. You might meet in your Ancient History class – and don't make the mistake of going to all your lectures – someone who will become a lifelong friend. That's what I should have done.'

I grasped the mantelpiece for some solidity.

'And you'll encounter arrogance on a scale unprecedented in your previous, decent, insular life. Could be the friends you make will be random exceptions. And you will find new ways to hurt.

'And you will learn how to become yourself. But goddammit, not everyone changes for the better. See? I'm a miserable bastard! The drink! The missed opportunities! Good God, don't you know how long it is since I held a woman close—? Ah, forget it.'

'Well, I – I better go. Thank you for the talk. The advice.'

'Disregard it! The only things you need to know are that a city – a city has more choices. That means more temptations. Means more likelihood you'll change from who you are. Think regularly about who you are. *What* you are. And don't for the love of God become like me.'

'But I—'

'But nothing. If you came to learn from me, then all you coulda learned was what not to become. But maybe that's a learning, too. A young man owes it to himself to be happy.'

He looked at me for a moment, actually held my gaze. Maybe something had got through. He started to turn and make for the door. My shambolic feet decided to follow.

At the door he turned to shake my hand. It was bucketing rain out there now.

Apparently I had something more to say. 'I once knew a girl – an Italian goddess with impeccable English and a hug that coulda nearly brought the dead back to life. One night I was with her and I used the phrase "driving rain". *Driving rain?* she said with a giggle. *Where is it going to, in little raindrop cars?*'

He smiled, shook my hand.

'And one last thing. What Picabia – you know his work? – said wasn't wrong. *What I like least in others...is myself.* You take care, Angus.'

He nodded, then turned to leave. As I watched him scuffle among the overgrown garden path, I still felt the warmth of his hand enliven my own, just as the cold in my hand must have transferred to his.

As he passed through my garden gate I had a sudden vision of him emerging on to Princes Street, in the natural urban ebb between two waves of street clamour, and I seemed to hear the distinct din of stressed engines and barking people and cursing and car horns and I recognised the long cacophony of the unhappy, among whom Angus walked, a man among men.

The League of Bald-Headed Men

Andrew Holmes

During the first half of the West End production of *Shrek*, staged at the Lyceum Theatre, and starring H, who used to be in Steps, something began to niggle at me.

It still niggled in the overheated interval, straining to get to the bar with my fat, unintelligent wife and her parents hovering behind me. That man there, in the dark suit. Another over there. Two of them in conversation to my left. There were, it had to be said, a lot of bald men in the bar tonight.

We were sitting up in the gods, of course. That meant one of our party having to contend with the inevitable restricted view. So, unable to see the show properly, I'd taken to staring at the audience – 'people-watching', my wife would probably say, like she'd invented the term. But she would have been wrong. I was working.

I hated my work. It was preferable to my home life, but only just. What I did, I was a proof-reader. I corrected other people's mistakes (my own I had to live with), so it was my habit to seek out, not just errors, but also unwelcome patterns and repetition.

In the end it was like one of those magic pictures you slowly pull away from your face until an image appears. I knew there was a pattern there; it was a matter of seeing it. And in the second half, I did. It said:

H who used to be in Steps, is a cock.

It was spelt out by the bald heads in the audience below me.

How many? I counted. One hundred and twenty of them, spread almost the width of the theatre. One hundred and twenty bald men sitting; their heads spelling out the sentence: 'H who used to be in Steps, is a cock.'

I sat back and laughed so loudly that I fancied Shrek himself paused and looked to the gods. I'd found them. The blogs and Internet rumours were right. At last it was my pleasure to meet the great League of Bald-headed Men.

From Wikipedia:
Roots and beginnings
Shrouded in secrecy and mystique, little is known about the early activities of the League of Bald-Headed Men or its founder, a cancer-sufferer named Pere Jaworzyn (or 'The Father').

Early events, which included 20 or more bald men entering a branch of Claire's Accessories on Oxford Street and asking to try on red woolly hats, were organised by text messages, though as the group's numbers grew, its activities (or 'events') were coordinated by email and a password-protected website.

At the show's end I stood on the pavement with my fat wife and my in-laws, looking out for the bald-headed men. There. One, two, three...I watched them muster nearby, greeting each other with spare inclines of their bare heads. Slowly and silently they flocked – it was almost Hitchcockian. By now, attention on the crowded pavement had begun to shift their way. The bridge-and-tunnel set asking themselves: what are all those bald men *doing*? Until a man approached the hairless group, bald as they were, dressed as soberly as they were, but somehow different, apart, and the bald men began to applaud him, quietly at first, then with greater passion as he drew near, clapping him on the back ('A triumph!', 'Spellbinding!') as he disappeared into their midst. It was him. Pere Jaworzyn. I informed my wife I wanted a divorce, and left to join them.

Over a pint in The Warm Stove I monopolised The Father. The other bald men looked resentful, as though I was the newest and most nubile member of their harem. The pub had been overrun by us.

I told him what I did.

His lips twitched the way Christopher Walken's lips do. As if to say, *Yes? And? Go on.* Wordlessly, he emphasised with a wave of the hand.

'It's because of that I noticed…There's an error in the sentence.'

Lip twitch. Yes. And. Go on.

'It's a sub-clause. 'H, *who used to be in Steps,* is a cock'. You see?'

Smiling indulgently, he said, 'I don't think I do.'

'There really should be an initial comma. There should be two commas in that sentence, so it reads, "H, comma, *who used to be in Steps,* comma, is a cock".'

'And what do you propose to do about it?'

I leant forward. All my life I have viewed the world with the same detachment with which other people watch television. From the other side. My whole life: the years of living safely, of saying yes when I should have said no, of taking the path of least resistance. Until I found myself in a nondescript house, half listening to a chubby woman's plans to fill it with drab things I had to pay for by working in a soul-crushing job I hated. All of that bottled-up bitter frustration went into my next six words.

'I want to be your comma.'

He sipped from his pint of Guinness and sat back in his seat, looking out over the sea of bald heads in the pub.

'Sorry,' he said, 'but I didn't catch your name.'

'Derek. It's Derek.'

'Well, Derek, I'm afraid you can't join the League of Bald-Headed Men.'

My shoulders sank. 'Why?'

'You're not bald.'

A droplet of sweat ran from my hairline and down my cheek. 'But I am,' I said. 'This...' I touched my hair, improvising. 'This is a wig.'

He regarded me, his lips turning up at the corners. 'Then remove it and let's see your head. Your bare head.'

'I can't,' I hissed, leaning towards him as if to impart a great secret. 'I use adhesive.'

He reached to touch my hair.

'It's a human-hair wig,' I invented.

His fingers probed my scalp.

'It's implants,' I improvised.

Later, I pressed polythene-wrapped flowers into my wife's pudgy hands and invented a story that wasn't nearly as pathetic as the truth. When I brushed my teeth that night I could hardly bear to look at myself in the mirror. He was right, The Father, I was not bald. It seemed so unfair.

The following day was Sunday. My wife was watching one of her *Alan Partridge* DVDs, which was less an exercise in watching and enjoying *Alan Partridge* and more to learn the lines for endlessly repeating at a later date, so I excused myself and went into what we call our 'computer room', a small room – I think the previous owners used to keep their Hoover in it. There, I busied myself on Microsoft Word.

On Monday, I approached two women who sat at the opposite end of the office to me. One wore a T-shirt with the word 'Bench' across it; the other was holding a cup of something hot that she blew into. Their conversation ceased as I approached, bearing a clipboard.

'Hello,' I said.

They both stared at me. 'I was wondering if you'd like to sponsor me,' I said, holding the clipboard towards them. On it were two or three names and figures I'd scrawled myself.

'Why, what are you doing?' said one.

'It's my local, The Falcon,' I explained. 'We're having a series of events to support a charity called Tiny Chances, which offers care to sick and abused babies.' I pointed at the Tiny Chances logo across the top of my clipboard. A line-drawing of two huge but caring hands protecting a swaddled infant. 'There are people doing sponsored runs. One lady is going to read a book. And someone's going to be walking in wellington boots filled with dog mess for a day.'

'And what are you going to be doing?' they asked.

'Shaving my hair off. Completely. To the wood.'

Leaving with their signatures, I suppressed my rapture until I reached a toilet cubicle, where I clenched my fists and screwed up my face in silent jubilation. The Father was right, I was not bald, and perhaps never would be. Not without cancer, a monumentally poor diet or stress-related alopecia. But in my heart?

In my heart I was as bald as a coot.

From Wikipedia:
National awareness
After a stunt in which members spelt out the words 'H, who used to be in Steps, is a cock', at a West End performance of *Shrek*, a photograph taken on a mobile phone appeared in a national newspaper, the *Daily Mirror*, under the headline 'Bare-headed cheek'. Shortly after, an ex-member appeared on a BBC2 culture show (albeit in silhouette) and it became clear that the League's clandestine status was under threat. 'We

began to get people wanting to join the League,' said Pere Jaworzyn in a rare interview, 'but people who had failed to grasp what it was all about, which was an expression of brotherhood. The League was supposed to be an alternative to support groups, but where the support and togetherness are not an overt thing – not something you sit around talking about – but implicit. They don't need constant reaffirmation. They just are. Which is the strongest kind of community.

'I guess people were attracted to that, for better or for worse. So I had men who were thinning on top trying to convince me they were bald. Men who had obviously shaved their hair, but badly, so you could already see the stubble coming through, *adamant* that they were bald. Then…at the other extreme, we had men who *were* bald and in theory would have been welcome to join, but who wanted to change the direction of the League. Wanted us to take radical action, like outing celebrities who wore wigs, targeting hairdressers. There was a splinter group in Leeds – that big Yul Brynner face they did. That was never what the League was about. It wasn't a political group. It was never about attacking the hair-world, it was about solidarity. This infighting and divisiveness that came about. They were anathema.'

Two months later I was called into Walter's office.

I knew immediately why I'd been summoned. It was nothing to do with my work, of course – he was at pains to point that out.

'It's…your hair, Derek.'

I passed a hand over my scalp. I'd asked the hairdresser for 'a number one'. My stupid, fat wife had glanced up from learning her DVD of *The Office*, glanced back at the television, then done a double-take at me, open mouthed with shock. 'It's not quite finished,' I informed her, enjoying her abject horror. 'I need to shave it yet, so it's nice and smooth.'

She told me she wanted a divorce, and I made my way to the bathroom. I'd been shaving it smooth ever since.

'I've had it shaved off for charity,' I told Walter.

'Really?' He pushed a hand through his own hair, which was full, it had to be said, like hair belonging to a man in a Gillette advert. 'But it's not just that. It's…your clothes as well.'

I glanced down at myself. Not a pretty sight. 'I'm afraid I'm going through a divorce,' I explained, evenly, 'and my wife's keeping the house. See, I'm living in a bedsit, and I haven't had a chance to buy an iron yet…And the launderette's often full…'

He nodded, as though understanding. 'And there's nothing else? Nothing else you'd like to tell me? Anything on your mind?'

'No,' I said.

He looked at me long and hard before seeming to decide and drawing himself up behind the desk.

'Derek, the money you raised to have your head shaved.'

'Yes.'

'What did you do with it?'

'It went to a charity called Tiny Chances, which helps sick and abused babies,' I told him.

'Yuh. Except that there is no such charity as Tiny Chances, is there? That helps sick and abused babies.'

I said nothing.

'Moreover, there is a pub local to your old home, but it's not called The Falcon, and they haven't held any fund-raising events recently, and they've never heard of you. Isn't that right?'

Still I kept quiet.

'You're a fraud, Derek,' stated Walter.

After he'd finished letting me go, I caught a whiff of my own body odour as I stood to leave.

From Wikipedia
The End of The League
Tragedy struck during the League of Bald-Headed Men's first and only foray into television advertising. This had been a

move opposed by Pere Jaworzyn, but members when polled voted overwhelmingly to appear. Jaworzyn himself is said to have taken part in the commercial reluctantly, claiming the money offered had, in the end, been simply too good to turn down. By now the group's leader was withdrawn, depressed by what he saw as a corruption of his original venture. He had become less involved in the League's events, which had themselves become increasingly commercially oriented.

I was eating baked beans on toast when I saw it.

I was eating baked beans a lot by then. A handwritten sign at my local shop told me they were on special offer, and I didn't give a toss that they'd given beans an apostrophe. So fucking what.

And then it came on the lunchtime news. The League had been in Portugal, or Spain – I forget where – somewhere they don't give a shit about health and safety anyway; somewhere they don't bother fencing off the edges to cliffs.

To make a human Pac-Man, most of the League had had their heads painted bright yellow. With several helicopters filming from above, the idea was that the human Pac-Man would create a stirring but quirky image as it raced towards the cliff edge gobbling up pills, stopping just short of the edge.

That was the theory anyway. But I think you can guess what happened. The human Pac-Man had gone over. Almost the whole thing. Three hundred members who were either killed by the fall, dashed on the rocks, drowned or lost at sea. Among them was The Father.

When the news was over I left for the library, where it took me fifteen minutes on the Internet to find the gruesome footage the UK news did not show. Fortunately, they are not so squeamish overseas. Courtesy of Spanish TV online, I watched the Pac-Man running pell-mell towards the cliff edge, already in the process of splitting up. Some of the bald men had seen what was coming and were attempting either to peel away or stop the charging Pac-Man. But the baldies had built up a head of steam. There was no stopping that Pac-Man, and over the edge it went. The camera, mounted to the helicopter, watched implacably as almost three hundred men with yellow-painted heads tumbled to the sea below, as though somebody had emptied a huge tin of sweetcorn off the cliff. It continued watching as the bald, yellow heads bobbed in the ocean. It watched as the waves crashed them into the rocks, or drew them farther out into the open sea, their arms flailing. It carried on watching, so for me it become a process of picking a head then following its progress, like the game Winnie-the-Pooh had played with raindrops, except with bald men dying.

I watched them die until eventually the footage simply stopped – even Spanish TV had had enough – and I sat back in the library chair, and found myself smiling, clicking to replay the footage. Serves them right, I thought. Fucking bald twats. Who did they think they were?

The City Never Sleeps

Helen Walsh

Every night, round about midnight, I slide open the big sash window in my living room, wedge a book between the frame and the sill lest the wind slam it shut and climb out on to the external fire escape. I steal up four flights of stairs, ducking as I pass under the windows of the people who live above me. I never pry but it still feels like I'm trespassing as I step through the vignettes of lives distilled in the squares of light that spill out on to the stairway.

I live in an old red-brick warehouse in the heart of the city. Right above me, there's a young couple, Vanessa and Nick. Nick's a high school teacher and Vanessa's a nurse. Vanessa is unfairly pretty. She's half Vietnamese, half Portuguese. Enough said. She works the night shift at the Royal. She gave me a shot of morphine in the arse once, the night I was wheeled in with a stab wound. It's funny – I'd lived below her for a whole year prior to that and had no idea she worked there. Nick is the kind of bloke that all girls want as a neighbour – generally, he keeps himself to himself but he was bold and inquisitive enough to interrogate the couple of youths he found lurking in the foyer last week. I saw the lads that same morning, hanging by the intercom. I was on my way out to work. They had nasty, weaselly faces. Black faces. I only mention that because it might help you understand why I let on to them and inadvertently let them in. I couldn't quite bring myself to call the police, wouldn't even allow myself to alert the other residents. That's middle-class guilt for you. Besides, there's nothing in my flat worth lifting.

Anyway, back to Vanessa and Nick. They've been trying for a baby ever since I fetched up here. I know this because their conversations fall in a pitch-perfect camber from their bedroom window into mine. It's not that I'm eavesdropping or anything, but they speak in that loud droning timbre that seems to have become the lingua franca of anyone who's spent time at a university. Too often I'm privy to Vanessa's monthly disappointments before her boyfriend is. Every twenty-eight days, regular as clockwork, I hear her crying on the toilet when she comes in after her shift.

Above them there's a Welsh lad, Llew. There were three of them when I first moved in and then there were two and now there's just Llew. I don't really know that much about him but of all the other residents who live in this block, he's my favourite. I like him because, like me, he often stays up as long as the night. I wonder if he's haunted by the same demons that stop me from sleeping and if the criss-crosses of amphetamine on the top of his vinyl player are the cause or effect of his insomnia. The other night, as I stole past, he was playing 'Sketch For Dawn' by The Durutti Column. I slid my head above the ledge of his sill and watched him pacing the flat for a while. I almost rapped at his window and asked to come in.

An old don occupies the penthouse above him. He calls himself Sanders but his mail reads Sanderson. His entire living room is ranged with wall-to-wall shelves that have warped under the weight of his books. One of his shelves is arranged in a dot-to-dot chronology of existentialist thought – Kierkegaard, Heidegger, Dostoevsky, Nietzsche. Sartre and Kafka. He never has visitors, least not of the platonic variety. His rent boy comes round every other Wednesday. I saw him hunched up over the old man once. The young lad was turned away and I couldn't see his face but his skin was so white, so pale, it looked like you could blow it away. I passed Sanders on the stairway last night. He grunted, not deigning to lift his gaze from the floor. He'd been caught in the downpour and his clothes gave off the musky tang of his books. Sometimes, in the summer, when the night air is cool, he'll throw his windows right open and that same smell will drift up on to the rooftop. And if I listen really carefully, I can hear the static of his old transistor radio hissing in the vent of my near-empty can.

There's always that sense of relief, that slight gladdening of the heart, when I find their lights still on. It's reassuring to think of all that life boring on below, especially when it's raining and cold and the city is threatening to shut down early. That happens sometimes, usually towards the end of summer or the start of the year when the students have deserted the city. I'm no better at dealing with it now then I was the first time it happened.

It was a Sunday, early in September. I could hear the signature tune of *Miss Marple* wafting up from the old don's flat. I was sat up here in my thermals and raincoat, casting yesterday's bread to the pigeons in the square below, when I noticed that the taxis bundling life away from the city were returning empty. It happened so suddenly – almost in the blink of an eyelid – the rain scattered the last drunken stragglers into the night, the pubs closed down, the taxis left. I heard the sound of the TV being snapped off and the brief electronic after-whirr seared my ears as it coasted along the rising veils of silence.

Manchester had closed down.

I ran to the edge of the roof, hoping to see the familiar bars of light from the flats below glistening across the metal stairway, but no one was up. Not even Llew. I was utterly alone – marooned in the dead, looted night. It was a terrible sensation that rubbed all over me. I could feel myself slowly drowning beneath the city's nightmares as they wended their way through the gutted streets, dredging up ghosts and other wraith-like creatures from the banks of the Ship Canal. It was all I could do to stop myself plunging headlong into the square below and opening up the veins of the city.

It was a ram raid that saved me, in the next street along. I heard the screech of tyres, the shattering of glass as it rained out of its pane and then an alarm ringing and ringing. I saw the blue lights of the police vans in the distance, weaving through the city's grid like Matchbox toys. By the time they arrived a sizeable audience had crawled out from their beds and amassed in the square below. Their voices floated up to me, rapid and adrenalised. I could smell the drift of weed. I felt safe, then. Safe enough to move away from the edge of the building where I'd frozen into a half-crouch, my legs spring-loaded and ready to jump. Even as the rubberneckers slunk back to their flats, and the glass was swept away, I was calm. There was still enough commotion to keep the city's heart waxing and waning till daybreak.

I moved here to be close to the city. I was raised in Yorkshire, a little farmhouse on the moors near Craggyfell. There's no light pollution there, none whatsoever, and when night falls it falls hard and heavy. As a kid I always had trouble sleeping, but when adolescence kicked in, there was nothing I feared more in the whole world than nightfall. You see, when it's midnight and the house has been sound asleep for the last two hours and you're wide awake, so awake that you feel chemically wired – and you know there's another six hours to go, six solid hours in the prison of the pure darkness that slips over the windows like a heavy black cowl so you can see nothing out there but the wall of night – all you have for company are the feral acoustics of the moors. Your head can turn on you. It's too much, all that silence – all that time, all that waiting in the restless fat of your paranoia. It can fuck you up. I tried everything – starting with the herbal remedies of valerian, melatonin, tryptophar, the onion cure which involves chopping up a raw onion and putting it in a jar by your pillow, the noise cure which made an unlikely bedfellow out of Radio 4 for a while, and then I sought medical help and whizzed through the whole gamut of harder drugs – Lunesta, Ambien, Eszopliconeto. I even tried smack. Nothing worked. So I came here, to the city, so I would never have to be alone again, and I sit up here to be part of the oxygen that pumps its heart so it never stops beating.

I come up here to keep vigil over the city. To make sure it stays up with me. And sometimes, if it drifts off, to jolt it awake.

On a clear night, the city can be great company – it regales me with its soaps and comedies and Greek tragedies. When something big happens, like the shooting outside the Dry Bar last week, I'll write it down as it's unfolding, then cast the notes loose on the streets before the first fissures of dawn crack through. It gives me a mad mad thrill to think of somebody finding them and reading them before they've been printed as news. I thought about sending them to a publisher once, all my 'Tales from the City', but the endings are rarely resolved; often they're carried off in the neon blue egress of an ambulance or swept up and burnished to urban lore only to surface briefly in the murky pools of the underworld, bandied around at a gentleman's evening, before sinking back down for ever.

There's a feeble moon tonight fighting through the low wash of pollution. The air is still dirty and wet from the morning's downpour. The tower blocks that stud the Salford skyline are still a murky serration. I can just about make out the jaundiced pinpricks of a few windows and I wonder if they are night-watching like me. It's out of term-time at the moment and so I have to be extra vigilant. It's past three and I can feel the blue-black layers of silence bearing down on my shoulders as they descend upon the emptying streets, finding every nook and cranny, slowing the city's heartbeat right down to a deathly pulse. The dance floors and smoky saloons of backstreet pubs have hollowed out now and I can hear the rattle of shutters being pulled down, the evening locked up and sealed away for ever. But I'm safe up here – for a little while longer at least. Human detritus still lurks in the city, spilling in and out of fast-food joints, lurching into roads to hail down already occupied cabs, some of them braving the sharp November night and walking it home. I can't see them, but I can hear the drunken bray of a girls' night out echo round the square below, the halting click and scrape of heels still sticky from the dance floor. A couple of drunken tussles flare up between them then bluster out into harmless riddles. As they near the edge of the square I hear their laughter freeze in the night breeze as danger peels round the corner and slaps them sober. I wait with bated breath for it to start up again. And it does – bolder, louder, stupid with relief. It isn't always like that, though. Sometimes the laughter doesn't return. I'll read about it the next day in the *Manchester Evening News*. A girl dragged into a car. Her mates looked on, horrified, too stunned to scream for help.

I guess I should go down now. I can hear the veils of silence building up, layer upon layer, sucking the life from the city's lungs. The low puttering of the generator from the pub across the road has dissipated in the cold snap and I can see the taxi rank is empty. There's still a few stragglers in the square below, flitting about like stunned bats, but they'll be gone soon – I know this hue of silence too well – this is the final refrain of a city as it shuts down to recharge its batteries. I should go down and keep it awake.

There are all kinds of things I do to keep the city awake. The easiest and by far the most reprehensible involves bricking a shop window or a posh car in one of the residential pockets. It never fails – an incessant alarm will always fill a street. But that's a last and desperate resort. Usually I just go down to the bus station and shake the tramps from their drunken stupors and force them to sit up and share a smoke with me. When it's really cold and they take shelter in the garbage sheds down by the canal I go and hang in the queer loins of the city. There's always some coked-up queen cruising the main drag, not willing to accept that the party is over.

If you're resourceful, if you're well versed in the ebb and flow of the city, then it's not that hard to keep the place breathing. The only exception is January, when clubland takes leave and the snow comes, drugging the landscape, smothering it with its blanket of silence. This is the nick on the calendar I fear most of all. I remember this one time – it had snowed heavily all through the day and come midnight the whole city was mute and empty. My panic spun me from street to street, corner to corner – but there was not a soul around. The snowballs I slammed into windows announced themselves with a barely audible thud. I launched the heel of my boot into the 7–11's window but it was frozen solid. I ran back to my flat, got a knife then went down into the square and stabbed myself in the leg. I slipped the weapon back in my handbag. The wound was superficial but deep enough for my veins to bleed hot life into the frozen arteries of the city and thaw the panic from my bowels. My screams drew people to the windows, and bang! In an instant the city was wide awake and breathing, its heartbeat picking out and mirroring the pulse of pain in my thigh. I saw the blue wail of the ambulance sliding towards me and it felt gorgeous. I felt so close to the city that night, as we guarded each other's secrets, unresolved to the people in the windows who came down with blankets and the random knife attacker whose footprints had already been washed away by the fresh skein of snow.

I latch on to a couple of junkies marching across the square on the balls of their feet, arguing in garbled coils, their eyes starting from their heads as though they might pop out. You used to be able to tell them apart – crackheads and bagheads – the crackheads with their rapid-fire march and the bagheads with their leaning tower of Pisa lurch. But now they're just synergised parodies of each other – a bit of white to go up, a bit of brown to come down. I've been walking alongside them for a good fifteen minutes and it's only now that they notice me, jumping back into their shadows, assaulting me with the foul paste of their breath. I peel off down an alleyway, feeling their dead bulbous eyes drilling the scrag of my neck, a splinter of anxiety worrying its way under my skin as I sense them making after me. But their hacking junkie cough on the next street down tells me they're back on their mission and I'm already a hazy, hallucinatory shiver. Down on Canal Street the night still thumps on behind closed doors. The gritter van is out on the street. My spirits lift. There's enough activity down here to take the city through its final few hours of need.

The rinsed-out bitumen of the sky fades to copper. I can hear the distant buzz of dawn traffic. I make my way home, my head slowing and easing, with each shifting inflection of morning. I pick up a paper from the 7–11. I pass Nick on the stairway. I run myself a deep, hot bath. There's just enough time to tally notes with the morning paper before I get ready for my shift.

The Aphid

Stewart Lee

The first three hairs had appeared upon my chin. Now I would accept my fate. At sunset I was to assume the role of the innocent fool, in an endless story, ludicrous, majestic and exhilarating. I was the seventh son of a seventh son, promised to Pan when at last a man, in a deal done in infancy. I was a hostage to tradition, a clown in a victim's hat. The old golden savages killed their philosophers, to free them of such unreasonable obligations. But we were in a second Dark Age and I was the vessel of the villagers' hopes. It was hard to live in the country. My death would ensure the rising of the crops, the budding of the blooms, the quickening of the sap and the swelling of the nanny goats. I walked a dark corridor, a tunnel of endless outstretched hands, pawing at me, repulsed and aroused in equal measure, priapic with horror.

The village clung to the rim of the mountain, between the threadbare meadows and the low roof of the rumbling clouds. The people were the spawn of the volcano itself, thick and impatient. I did not feel for my compatriots. They sang of legends. I heard only destruction. 'We have the power,' whispered the priests, in secret, 'we must not misuse it. Kill the ugly duckling.' A stupid man, gratefully running towards the spear, would have been ideal. Idiots clamoured for authenticated fragments, a twist of thread from the hem of my garment, a lock of hair. But my former friends shunned me and thought me unclean, soaked in blood, set aside for the hairy host. They kept their distance lest my ill stars should infect them. And from my eyes they could see I knew.

There were no scholars here, no palaces, no lawyers or surgeons, just magicians and dungeons, and I'd been in the pot too long. I had come to deplore my God, with his incomprehensible mutterings, his inconvenient commands. The hoofed idiot, he knew better. He could have saved me with a gesture, come out of the green and be seen. 'Fate is fixed,' said the covert intellectuals, 'and life is cruel and hard. It does not compensate,' but to no avail. I was due to die at the rising of the constellation of Cerunnos. The firmament was both my enemy and my friend. It set my death date in stone, yet, as the moon rose over the Pass of Snakes, I called for an escape route and the stars showed me one. I had observed the razor route over the crags and out into the valleys below, flickering in the waxy light. It was the path from which the traders came, a road that made the villagers shrink in fear.

The tales of terror, which my father told me, had never scared me. Before the moon fell, I had to create a new regime, or die by another man's. On the morning of the day before my execution, racked on my bed all night long, I woke into a richly decorated room.

'Those flowers. Take them away,' I commanded, 'they're only funeral decorations.'

'Do not fear, son. Think how great is Pan's golden assurance,' my father offered. 'Besides, there is not much more time to go. Just fifteen hours for the good of the soul.'

But his platitudes were irrelevant. I had already decided to rewrite the old, endless story. This time, the hero would run into the mountains. The hero would go into the mountains, through the Pass of Snakes, to the valleys below, and the moon would rise over the village and throw shadows upon an empty circle.

'Cast the runes against your own soul, Father,' I said to him at last from my perfumed bed, where he sat with me counting down the hours, 'I shall flee, before the villagers come for their due.'

'You must do as you see fit,' he said. 'Hurry now. Take these gold coins. Know only this. Avoid fat aggressive men and handsome aggressive men. In conflict they disappear overnight with bad backs. Peace is a kite you will never catch. And many have found pleasures in curvaceous women, their undulating curves upper and lower. But what you really need is a glass of cold water. Should you lie or cheat or rob, understand that your decadent sins will reap discipline.' Then he washed the dirt from my eyes. 'All devils are exorcised,' he said. 'Here, let me kiss you. Now go, before they miss you.'

A spiritual king has to rise or perish. And so, my heart clanging in my chest, I slipped between the priests and scurried to the scree slopes, gaining the cover of the crags as the sun set. As I reached the ridge I saw the panic below, as the people scampered from hut to hut, searching for the sacrifice.

'Dear Lord, obstruct their abject search,' I prayed under my breath. 'Let them learn that assumptions do not bring a harvest.'

My feet flapped on the flinty path as I descended to the high valleys. Through alpine meadows and into the moorland I ran, my thoughts only for the core of myself, my family forgotten. For the first few days of my flight I did not dare to rest and pushed on across the peat fields, over the beige heather encrusted with bluebottles, butterfly bedecked, where ecstatic midges hovered. After a week, cooled with brackish water and sustained by shrivelled berries, I left the moors behind me, slowing to a gentler pace in the flood plains, and headed west. There, tinkers told us, were great cities, thousands strong, where I might escape my fate, become a no-man and live by my own rules. They say happy memories leave a bitter taste. I can never go home. Luckily I have no happy memories.

By moonlight, I passed privet bushes and wide-leaved foliage. Faeries flew from the trees, it seemed to me, and wild rose bushes bloomed in the blackness. I fancied I felt Pan's jealous breath upon my neck and thought I saw the burrowmen, and ape things, upon the road ahead. Fiends were on the loose and they followed me through the fields, rubbing their straw hands together, their turnip hearts black with malice. There were worlds of silence in my ears, my head numb, my feet numb, and crow's feet under my eyes. Day by day, the moon gained on me. Perhaps I was a fool to imagine I could outrun astrology, a fool to imagine the stars could be stopped in their tracks. Day by day, the moon came towards me. I slept in ditches, where its cyclopic eye would never see me. The sun rose once more and I awoke, the mountains shrinking at my back. O'er grassy dale and lowland scene I ran, thick skinned, slit eyed, until I saw a red church on a hill, ruined and abandoned, the first sign of human habitation since my flight began. The formless moors gave way to fields as I travelled farther west, into the arable lands, where livestock hugged the high ground and blackbirds shook the hedgerows. The goat god's sighs grew quiet and distant and as I forded a river into the flatlands I wondered if he'd set me free.

Then, on the horizon, a wooden house, a windmill turning and a column of smoke, the smell of bread and bacon. My fatigue enveloped me and I sank to my knees. The landscape refolded behind my eyelids, cracking my mind. Clouds rushed by. I heard the distant laughter of a girl. My face fell slack and my kidneys burned in the small of my back. I lay with my left cheek against the soil, a rabbit's skull on my right, at eye level with the insect world. Three green moths shivered. Cockroaches mouldered in the ground.

Tonguehorns belched fire. Then I heard horseshoes splacking and saw a blood silhouette through the ceiling sky.

'Frankly, I have never been keen on Parmesian carrots with mushrooms.'

I heard the voice of a young woman, grumbling in an unfamiliar accent, and the sound of a plate being pushed away over the surface of a wooden table.

'It's pumpkin soup and mashed potatoes that I want for my Halloween tea.'

'There is no pumpkin soup, love,' said an old man's voice, 'and there's no fucking mashed potatoes neither. And it isn't Halloween yet. If it were Halloween, you'd be ready. And anyway, you have to eat what Cameron says, no two ways about it.'

The girl continued unashamed. 'But pumpkin soup and mashed potatoes have always been my dream. The physician moans about vegetables, but to be frank what I'm keen on is pumpkin soup. Pumpkin soup and mashed potatoes.'

I opened my eyes, and found myself slumped in a hard wooden chair.

'Ah,' said the farmer, turning away from a black stove set into a stone wall, 'you're awake.'

His face was creased and crumpled, his hair a rats' nest of straw. His eyes were brown and watery, his fingers a pointed yellow, but he was well dressed, his trousers neatly pressed, a grey shirt, ironed and buttoned to the neck, and shiny shoes.

'You are a lucky bastard,' he continued. 'I'm the sort that gets out of the bath with a dirty face but you,' he approached me and prodded my chest with a thin finger, 'you, cock, you are lucky. You were lying on the ground, all thin and white and dislocated. If my daughter hadn't found you, you'd be dead.'

The farmer's daughter leaned into view and blocked out the

sun that streamed in at the window. My vision was still blurred but she was too much to take in, three times the size of her father, a pretty doll's head set atop a barrow mound of meat, like something beautiful fattened for slaughter.

'Here,' she said, pushing her plate towards me. 'Eat yourself fitter.'

But I had never been keen on Parmesian carrots and mushrooms either. What I really needed was a glass of cold water.

The farmer did not ask any questions, but explained that I owed him my life. He led me to a rough and simple room and told me I was to be set to work in the fields to repay my debt.

'There's beer in the cellar,' he said, 'but mind you don't drink more than ten pints a day. That's no more than a working man should.'

By day I grasped a scythe and felled sheaves of corn and barley and took the bundles to the barn. The sun lengthened the shadows of the stalks, even as I struck them down. The work was hard, but I could frolic around all night in the green grass behind the house and I was not unhappy. I returned to the farm for meals when summoned by a bell, where I sat and watched the farmer's daughter eat portions five or six times the size of those I was offered. The farmer stoked her like a furnace, returning to the stove every time she cleared her plate, reedy hand-rolled cigarettes shrinking in his mouth as he sucked them thin in concentration and continued cooking. He himself ate only dry biscuits, but he prepared the girl the most sumptuous foods, of which I was allowed a small share. At the end of each meal, the farmer's daughter leaned back and opened her mouth, while the farmer poured a gallon of cold grey-green gruel into her mouth through an iron funnel. I was puzzled by the situation. At night, as I lay huddled beneath blankets, the father's footfalls echoed along the farmhouse corridors, back and forth between the bedrooms. And I dreamed of his daughter, stumbling towards her, as if in flight, my knees knocking.

'Dare you enter my house?' she asked.

I did not.

One afternoon, I misjudged the swing of my scythe and the blade buried itself in my thigh. I limped back towards the farm to bandage it. Blood ran down my bare legs and sloshed in my shoes. A black open-top car was parked by the barn. I crept behind a low stone wall to observe its owner. The farmer stood speaking to a stranger, dressed in a black suit and a black hat. Money changed hands, an indeterminate amount in different currencies.

'The serum gives results,' said the visitor, unloading a crate from the seat of his car. 'Feed her with the finest grain solution. And remember the importance of vegetables.'

'Aye, Cameron,' said the farmer, 'thank you.'

Cameron turned his back and walked into the fields with no apparent purpose, kicking at stones and pebbles. The farmer fumbled with a padlock and drew the heavy doors shut. I waited for him to leave and slid on my belly towards the barn, pressing my eye to a crack in the boards. Inside, between bails of straw and sacks of grain and vats of fermenting solution, a low light cast thin shadows over rubber tubes and iron grilles and layers of plastic sheeting. I heard a sound behind me. It was Cameron, the visitor, swigging spirits from a silver flask. He leaned forward, moved my head aside and took my place at the spyhole.

'Nothing does any good,' he said, with an air of apparent regret. 'I used to grow things, but now it's just faces and brains.'

He offered me his flask. I shook my head.

'Now it's just faces and brains.'

Months passed but, whatever the season, the stalks still sprang up in the fields. My labours were apparently endless. I brought fresh bundles daily to the door of the barn where the farmer gathered them for grinding into the grey-green gruel, but within weeks the fields were full again. The farmer's daughter often rode out to watch me, sitting silently behind me astride a buckling mare as I sweated and strained. We said nothing, but we seemed to have an understanding. One day I came upon her squatting to relieve herself in a clearing of crushed stalks, her head thrown back, her haunches taut. Something was imminent. And from the way the farmer's daughter's eyes appeared to flash at me, I wondered if she was disporting herself for my benefit, or to please herself. And then I realised I did not care, and hid myself among the stalks to delight in her nakedness, untroubled by notions of its intended audience. In truth, these were the finest days of my life.

One evening, in late summer, my labours for the day finished, the farmer's daughter and I walked wordlessly to the perimeter of the farm and looked back towards the mountains, towards the life I had left. The girl had grown bigger in the six months I had served her father, but she moved slowly and surely, with a grace and dexterity that seemed inappropriate to her size. I, however, hurried eagerly through the rocky ground and caught my feet in rabbit holes. Then, amid the sunset squawking of crows, we heard another sound, threading the breeze. Out in the scrubby grass beyond the wheat fields, the farmer stood perched upon a low wall, a small wooden pipe pressed to his lips. He blew tunelessly into it, pausing between notes as if awaiting a response. But it grew dark and he turned and headed back to the house, his hand in his left pocket, his shoulders sunken.

'What is it that he wants?' I asked the farmer's daughter, not expecting her to reply.

But she did.

'Many years ago, my father left his home for the clough, and said goodbye to his infertile spouse,' she explained. 'We all have the desire to leave something of ourselves behind in the world. That is only natural. A deal was struck, and now it must be honoured.'

The next morning, I smelt pumpkin soup boiling on the stove and realised October must almost be upon us.

Winter came and the fields grew cold and frosty, but still the stalks sprang up, even through the thick snow. I never saw the farmer's daughter again after the day she spoke to me in the fields. The farmer and I ate alone in silence, dry biscuits mainly now that the girl was no longer with us, with occasional bowls of thin, watery soup. The farmer said little and spent all day in the barn, returning to the kitchen at mealtimes to unlock the biscuit barrel. His demand for grain to grind grew. I slashed at the stalks all day, but he was always disappointed, and drove me on into the dark. Now I harvested by moonlight, and he worked through the small hours too, dragging the bundles I brought him into the barn, pausing only for periodic visits to the perimeter, where he played his pipe to the empty air.

One winter's night when I was working at the fringes of the farm, where the fields give way to the wilderness, numb with cold, my fingers frostbitten and frozen to the shaft of the scythe, I saw a figure moving towards me among the trees. My instinct was to hide, but something compelled me to stand my ground and meet the stranger head on. The shadow approached from the trees and came to rest a few hundred yards from me, perched on the remains of a crumbled wall. The brown skin of his bare torso shone in the moonlight. The fur on his legs rippled in the night breeze. Sweat hung from his body, splendid droplets on strings. Toes cloven. Teeth squirly and pointy. The tattered velvet cape that fluttered around his shoulders gave him an intermittently gaseous quality. He moved between liquid, ice and vapour, at a speed of three thousand times per second. I had imagined him smaller, somehow, but his body was vast, his chest three times the breadth of my own, his neck a thick log of black meat. Spindrift cloud passed between us and, despite his sudden solidity, he threatened again to melt. But his eyes met mine for a moment and I held his gaze. Then, with a flick of his tail, he was gone.

Cameron came each day now and eyed me with suspicion. Perhaps he regretted what he had said when he offered me whisky in the field. One day in early spring, he arrived later than usual, and the farmer ran out to meet him, waving his arms agitatedly. Something was afoot. I secreted myself among the stones behind the barn, squashed my face against the knothole and settled down to watch. The farmer stood without, blowing his pipe at the setting sun, pressing it to his mouth. Then the doors closed once more and through my slit, in the lamplit barn, I saw Cameron and the farmer, clad now in ostrich headdresses, their faces covered with feathers, orange-red with blue-black lines. The farmer kicked over a row of chicken-wire cages, stuffed with squealing poultry and fidgety rodents. He unleashed the clasps of the containers. Things were brought forward and eaten alive. The farmer's feathered features became layered with blood and fur. Marrowbones were sucked. Cameron performed an obscene dance. The farmer curled on the floor like a snail then rolled on his back and waved his legs in the air as Cameron filled his mouth with straw. They passed the wooden pipe between them, blowing it and laughing until, eventually, they turned their attention to a shape at the back of the barn. Through the darkness, I could just discern its bovine bulk, hanging from rubber tubes, its kicking legs sliding on tarpaulin. From the back it looked like a household pet, a kitten, a puppy, a rabbit grown fat on fondness, but, when it twirled round on the tangled threads, it was revealed to be a three-legged black-grey hog, its flanks twenty feet across, with coiled protuberances and dangling veins. Its colours glowed, ancient and newborn, hissing and kicking, its hackles rising like those of a rat trapped inside a warehouse by a city tide, with brown sockets and purple eyes. A dull orange head lolled on the body, topped with a sprout of hair, ridged, segmented, and, as it turned again, I saw a small pinched face squealing at the centre of a pumpkin-like expanse. The farmer's daughter. Her features were compressed by pumpkin meat, clogging her like a fungus, and she laughed, a lost soul trapped in a Halloween lantern, the body a tentacled mass.

The oil lamps flickered dimly and Cameron lit a match. Fur and feathers floated down and, outside, something scratched around, pawing at the frozen ground. The farmer's daughter did not make a sound. Cameron shivered, his ostrich feathers shaking, and his butterfly stomach rumbled.

'It is approaching,' he said.

Pumpkinhead grew rigid in expectation but she did not seem afraid. And then, untroubled by lock or latch, silent and unseen, the visitor was in the barn. Six hundred pounds of gas and flesh, robes in tatters, it was approaching. Toes cloven, teeth squirly and pointy, gutter sweat, approaching. With lips and tongue abhorrent and knee cups curly, it was approaching. Cameron snatched up a chicken carcass and waved it at the thing, which hobbled on its hoofs, while the farmer blew low notes on his pipe. It seemed they had done this before. The creature followed a trail of smashed rats and broken poultry along the floor of the barn, along a pre-arranged route towards the farmer's daughter, in her pumpkin state, betrayed. And I looked on and remembered the moon, pursuing me across the moors. But perhaps it had not been chasing me. Perhaps I had not been its quarry. Instead, might it not been have urging me onwards, towards this hour, the clown in the victim's hat, ready to make his mark.

When I fled the village on the day of my death it was not an act of bravery, but an act of cowardice. But, looking back on the moment that I kicked my way through the wooden wall of the barn, snatched up the oil lamp and flung it into the dry pile of straw between the goat-man and the farmer's daughter, I am rightly proud of my courage. Cameron and the farmer fled towards the doors in a flurry of ostrich feathers, but the beams above them turned black and crumbled while they struggled with the lock. Cameron was struck on the side of the face, his headdress no defence, and the farmer fell a second later beneath a rain of falling cinders. Pan's eyes met mine once more through a wall of flickering flame and then he accepted his defeat, dissolving in a haze, a cloud of steam where he once had been. I fought my way through the burning straw towards the rubber apparatus which had held the farmer's daughter, but the bonds hung bare and the wall behind her stall had collapsed. Pumpkinhead had escaped.

Behind the barn I followed her trail, a twenty-foot-wide swath of crushed stalks heading away from the burning building, growing ever narrower in the night as it reached the farm's perimeters until, finally, by the low wall where we had watched the stars together, it could no longer be discerned. Then I beheld her, as if in flight, a leafy winding spiral, ablaze in the sky, bedecked in lace, the pumpkin skin falling from her face, two feet tall and shrinking as the wind carried her away.

The sun rose. Cameron's car sat behind the smouldering barn. I climbed in and turned the keys and it spluttered into life. But I'm not going back to the slow life, where every step is a drag. Instead, I will drive west, to the great cities, thousands strong, where I will escape my fate, become a no-man, and live at last by my own rules.

Touch Sensitive

Richard Evans

Outside the seventy-seventh-floor window, snow falls from a cast-iron sky on to a white blanket street, somewhere far below. The city of Kobe is frozen, still as a day from a forgotten ice age. Street lamps peer out, only their tips visible above three or four metres of powder, lighting avenues and boulevards that can no longer be traversed.

Inside the apartment's sealed cocoon it is warm and safe and Takumi Hanada changes his focus to catch his reflection in the windowpane. His features are thin but healthy, lined but not weary, and his short, grey hair is receding slowly, never to return. He turns on his television set to see date and time appear on the flat-panel screen, a subtle reminder of the inexorable procession of numbers. It is 24 January 2030 – just one more week until his sixty-fifth birthday, an anniversary that Takumi doesn't want to think about, much less celebrate. In his mind's eye, an hourglass is slowly running out of sand. He shrugs the image away, sliding into his easy chair while the living room bathes in the television's clarity and definition. Mood sensors adjust the glow from table lamps to lift his sombre frame of mind and the television responds by offering a range of comedy shows for his consideration.

Takumi studies the array of choices but it is the faint whoosh of the *Übertron*, a monorail system linking the spires of the city's numerous skyscrapers, which attracts his attention. It is the only form of transport during the harsh months from November to March, the network of pod-like compartments tirelessly shifting goods and people, a vital blood flow that keeps the ice-covered city alive, somehow. Takumi wonders idly whether it has brought a visitor today, and within an instant an ethereal sound ripples the air and a thumbnail image superimposes itself on the TV screen. A youthful face is waiting at his apartment door. It is Nanami, his only daughter, and Takumi pushes a button on his remote control to let her in.

'Hey, Dad, how you doing?' She peers round the living-room door and winces at the TV blaring from the corner. 'No wonder you're going deaf.'

'You finished work early.' Takumi breaks into a broad smile. 'Come over here and give your old dad a hug.'

He strokes her wavy black hair and feels the cold skin of his daughter's cheek touching his face. The sensation gives him goosebumps.

'Nanami, you're freezing! Why don't you wear the scarf I gave you?'

'Dad, don't start…' She pulls away to slip out of her red overcoat and Takumi performs an unconscious scan, checking for signs of weight loss and for any fresh scars on her wrists. His daughter has an anxious, birdlike physique but he cannot miss the smile that is lighting her pretty face as she slumps into a brown leather easy chair.

'What's up?' Takumi frowns at her.

'Well, I know it's not your birthday for another week…' She carefully slides off her black gloves one finger at a time. '…but I got your present a little early.'

'Oh, you did, did you?' Takumi moves to stand by the window, feigning indifference.

'You want to see it?'

His curiosity is so great that he mutes the TV.

Nanami calls out to the apartment's hallway. 'Amika?' She waits a second. 'Amika – you can come in now.'

Takumi watches as the living-room door creeps open. His face widens in astonishment when a young girl, barely fifteen, stands in the doorway, straight black hair framing her delicate, almond-shaped face. A symbolic red ribbon is tied around the waist of her green silk dress and she holds a small brown suitcase in her left hand. He looks at his daughter for an explanation.

'It's not what you think.' Nanami lowers her voice conspiratorially and speaks from the corner of her mouth. 'She's not a "she" – she's an "it".'

Takumi shakes his head in disbelief. 'You've got to be joking.'

'You want me to open her up so you can see inside?' From inside her coat, she produces an instruction manual with Amika's full-colour face dominating the cover.

He scans the document briefly, seeing notes and diagrams that make him peer even more closely at Amika.

Nanami continues her sales pitch. 'She'll help you look after this place, keep an eye on you in case anything goes wrong. She's eScape compatible, she'll do the ironing – she'll even play that old keyboard of yours.' She gestures to a neglected electronic instrument in the corner of room.

Takumi narrows his eyes. 'Is this your way of telling me I won't be seeing as much of you now?'

Nanami sighs. 'No, Dad, I'll be around every Sunday like always. It's just I want you to be OK when I'm not here too.'

'Must have cost you the earth.' Takumi throws more obstacles in Nanami's path, trying to maintain his air of indifference. 'How can you afford it?'

'I got a bonus – plus they're not half as expensive as they used to be.'

Takumi folds his arms as he watches his unwelcome guest coldly. 'I can look after myself perfectly well. I've got everything just the way I like it.'

'Come on, Dad, just give her a chance…' Nanami's eyes plead with him. 'She won't bite.'

Amika slides the closet door shut and places her hands gracefully upon her narrow hips. Her fingers are long and slender, her olive skin indistinguishable from that of a human counterpart. Takumi is transfixed by the covering of soft hair on her exposed forearms and, lost in silent amazement at the levels of detail present, it is some moments before he notices that her lips are moving.

'I've put the laundry away now – is there anything else you'd like me to do, Takumi?' She has raised the pitch of her voice a semitone.

'Pardon me?' Takumi realises he must have missed her question first time round. He breathes in deeply. 'No…I don't think so.' He checks his watch; it is only 11 a.m. and the day is going so slowly that he wonders whether time itself is winding down.

She seems to await his instructions for a few seconds, settling into a routine of blinking and smoothing out the fabric of her green silk dress. Takumi can't figure out whether she is thinking or not. He runs through a list of his favourite activities – reading, correspondence, tending his aquarium – wondering what his young guest might enjoy. Glancing out of the living-room window to check the weather, he arrives at a decision.

'Do you operate outdoors?'

She smiles demurely. 'As long as it isn't colder than minus twenty degrees Celsius or warmer than sixty.'

'Well then, we could go up on the roof. Nanami used to like that when she was little – there's a marvellous view of the city and the mountains.' Takumi frowns at her thin clothing and waves a dismissive hand. 'You might need a coat.' He shrugs at her. 'If you can even feel the cold, that is.'

Takumi holds the elevator door open and waves his companion out to the roof terrace. 'You go first.' He watches her step cautiously forward, wrapped in a black cashmere jacket, her movements unsteady like those of a newborn animal. He finds himself reluctantly adopting a paternal tone as she passes him. 'Be careful now – it can get very slippery up here.'

Amika nods lightly and smiles as she crunches her way out across the snow-covered surface. She studies a horizon that is filled with an array of skyscrapers, some biomimetic, some traditional, each connected by the *Übertron* rail and all frozen beneath an opaque grey sky. In the distance, the ice-bound, serrated peaks of the Rokko Mountains form an austere backdrop.

'This *is* a great view,' she calls to him.

Her voice is carried by the bitter wind whipping in from Osaka Bay, and Takumi has no idea whether she understands the meaning in what she says.

His gaze follows the path of Amika's small footsteps from the doorway to the waist-high wall around the terraced roof, her lightweight frame barely making an impression on the compacted snow. He waits another moment, stealing some residual heat from air-conditioning vents and the cladding around the building's fuel cell, before sinking his feet into the snow, hands tucked neatly into his slate-grey duffel coat, synthetic boots disappearing reassuringly into the powder.

'I used to be afraid of heights.' He talks over the billowing easterly wind. 'For the first six or seven years that Nanami and I lived here,' he nods towards the elevator, 'I couldn't get past that doorway there.'

Amika tilts her head to one side, as if listening intently.

Takumi shrugs and then offers a self-conscious smile. 'Then I realised that I would be all right as long as I didn't jump off.'

She peers over the edge. 'It's certainly a long way down,' turning back towards him, her brown eyes meeting his, 'and I wouldn't want you to fall, Takumi.'

The concern in her words takes him by surprise, an unexpected chip at something implacable inside him. He looks first at the snow falling from above and then down at Amika.

'You're getting wet.'

She lifts her hand lightly to her head, searching for the moisture and finding the remnants of a snowflake stuck to her fingertips. 'Yes, I am. My sensors are working and it feels funny.' She giggles at the notion.

Together, they watch as the snowflake dissolves into clear water in her warm hand.

The sound of a concert piano fills the apartment late into the evening. It is rich, elegant and resonant. Takumi watches Amika's hands move expertly around the electronic keyboard and then closes his eyes, to be carried away by the soundscape that she creates. Chopin's *Étude in A flat minor* is both wistful and passionate at once in her flawless hands. It has been an unexpectedly good birthday and, for some moments, Takumi forgets where and when he is – the march of time is blissfully absent as the music transcends the invisible frame that defines Amika in his mind. She finishes the piece and he opens his eyes. He is alive on a wave of wonderment.

'That was beautiful. As good as the first time I heard it in San Francisco nearly twenty years ago.'

A sweet smile flickers across her lips. 'I'm glad you liked it.'

Tranquil in his chair, he breathes more deeply than he has in months, or perhaps years. 'That keyboard hasn't been played since Nanami had lessons when she was a little girl.'

Takumi falls silent.

'You talk of her often.' Amika's voice is soft. 'Do you miss her?'

He studies her from behind tired eyelids. 'I do not mean to be so repetitive.' He feels embarrassed. 'I think I miss being a father to her. It was not easy between us after her mother died.' He sighs a long sigh. 'I didn't get everything right.'

Amika turns the keyboard off carefully, barely making a sound. The apartment is entirely still around them, and the snow outside muffles any murmurings from the city.

'It is late and I think I will go to bed now – if you don't need anything else?' She stands up attentively.

Takumi moves involuntarily in his chair. He is uncertain of what he wants to say. He starts to speak. 'Might I...'

'Yes, Takumi?' She waits for his answer, hands clasped demurely in front of her waist.

He looks at her, and then down at the backs of his thin hands. 'Nothing. You go to bed.' He shakes his head. 'I think I must be a very tired old man.'

It is 2 a.m. Takumi cannot sleep. Something invisible and relentless is keeping him awake, an angry ghost that will not let him rest. He steps from his bed and throws on his silk dressing gown as he crosses the cold wooden floor. In a moment, he stands at the door to Amika's room – Nanami's old room. He watches his right hand knock lightly on the varnished wood.

Amika's face appears in the doorway, delicately framed by the ambient light from a bedside lamp. In her white satin pyjamas, she looks as neat as she did when she went to bed, and Takumi wonders whether she has rested at all. She blinks patiently and he doesn't know where to start.

'I cannot sleep and I was wondering…' He smiles at her. 'You may think me foolish, but…' his voice is little more than a whisper. '…But might I read a story to you in bed?' He points to a shelf of children's books on the wall by her bed. 'There are many to choose from.'

She steps to one side for him to enter and smiles. 'I would like that very much, Takumi.'

An old habit makes him look once over his left shoulder as he steps inside. He presses the bedroom door firmly shut behind him as, finally, the angry ghost takes control.

A steel door slides shut behind him and Takumi sits down behind a glass panel. His skin is irritated by the harsh fabric of the prison's one-piece, lime-green jumpsuit, starched to give maximum discomfort. His stomach rumbles but he has no appetite. The chair he sits in props him up but gives no support to the small of his aching back. It is one of many placed in a long row inside a large, windowless hall that reverberates with the sound of subdued conversations. Manacles bind his hands together tightly. He lives in fear of them, as they can emit vicious electric shocks to punish any perceived act of disobedience.

Nanami enters and sits opposite. They are separated by the thick pane of glass, which is perforated by a series of small holes that allow them to communicate. Burly, stern-faced guards watch over the proceedings, ready to respond to the slightest misdemeanour. The room is noisy but Takumi and his daughter are silent. She has removed her red winter coat and has on a white, short-sleeved blouse. With a furtive glance, he can see old purple scars from wounds repeatedly cut into her slender forearms, wounds that are yet to fade. He feels a surge of emotion swelling in his throat and his head hangs down against his chest. The air between them is thick with ancient, unspoken emotion.

'How have you been?' She speaks quietly and does not make eye contact.

Takumi ignores her question. 'I didn't hurt anyone.' His voice shakes with pent-up feeling. 'She's a machine – she cannot even be hurt, so why am I here?'

Nanami's voice stays low and resolute. 'Dad, she is fashioned to look just like a child. When you touched her…that way…it was recorded, stored in her memory.' She pauses for a moment. 'And her memories are uploaded to a central database every night. They think that if you did that to her, then you will do the same to a human child.'

Tears swell in Takumi's eyes, before making their way slowly down the lines of his ageing cheeks, like the first drops of a rainstorm. 'I see now why you bought me the robot.'

Nanami doesn't answer.

He places his head into his tired, bound hands and begins to sob freely for a minute or more. Eventually, he finds his voice again.

'After your mother died,' he speaks slowly and clearly, 'after she died, I would get so lonely.' He shakes his head at the memory. 'The night-times were the worst.'

Nanami begins to sob too, her frail body trembling as tears flow down her face. Finally, she looks up, her eyes red and angry. 'It was the night-times that were the worst for me too, Father.'

My Ex-Classmates' Kids

Matt Thorne

I was delighted when my wife left me. It'd have happened a lot sooner if I hadn't held out for the house. I just had this suspicion there was no way she'd let me keep it if we went through a conventional divorce settlement – even though the mortgage was in my name and we didn't have any kids – so I had to come up with a large enough lump sum to pay her off. And my gambling is a day-to-day thing, a way of life; I'm not looking for the big score, which meant I had no choice but to go to the moneylenders, or rather one of them, my sort of mate Mike, and get him to give me seventy-five grand. The embarrassing thing is, I had to pretend I wanted it for a bet; if he'd known I was giving it to my wife he'd have broken my legs there and then.

So either you already think I'm a wanker or you're wondering what sort of house is worth that sort of risk. And you'll only understand this if you're a certain sort of person, but I think my house is perfect. It's an eighties detached house, a show-home, the only one in an abandoned development not far from Banjo Island. There were supposed to be twenty houses here, running along both sides of the street, but as soon as they finished the show-home, a car

caromed off the road and stapled three builders to a concrete wall. I
read about the incident in a local newspaper and assumed it'd make
no difference to my future accommodation. If I'd been in charge
I'd have stuck a memorial plaque on one of the new houses, or
granted free homes to the widows and their children, but I doubted
the contractors would share my largesse. I'd inspected the show-
home, put down a deposit for my house in the estate and assumed
nineteen other couples would've already done the same.

But then I got the call. The estate was being abandoned, no more
homes would be built, my deposit would be returned to me at the
end of the month. I couldn't believe it. It seemed astonishing that a
bunch of contractors would prove so sentimental. One time when
I was arrested, the policemen decided I was all right and spent the
whole journey back pointing out spots where violent murders or
accidental deaths had occurred: if they pulled down every house
where something horrible happened, there'd be nowhere left for
anyone to live. OK, ordinary people might get a bit freaked out by
this, and I can understand the logic in levelling the lairs of famous
serial killers, but these were brand-new homes, and this was just
one unfortunate accident that happened before the houses were
even built. Even if ghosts did exist, the worst these dead builders
might offer was a few phantom wolf-whistles. It wasn't hard-
hearted to favour the living. All I could assume was that this sort
of accident was liable to occur again, or revealed some flaw in their
planning, exposing a danger they'd never considered. But even so,
they'd already been given permission to build these houses. Why
stop now?

What about the show-home, I asked, what's happening to that?
The caller didn't know, assumed it'd be pulled down. After a brief
discussion with her boss, I persuaded them to let me have it, and
moved in a fortnight later.

Amy didn't share my enthusiasm. She was grateful that I'd found her somewhere to live, but thought it was creepy that our new home was on an abandoned estate. We were yet to be married at this point – I was seventeen, but she was only fifteen, and there were still two months before she came of age – and I spent the run-up to our wedding in the house on my own, getting used to its dimensions. The money for the house had come from my grandfather, who died when I was sixteen. The old man was a miser, but thankfully didn't donate the cash he'd squirreled away over a lifetime of hard work to the Battersea Dogs' Home. Instead he bequeathed the money to my father, who in an unprecedented display of drunken generosity split it into three, giving a third to me, a third to my brother, and keeping the rest for himself. I knew it was only a matter of time before Dad gambled his share away, so I thought it was important to use the cash for a deposit and turn Granddad's pounds into property as soon as possible.

The only thing Amy liked about the house, once she'd moved in, was the hot-air vents it had in each room instead of radiators. She'd pull up the grey metal slats, take off her knickers, tent her jumper over her knees and send so much hot air up her backside that she eventually gave herself haemorrhoids. The whole time she lived here – eighteen years, in total – she was constantly moaning, getting me to do DIY every weekend, which to my mind defeated the purpose of buying a new house, and didn't change anything, as the house defiantly shrugged off any alterations. At first I tried to appease Amy by getting her schoolfriends to come round as often as possible. We threw parties every Friday night, even though in those days I had a civilian job in Great Mills, and was always exhausted by the end of the working week. Amy stayed on in the sixth form for a few months, but her heart wasn't really in it. It wasn't that she found A-levels any harder than O-levels, but she didn't really feel she belonged. Most of her closest friends had already left school, and she fell victim to the kind of social exclusion that separated her from the few who were going to go on to do degrees and get good jobs. I don't mean to get all sociological about this; time was the biggest factor in shaping Amy's destiny. A few years later and almost everyone was going to university, certainly any girls of Amy's intelligence. I might even have considered it myself, in spite of everything I said to Amy about how it was a waste of life. I reckon I've read more than most students, but it might've been nice to have a bit of direction now and then, although I've never had a long enough attention span to stick to one subject at a time.

When we started having parties there was something gloriously adult about it; we felt stupidly sophisticated for a bunch of West Country teenagers. Other students in the sixth form would try to crash our parties, but I'd go over and politely inform them they weren't welcome, and they'd usually leave without complaint – something of a surprise with party-hungry locals in a quiet Bristol suburb. Not to be deep, but they knew they hadn't made the transaction we had, and didn't deserve to share in our payment-plan false luxury. This was 1987: I'd change out of my Great Mills overalls into a suit to host the parties and no one ever said I looked like a twat. I remember earnest conversations about Black Monday, even though the only person I knew who invested in the stock market was my dad, who phoned me up every day to tell me how well he was doing in the week before the crash, and of course lost everything, just as I predicted, appearing on my doorstep to demand I get a loan and give the money to him.

After Amy stopped going to school the parties got smaller and smaller until there were only half a dozen of us. Even then we kept going and probably would've done so for at least another year if it hadn't been for an awkward incident between me and Amy's friend

Kerry. This is what happened. Coming out of the upstairs bedroom, I ran into Kerry, who was standing on the landing and plucking at the crotch of her pink trousers. She blushed when she saw me, bashfully hiding her face behind her dirty blonde curls.

'Can you help me?' she asked, stepping backwards.

'Of course. What's wrong?'

'I knew I shouldn't have worn these trousers again tonight,' she said ruefully.

'They are lovely trousers.'

'Aren't they?' she said, pleased. 'I just refuse to believe that they're broken.'

I always felt nervous around Kerry. I'd never have been friends with her if it wasn't for Amy. It's hard to describe my feelings without sounding snobbish, and it seems ludicrous in retrospect, but there was a strange social barrier between us. It was my mother's fault. From the age of twelve onwards, after something happened between me and my dad that I don't want to write about here, I became a mummy's boy, and although she'd grown up a few streets away from my father, early in their courtship he'd let slip that just a couple of generations back his family lived on Goat Alley, Bristol's most notorious slum. After this discovery, she always considered herself a few social notches above his family, and everyone she encountered in our neighbourhood. Her powers of indoctrination were so great that I felt the same way she did about most people. Obviously my love for Amy meant I ignored anything bad she said about her, but I would see her supposed flaws reflected in some of her friends, especially Kerry and her boyfriend Vince. But at the same time I found Kerry incredibly attractive, and this combination of disdain and desire rendered me awkward around her.

'What should I do, then?'

'Can we go into your bedroom?'

'Of course.'

We did so. She perched on the edge of the bed. 'I'll lean back and you pull.'

'OK.'

She guided my fingers under the flap and up to the small nub of a zip at the top. Once I'd located it, she arched backwards on the bed. I tried tugging, but it wouldn't budge.

'OK?' she asked.

'No. I'm worried if I pull too hard I'll break the zip.'

'I think it needs more of a jiggle than brute force.'

'Right,' I said. 'Is it OK if I put my legs around yours?'

'Of course...if you think it'll help.'

I clamped my thighs around hers, placing my hand on her soft belly. She held still as I tried again. Miraculously, this time the movement worked and the zip came down. I pulled it down slightly farther than necessary, exposing her pink knickers. I suppose it was inevitable that Amy should choose this moment to walk through the bedroom door.

Amy understood that what had happened was relatively innocent, but didn't risk making a joke about it in front of Vince. She was cold with me after everyone else had gone, and I knew that she understood that the temperature of my friendship with Kerry had changed. That essential distance between us had diminished, and it was now possible that either one of us, if bored or resentful, might try to take things farther. I wasn't surprised when she suggested that we didn't bother having a party the following weekend and just stay in with a video and a Chinese takeaway instead. From then on, she always saw Kerry on her own, and I'd have to go to the pub with Vince, who was good company inasmuch as he could drink seven pints without getting sentimental, but was scarcely more interested in me than I was in him. Still, I was touched that Amy cared enough about our marriage to remove the possibility of temptation, and as a mark of respect I didn't sleep with anyone else until over a year later and made certain it was someone she'd never meet.

This was the time when we should've had a baby. But no matter how hard we tried, it just didn't happen. In retrospect, I suppose it might've been our lifestyle, but even if it had helped our chances of conceiving, I doubt either of us would've wanted to ditch the drink, cigarettes or recreational drugs. When I lost my job at Great Mills I couldn't be bothered to find another one and it wasn't long before I followed my father into what we both bitterly referred to as 'the family business'.

When I was a toddler, my parents went up to London to visit my godparents. It was a cosy two-couple friendship – my parents were godparents to their slightly older son and they'd returned the favour with me – and on this evening they put me and Jake into a playpen together and went downstairs to get pissed. Halfway through the evening, my father heard me wailing and the two couples came up to check I was OK. Discovering that my godparents' son was tormenting me by repeatedly bashing me on the head with a plastic hammer, my father demanded that his father make him stop. But my godfather refused to tell Jake to stop hitting me, saying it was only a plastic hammer, couldn't hurt that much, and I should stop being so sensitive. This incensed my father and the two men ended up having a violent fight. After Dad had beaten up his friend, they grabbed me from the playpen and drove all the way home that same evening. I don't know whether it is the real memory of this traumatic event, or the fact that it was clearly such an important incident for my parents that they kept repeating the anecdote and it subsequently lodged itself in my memory, but since that day I've had a terrible fear of being hit on the head with a hammer. Of course, no one *wants* this to happen to them; but I worried that the fact that this was such a vivid terror would make it somehow more likely to happen to me than to the average person.

My parents may've been antisocial, but I'm not much better. I only have one real friend, my mate Friendly. Barry came up with his nickname, claiming it was the name of Edward Woodward's only confidant on the 1970s TV show *Callan*. But when we finally went round to Barry's house to watch the repeats he'd taped off Channel 4, we discovered the character was called 'Lonely', not 'Friendly.' By this time it was too late, the nickname had stuck, but we did rip the piss out of Barry for believing that a smelly stool pigeon in a hard-boiled spy show would have such a soppy name.

Friendly is the same age as me, and also comes from a long line of working-class wastrels – although it seems ridiculous to call either of our families working class as there's always been precious little work going on. He's different to many of the other people I meet in my daily shuffle from betting shop to pub to different betting shop to different pub as he's always got a book (the kind you read) on the go, can occasionally be persuaded to spend a morning or afternoon in the cinema as a break from the normal routine, and is an incredible cook. I didn't discover this last talent until Amy left me and he started coming round every Saturday.

On the night I first met Alison he'd cooked me a delicious chicken curry and as usual we'd sat down to watch *The Shield* when he commented on the distant music that was loud enough to hear through the double-glazing.

'Yeah,' I told him, 'I don't know where it's coming from. It's started a bit earlier tonight but it gets really loud later on. It's the same every week and usually keeps going until Sunday afternoon.'

'But there aren't any clubs anywhere near here.'

'Well, the one possibility that did occur to me is, you know that abandoned infant school.'

'My old infant school…'

'Yeah.'

'Anyway, I was driving past there one night and I saw some lights inside. Maybe it's been turned into a squat.'

'Could be.' Friendly was silent for a moment, and then said, 'Let's go there.'

'What?'

'After *The Shield*. Why not? We've got nothing else to do. And you're a single man now.'

'Sshh…' I hissed. 'It's starting.'

Friendly laughed at me when I asked him for five minutes to get ready before we started our music hunt. He's one of those fortunate men who needs little in the way of personal grooming besides shaving once a week and running a wet comb through his mostly grey hair. He also had an uncanny skill for picking out clothes that only improve with wear. Friendly's clothes seemed so much a part of his personality that if one day he decided to stay home and send his jeans and jumper out without him I doubt any of us would've noticed. I rarely felt at home in anything I wore, and every time I had a sizeable win I bought a new shirt. The main problem was that I liked being smart, but as most people my age dressed like giant toddlers, I ended up looking like the old dossers instead. All I lacked was piss stains on my crotch and some sort of hat.

'Are you wearing aftershave?' Friendly asked, as I came back downstairs.

'Fuck you.'

After we'd been walking for a while, it became obvious that I was right and the music was coming from Friendly's old infant school. What sounded like innocuous techno from a distance became stranger the closer we got. The school's doors were open, but the lighting inside was minimal. It was obvious they were afraid of attracting the wrong sort of attention.

'They're not going to let you in,' said Friendly, 'they'll think you're a policeman.'

I ignored him, worried this might be true. Hardly anyone lived near the school, but I couldn't see this place surviving for long. There were close to a hundred people packed into the hall, and word was bound to spread. We waited in the reception area as a Scottish man with curly black hair collected five pound notes from the queue.

'What sort of music is this?' Friendly asked the girl in front of us.

'Oh, y'know,' she said, 'noise.'

I expected Friendly to make a sarcastic comment, but he didn't reply, handing a ten-pound note across for both of us. We pushed into the hall, and Friendly looked around for a bar. A man in a manky green T-shirt noticed his anxiety and told him, 'You have to buy tickets from the Wizard, then swap them for cans of Stella.'

Friendly rolled his eyes. 'And where do I find the Wizard?'

'He's about. Probably dancing. You'll spot him easily enough. He's nearly seven feet tall, he has long white hair, and he's wearing a large blue hat with gold moons and stars on it.'

'Of course he is.'

The man didn't seem to notice Friendly's irritation, and happily drifted away from him and back into the crowd. I stayed where I was as Friendly went off to look for the Wizard. I realised what I thought was a DJ was actually a guy playing a drum kit along to a laptop that was producing what sounded like the music from an old-school computer game. The rebarbative nature of the noise didn't stop people dancing, and I was impressed to discover a scene like this in suburban Bristol. I felt completely at sea here, unable to tell anyone's age or social background. While I waited for Friendly to return, I watched two women dancing together slightly apart from the rest of the crowd. I hadn't slept with anyone since Amy left me, and in the two years when things were bad before she finally went I was so horrible to her that we hardly had sex anyway. I'd always assumed that as soon as Amy moved out I'd be so desperate for female company that my desire would force me to find someone to fuck – but although I stared at every attractive woman I passed on the street, so far I hadn't properly pursued anyone. Friendly was good with women. He had the occasional dry spell, but usually had a girlfriend, although the women tended to move on when they realised how deeply he loved his lifestyle. I'd hoped we'd go out on the pull together, but before tonight he hadn't offered. I wondered whether he'd be prepared to play wingman to help me with the taller of the two women. Going on his past form, I thought he'd probably be more interested in her friend, and this could be the perfect pair for the two of us.

Friendly returned with the beers. He noticed where I was staring and smiled. 'Shall we go over?'

'I don't know,' I replied, 'I'm not sure it's that sort of place.'

He laughed. 'You're right. I'm sure this is the kind of club where pretty women prefer being ignored. Come on.'

I followed Friendly over to the two women. It was hard for men to dance to this sort of music without looking stupid. It wasn't particularly aggressive, but it was so fast and jerky, continually building up to increasingly manic peaks, that if you didn't thrash about at least a little you looked like you weren't making an effort. The women could get away with a slightly speeded-up version of normal dancing, but I knew if I did that I'd look like a disco dad.

Now we were closer to the women I realised they were much younger than I assumed, possibly only in their late teens. I tried to signal to Friendly that I'd changed my mind, they were too young for us, but he ignored me and tried to make eye contact with the shorter blonde woman. He'd started to jig about a bit, but he was making an even worse job of it than me, like a sailor in a silent movie. I expected both women to find us incredibly embarrassing, but Friendly at least seemed to be making a good impression. After reaching a crazed crescendo, the drummer stood up from behind his kit and turned off his laptop. Relieved to be able to stop dancing, I moved behind Friendly as he asked the blonde, 'What was that guy's name?'

'The drummer? Duracell. He's French, I think. But the music he's covering is mainly Lightning Bolt.'

Friendly didn't pretend he knew what she was talking about, saying instead, 'It's great to have something like this in Bristol, isn't it?'

She seemed surprised. 'But there are loads of things like this.'

'Oh yes, I know, but you have to know where to look, don't you?'

While they were talking, I stared at the dark-haired woman, trying to think of something to say. I'd barely sipped my beer so it couldn't be the drink, but this woman was more beautiful than anyone I'd ever seen before. I know these things are subjective and I should just tell you to picture your first crush and favourite film star rolled into one, but I'm going to risk trying to describe her. I've always had a thing for women who dress badly (I'd actively encourage Amy to buy clothes that didn't suit her, and in the old days, whenever our sex life needed perking up, we'd go to some charity shop or cheap wholesaler and I'd pick out outfits that made her look like a crack whore) and this dark-haired woman had thick, wide white shoes that wouldn't disgrace Daisy Duck, a floral dress slashed and altered in wholly unflattering ways, and an ugly pair of red glasses. I think the reason why I like women in bad clothes is because it immediately makes you want to undress them. And also because it often indicates a pleasing absence of vanity. Now I read back this description, I realise I've made her sound like Su Pollard, and should quickly add that her peculiar outfit only intensified her beauty.

'I like your glasses,' I told her, and she smiled at me in such a way that I worried there might be something more considered behind her ugly clothes than genuine poor taste. It was too dim and too crowded inside the infant school to really get a sense of how everyone was dressed, but I was concerned that this blind-woman-let-loose-at-a-jumble-sale look might be part of a general club trend. What had finally driven me away from clubbing in the first place were the dark years of the mid-1990s when Bristol succumbed wholesale to the easy-listening revival, and all the city's big clubs gave over their weekends to nights called things like World of Cheese, all filled with students dressed in their parents' early 1980s cast-offs dancing to the theme from *Grandstand*. The possibility that this scene had gone underground and passed through some inexplicable transformation into this noise stuff chilled me. But her friend seemed normally dressed, so I decided not to worry and asked her her name.

'I'm Emma,' she told me, 'and this is Christine.'

Emma and Christine had a serious amount of cocaine on them. Like most suburban men my age, I'd long since grown bored of the drug, but there was something about being invited to the toilet by an attractive young woman that rekindled the faraway days when it'd still been exciting. Amy and I made a point of taking our drugs separately, as neither of us liked each other when we were off our heads. Doing coke together only seemed to intensify the unhealthy elements of our relationship, and I always preferred to do it with at least one woman I fancied in the assembled company. The novelty of being inside a derelict infant school was most pronounced in the toilets, and although the plumbing had either been abandoned or wasn't equipped for this many adults and there were wet trails of sewage across the cracked tiled floor, there were crowds of people just standing around chatting in the lavatories. Maybe they were trying to get away from the noise music. But there were more than enough pairs in the cubicles for no one to comment when Emma and I slipped into one together, even though the hardboard walls were so small that it was easy for everyone else to see what we were doing.

I think it was the way she made a fuss about flushing the toilet to hide the sound of our snorts that made me want to snog her. The idea that she would worry about decorum in such a disgusting environment was so touching, and I found myself wrapping my arms around her, pushing her up against the toilet wall and losing myself in a prolonged kiss. When I broke away, she said, 'I think you're great,' and I couldn't tell whether this was a compliment or a brush-off. So I kissed her again and hugged her and when she wrapped her arms around my shoulders I started kissing her neck. Amy had always loved this, and I hoped it might work on Emma as well. It seemed to prompt the desired response and she pressed her body against mine. I wanted to touch her small breasts, but I was so worried about either tearing or getting tangled up in her slashed floral dress that I limited myself to gently cupping them through the material. We'd reached the point now where I thought she'd probably be disappointed if I didn't at least try to have sex with her, so I stood slightly back and reached up under her dress. I pulled down her knickers, hooked them over those ridiculous

Daffy Duck shoes and put them in my pocket along with my wallet and car keys. I wanted to go down on her but couldn't bring myself to kneel down in the effluent. Maybe I was being silly: this was toilet sex; surely she'd forgive me for not offering the full service? I gently touched her for a while and when I sensed she was getting impatient, I unzipped my trousers and let her guide my cock inside her. Everything about the situation was embarrassing, but the worst thing was that all the cubicles were joined together and every time I thrust inside her, even gently, the whole structure shook. Emma didn't seem to care, which delighted me, as Amy had been self-conscious when we'd had sex in public. It's not always easy having sex standing up, and I was pleased we were accomplishing this so successfully. It was requiring real effort from both of us – Emma's eyes were screwed up with the strain – but we kept going and soon I lost any sense of the people standing outside the cubicle, and when she whispered, 'I'm coming,' before releasing a low guttural moan, I was so pleased that I came too. The two of us nearly slipped to the floor, but managed to stay upright, and as I stepped away from her I heard the people in the toilet burst into a round of applause.

By 6 a.m., I'd even started to enjoy the noise music, although I have to say that the highlight of the night for me – aside from the sex, of course – was a performance by a group of deranged women in Victorian dresses, all of whom had long matted brown hair, and sat in a circle pushing broken, blinded dolls back and forth across the floor. Friendly thought this was terrible, but I argued that it was amazing. I didn't admit that I mainly thought this because they were doing it to a more minimal soundtrack.

I couldn't tell if Friendly and Christine knew that Emma and I had fucked in the toilet, or if they had tried something similar on any of their cocaine trips. In an egotistical way, I loved knowing that my sperm was dribbling down Emma's thighs as she thrashed about to this terrible music, and that someone clearly so much younger had found me attractive.

We left the club at noon the following day. Emma and Christine wanted to go into town for a club that ran from Sunday afternoon until midnight, but even with the promise of more cocaine (which showed no sign of running out), I couldn't face it. We didn't swap numbers as I went home to crash out, but as Friendly went off with the two girls, I was optimistic I'd get to see Emma again.

I awoke late Sunday night, feeling like a new man. I knew nights like this only had a beneficial effect on you if you had them rarely, but I couldn't help wondering when I'd see Emma again. I looked at my watch. It was half past ten and I even considered calling Friendly on his mobile to see if he was still out with the girls, but I worried that if I joined them now, and witnessed Emma at the end of such a long bender, it might kill any burgeoning romance. I was about to go out for some fried chicken instead, but as I picked up my trousers from beside the bed, I found Emma's knickers scrunched inside my pocket and had to stop to examine them. I was proud of myself for swiping her underwear without her complaining, or even seeming to notice. I liked this about Emma; it didn't matter whether she'd been too laid-back to ask me to return them, or simply absent-minded, either way it indicated that she was the sort of woman I wanted to be with.

I hadn't really looked at her knickers before putting them in my pocket – she may've been the first new woman I'd slept with since leaving my wife, but I'm not that gauche – with the sense of delaying a treat for later, like putting aside a good book midway through an exciting chapter. I'd assumed that with her love of wacky clothes, Emma's underwear would be particularly interesting, but now I saw they were simple ivory-coloured silk knickers with a shell lace trim. But there was something disturbing about them: stitched into the back was a small name-tag with her name written in green thread: EMMA DONALDSON. I'd been fairly unperturbed about Emma's age until now, but it seemed shocking that I'd slept with a girl young enough still to have a name-tag stitched into her knickers. Who had stitched it there? Her mother? I didn't want to know. And then there was her name. It seemed familiar. I walked over to the laptop I used almost exclusively for downloading porn, accessed Google, and typed it in.

Emma Donaldson turned out to be a retired Scottish tennis player, once ranked thirtieth in the world. But it was obvious this wasn't the woman I'd met in the noise club. Maybe it was only her surname that was familiar. I'd known a Donaldson once, I was sure of it. I couldn't remember if this Donaldson had been a man or a woman, but they'd definitely been significant to me. My memory often worked like this, feeding me fragments. I couldn't really explain why, but I suddenly felt uneasy, and I threw Emma's knickers back on to my pillow, got dressed and went out for my fried chicken.

I saw Friendly in the bookie's the following morning. He looked shattered, and I felt glad I'd left him and the girls when I had. But he was happier than I'd seen him in ages and he didn't seem to care when he lost every bet he made that day. He even made a stupid one with me about whether I'd be able to eat three sandwiches at lunch, a challenge that wasn't remotely difficult. I asked him if he'd made any plans to see Christine again, and he told me both girls were coming round to my house on Wednesday evening.

Christine and Emma showed up at nine o'clock. Christine seemed much more attractive than I remembered her being the first time I met her, and she was wearing a pink T-shirt on which were written the words 'Last night I had a nightmare I was a brunette' in silver lettering. It was such a relief to see them: I'd been with Friendly most of the day and we'd run out of conversation. Emma wasn't dressed at all weirdly tonight, confirming my suspicion that she'd only disguised herself as a geek for the noise night. I wondered whether she'd be angry if she knew it was her strange clothes that had initially attracted me to her. But I'm not so perverse that I was disappointed to discover that she was equally luminous in conventional clothes. In fact, if she'd been dressed the way she was tonight the first time I met her, in simple – though no doubt expensive – blue jeans and a silver scoop-neck T-shirt, I would've thought her too far out of my league to approach.

'Shall we have a drink, then?' suggested Friendly.

'Do you have any vodka?' asked Christine.

'Of course,' he told her as she went through to the lounge and sat at the dining table. Friendly walked across to my drinks cabinet and poured two vodka-tonics for the girls. I felt strangely touched as I observed the caution with which he carefully carried them back. This was the first social activity my house had seen in years, and Friendly's proud smirk made me wonder whether he was thinking the same thing as me: maybe these two women were our reward for all the deprivations we'd suffered over the last decade and a half. I'd suspected Friendly would be a good wingman, but it'd never occurred to me that he'd be so into double dates. Almost overcome, I had a sudden vision of an alternative future for the pair of us. Instead of spending the remainder of our days staggering around betting shops until one of us had a heart attack and abandoned the other to suffer the in some ways worse fate of becoming the sad loner everyone else avoided, endlessly retelling boring stories about his dead best friend, maybe we'd marry these much younger women and change our lifestyles and be the envy of everyone we left behind. Barry would denounce us in the pub, barely able to say our names aloud owing to the acidic envy it would induce in him.

Friendly gave the girls their vodkas, and got us beers from the fridge. Christine and Emma were sitting next to each other and Emma collapsed against her friend's shoulder in embarrassed giggles as Christine said, 'Emma wants her knickers back, you dirty perv.'

Although the lack of sophistication in Christine's voice disappointed me, I had been prepared for this. I told myself not to be upset that Emma had evidently told her friend about at least some of the things that had happened between us, and that it didn't necessarily mean she'd gone off me. The two women were clearly very close, and young, and her tone hadn't been that insulting.

I took Emma's knickers out of my pocket and gently tossed them across the table at her. Although I'd lost count of the number of times I'd ejaculated into her knickers over the last few days, I'd put them through the washing machine twice and triple-checked I hadn't left any stains in them.

'Thanks,' said Emma, smiling. 'I don't really care, though. You can keep them if you want.'

I feigned bemusement. 'Why would I want your knickers?'

Emma looked momentarily hurt by this, which pleased me as it showed she still cared. Christine seemed to sense she'd lost control of the situation and demanded, 'So how are you two old giffers going to entertain us tonight?'

Friendly grinned, and in quick, deft movements, plucked a packet of playing cards from his pocket, broke the seal and started shuffling. 'How about a game of strip poker?'

'You dirty cunt, you're as bad as he is, stealing her knickers. Well, if that's what turns you on. But I bet it's going to be a lot more embarrassing for you two to strip off in front of each other than it will be for us. I've seen Emma naked more times than I care to remember.'

He shrugged, and started dealing. I couldn't help feeling uncomfortable with this situation. I'd never seen Friendly acting in this sleazy way before – he was usually such a gentleman – and I couldn't work out whether he was responding to some perceived challenge in Christine's behaviour, or whether he was behaving like this because they were young and he thought it didn't matter. He suddenly reminded me of Richard O'Sullivan in *Man about the House*, and I had a vivid flashback to a particularly grim episode where Richard taught Paula Wilcox how to play strip chess. Before even looking at her cards, Emma opened her handbag and pulled out another ridiculously large packet of cocaine. It was closer to the quantity you'd see in a dealer's suitcase in a gangster movie than an amount anyone I knew would have the money to buy on a regular basis, but once again she seemed completely blasé about it.

Realising that without some sort of system we'd all be naked before we'd even finished our drinks, I brought out my wheel of chips and gave everyone a small pile and told them that once they'd run out they'd have to exchange items of clothing to get more. This slowed things down, and by ten o'clock Christine was sitting topless, I'd taken my shirt off, Emma's shoes were placed on the centre of the table and Friendly had removed his watch. After he'd snorted another fat line, he asked Emma, 'Are you really rich, then?'

'What?'

'All this coke. How can you afford it?'

'Oh,' she laughed, 'I thought you knew. My dad's a dealer.'

'Really?' asked Friendly. 'Maybe we know him. What's his name?'

'Well, if you know him, you'll know him by his nickname. Jumbo.'

I froze. 'Jumbo the Elephant or Jumbo the Egg?'

'What?'

'Has he got a long nose?'

She laughed. 'What?'

'A really long nose. Like a cock in the middle of his face.'

'No,' she said, 'of course not.'

'He's bald?'

'Yes. Do you know him?'

Friendly and I exchanged glances. 'No.'

'Hey, do you know my parents?' Christine asked, perking up. 'Kerry and Vince?'

I shook my head. I didn't know whether she believed me, and prayed my ex-classmates never discovered that their daughter had played strip poker at my house. If Kerry found out, it would be sad and shameful; if Vince was the one she told I'd probably be in serious danger. But neither prospect was anywhere near as terrifying as what might happen if Jumbo the Egg – who'd been christened, I now remembered, Jamie Donaldson – learnt that I'd had sex with his daughter.

After the girls had gone the following morning, I confronted Friendly. 'You realise you're in as much shit as I am?'

Friendly laughed. 'No, I don't think so. I never really knew Kerry and Vince. They were your friends. And Christine doesn't know my real name.'

'It doesn't matter. Everyone knows you're called Friendly.'

'Why are you panicking, Paul? It's just a bit of fun. Do you really think Emma and Christine are going to want their parents to know their daughters are hanging around with a couple of deadbeats like us? It's just a bit of fun for them. It'll carry on for a while and then it'll stop. Which reminds me, when the girls get bored do you want to swap?'

'Swap?'

'Yeah, I know you're a bit squeamish about stuff like that, but Christine told me she thought your cock looked impressive when you stripped off last night and I thought if I called her bluff it might prolong things a bit. And I thought it might be exciting for you to sleep with Kerry's daughter, especially after what you told me about always fancying her.'

'I didn't tell you that.'

'You did, years ago. Don't you remember?'

Friendly always remembered our pissed conversations, and worryingly, had no sense of what should be considered inadmissible evidence. He'd hit so many raw spots that I had no idea how to respond. Any previous notion of us settling into a matey foursome had now been obliterated by the realisation that Friendly was viewing this situation as if he was acting in a Ben Dover DVD. Even his nickname now had a sleazy ring to it, and I wondered whether I'd made a mistake spending so much of my life with this man. Maybe this was the sort of mentality you developed over a lifetime of casual relationships. Perhaps it was only married men, or formerly married men, who took sex so seriously. He was offering the chance to sleep with Christine as if it was an exotic treat, like a pimp offering an ugly middle-aged man the opportunity to deflower a genuine virgin. And the worst thing was, it did appeal to me, and I knew that even if I didn't take him up on the offer I'd be masturbating to the memory of Christine's laid-back lack of interest as she removed her knickers in front of me after losing the last of her chips.

'Oh, I don't know, Friendly. Let's see if we're even still alive in a couple of weeks.'

We'd arranged to see the girls again the following Saturday. They were going to the noise club again and said they'd come round to pick us up after *The Shield* had finished. I was expecting them to be late but almost as soon as the credits ended, the doorbell rang. I went to let them in.

Jumbo had put on a lot of weight in the last twenty years. Once he had looked like Daredevil's nemesis Kingpin; now he was more like Jabba the Hutt. Vince and Kerry were standing behind him. I noticed Jumbo was carrying a hammer.

'Vince,' he said, 'go inside and get Friendly. Paul, come with me to the car.'

He put a hand on my arm, and led me to his car, the only vehicle in the whole street. Surely he knew about my empty development? He must've been aware that this was probably the best place to do anything he wanted to me and Friendly without being discovered. Still, I didn't want to risk arguing with him, not while he was carrying his hammer, and climbed into the back seat. Kerry slid in alongside me, and even in the midst of my terror, I couldn't help noticing that she had aged so much better than Amy, and in many ways was arguably a more attractive woman than her daughter, if you weren't obsessed with youth.

'I didn't know Christine was your daughter,' I told her. 'Not until the last time they came round.'

'Would it've made any difference?' she asked.

'Of course it would. And I didn't do anything to her. It was Friendly.'

'Don't worry,' she replied, 'he's coming too. And you should know that Amy knows all about this and fully endorses what's going to happen.'

'What's going to happen?'

Her voice became distant. 'She helped us decide what to do, y'know. She was the one who told us that you were terrified of hammers.'

Kerry's dead-eyed expression was so frightening that I didn't want to look at her any more. I stared past her to watch Jumbo and Vince bringing Friendly to the car. He was completely silent, which worried me, as it meant he must've realised he couldn't talk his way out of this situation. The back door opened and Friendly was thrown in alongside us. Jumbo and Vince got into the car. Jumbo started the engine, and Vince swivelled round in his seat and said, 'Bet this isn't what you two expected to be doing this evening...'

'Vince,' I said, 'I know how this looks, but neither of us meant any harm. You know what it's like...'

'Yeah, I know what it's like, forcing seventeen-year-old girls to do drugs and play strip poker...'

'Emma had the drugs,' I protested, 'she made us do them.'

Jumbo's eyes met mine in the rear-view and he told me, 'Keep talking like that, Paul, make this easy for me.'

Friendly gripped my arm and I realised the smart thing to do was shut up. It was clear these parents didn't want to hear anything bad about their daughters. Maybe Jumbo didn't even know his daughter was stealing drugs from him. But if I didn't say anything, how could we escape? It wasn't possible to open the car door and throw ourselves out, and although there were two of us, there was no way we could overpower the three of them. I didn't have a mobile on me, so there was no way I could surreptitiously call the police, and even if I had, when they showed up and saw Jumbo, he'd probably have a quiet word with them and they'd leave us alone.

After we had been driving for twenty minutes, I realised where we were going: the abandoned quarry. Possibly the only place safer to conduct unseen business than my empty street. I'd heard rumours about things that Jumbo had got up to here before, stories passed on in whispers which clearly someone (probably Jumbo) had once thought were funny, but had lost all humour by the time I heard them, sounding instead like the highlights of a sick horror film I was glad I wouldn't have to watch.

We drove into the quarry and Jumbo parked the car. There was a horrible black sweaty tension in the car, and I could tell both men were silently steeling themselves for what they had decided to do to us. I don't know if they decided to punish Friendly first because they thought his sins were worse than mine, or because they thought it would be more unpleasant for me to have to hear what was happening to him before they got to me.

As Kerry had told me that they were going to hurt me with a hammer because they knew how frightened I was about this happening to me, I wondered whether they would have a similarly appropriate punishment for Friendly. Maybe, I considered, they might castrate him.

Jumbo left the car headlights on so I could see what was happening to Friendly. The first blow was worst; Friendly gave out a terrible scream as Vince dealt him a full-powered thwack to the side of his head. At first, Jumbo held Friendly in a powerful grip so Vince could concentrate on his aim, but he soon let him slide out of his arms and on to the quarry floor as Vince succumbed to a horrible frenzy, every hit sending another fresh spray of blood up over his twisted face. As I watched this man trying to destroy my friend, I realised Vince had always had this capacity for violence within him, and suddenly I understood why we'd never really connected when we spent all those evenings together in the pub. It was obvious he'd done this kind of thing before. Although it wouldn't do me any good now, I was suddenly grateful that he'd never found out about the time I'd helped Kerry with her stuck zip. Soon Friendly was making no noise whatsoever and I was convinced he was dead.

When they returned for me, I knew I was going to die. I prepared for it, and asked for one small mercy. 'Jumbo,' I said, 'I understand why you want to hurt me, and I know you want this to be as horrible as possible, but is there any way I could persuade you not to use the hammer?'

He laughed. This clearly amused him. 'What should I use instead then?'

'I don't know,' I said, before suggesting, suddenly hopeful, 'your shoe?'

He stared at me for a long time. The only reason for going along with my request was because it presented him with a challenge: could he do as much damage to me with his shoe as Vince had done to Friendly with his hammer? I fully believe that if he had been wearing Doc Martens instead of giant floppy trainers, I wouldn't be here today. He took his time, carefully breaking my nose and my fingers by grinding the heel into the flesh, and having a good go at my skull, but ultimately he could only cause me so much pain, and when he'd finally exhausted himself, he gave me one final slap across the face, and went to rejoin Vince and Kerry in the car.

Contraflow

Matt Beaumont

Letter

Dear Sir/Madam

This might seem an unusual complaint. Not so much a complaint, actually, more a question with a gripey edge to it. I live across the road from a pub – The Crown. You may know it. It was recently refurbished. Now, I suppose, it's a gastropub. It can be noisy at times, but since it has been part of the neighbourhood for considerably longer than I have, I really can't complain.

However, three Sundays ago I was awoken (at just after ten in the morning) by the sound of music – specifically, religious music. Investigation revealed that The Crown had been taken over by something called The Sunshine Congregation. According to the sign placed outside, 'Jesus welcomes all', though I don't believe Jesus was literally present. They have been at The Crown for the two subsequent Sundays.

Anyway, my complaint/question: under the terms of his licence, is the landlord allowed to hand over his premises (presumably for money) to a church group outside regular pub hours?

I look forward to your response.

Yours faithfully
Steven Trafford

Letter

Dear Mr Trafford

I apologise for the delay in responding to your query. However, you directed your letter to Environmental Health. It has since been passed on to me in Trading Standards, the department that deals with the licensing of public houses.

In answer to your question, the landlord of The Crown is within his rights to allow church groups to use his premises provided they do not engage in the sale of alcohol outside prescribed hours. If you feel that the church group is behaving in a manner that constitutes a noise nuisance, then you should direct your enquiries to Environmental Health.

I hope this is of assistance.

Yours sincerely
Elenor Poulou
Trading Standards Officer

Classified advertisement

'Love ye therefore the stranger:
for ye were strangers in the land of Egypt.'
Deuteronomy, 10, 19

The SUNSHINE CONGREGATION invites all to its weekly Sunday service, held from 10 a.m. at The Crown, 2 Grove Road. Tea, coffee and worship. Children welcome!

For further information, contact Rev. C. Scanlon [number withheld for legal reasons].

Letter
Dear Ms Poulou

Thank you for your letter, though it was of little assistance. I originally wrote to Environmental Health precisely because I felt that the behaviour of The Sunshine Congregation constitutes a 'noise nuisance'. Frankly, I object to being aroused from my Sunday slumbers by any music, but especially by songs with titles such as 'Hail, Ye Sighing Sons of Sorrow' and 'Blow Ye the Trumpet, Blow'. If they merely mouthed the hymns, I could probably tolerate the invasion of my immediate living space by cultists – mute cultists would be acceptable.

I will be writing again to Environmental Health as a matter of urgency. Several weeks have passed since my original correspondence and the congregation at The Crown has swollen alarmingly (and noisily).

But while I have the attention of Trading Standards, surely holding a church service on licensed premises constitutes a 'change of use' under planning laws.

Yours sincerely
Steven Trafford

PS: Alcohol is being consumed during these Sunday morning rituals, though whether the minister is accepting money in exchange for the Eucharist is not clear. Please advise if you wish me to investigate further.

Letter
Dear Mr Trafford

Further to your telephone call, I have spoken to the environmental health officer that visited you. He is not prepared to alter his view that the noise level outside The Crown public house did not reach an actionable level. Though his report described the singing during 'Awaked by Sinai's Awful Sound' as 'lusty', he felt that it could not be defined as a 'nuisance' under current guidelines. Therefore, after much consideration, I am not prepared to sanction a second visit.

On a final point, the officer concerned does not need to have his 'f*****g ears syringed by Dyno-Rod'. I must remind you that abuse of council officials is a matter that we treat with utmost seriousness.

Yours sincerely
Simon Wolstencroft
Director, Environmental Health

Letter
Dear Mr Trafford

At your request I have looked into the terms of the licence granted to The Crown. The performance of live music is permitted so long as it is not amplified. There is no reference to particular music types, so the licence does not prohibit the singing of hymns, psalms and suchlike.

If I may make a suggestion, have you thought about approaching the worshippers and speaking to them? You will probably find that they respond positively to a reasonable request to quieten their singing a little.

Yours sincerely
Elenor Poulou
Trading Standards Officer

Letter

Dear Ms Poulou

Yes, talking to them was the first thing I did. In response to my polite request that they shut the fuck up, they grinned their idiot Christian grins and handed me a pamphlet. Its cover announced that it contained 'Good News'. Believe me, it did not, outlining as it did a schedule of services that stretches some considerable way towards eternity.

There is nothing 'reasonable' about these people. How is it possible to have a rational conversation with those who eat crackers in the belief that they're the flesh of a man dead these past two thousand years?

I will no longer put up with the obliteration of my Sundays by joyous song. It is the day of rest for God's sake. (Why oh why am I invoking the name of that arse – or should that be Arse? See what they've got me doing?) If you're not prepared to act, then I have no choice but to take matters into my own hands. Or in the words of the Sunshine Bastard Congregation, 'When the storm in its fury on Galilee fell…'

Steven Trafford

Letter

Dear Mr Trafford

The Archbishop thanks you for your letter. In answer to your query, the Church of England's premises are unavailable for use as public houses, certainly on Sundays, which you must appreciate tends to be our 'busy' day.

Have you considered buying a disused church and converting it for your purposes? Perhaps our Property Management office could be of assistance in this regard.

Yours sincerely
Reverend Yvonne Pawlett
Office of the Archbishop of Canterbury

Letter
Dear Mr Trafford

I must ask you to desist from further correspondence with Ms Poulou. As a committed Christian, she found your last letter both disturbing and offensive. I must also inform you that I have passed it on to the police who are examining it in the light of the new legislation re incitement of religious hatred.

Yours sincerely,
Marc Riley
Director, Trading Standards

Hand-painted sign (pig's blood on cardboard) placed outside 3 Grove Road

'*Shove it up your ass, you faggot!*'
The Exorcist, 1973

The BEELZEBUB FOUNDATION invites you to its
weekly service, held from 10 a.m. at 3 Grove Road.
Tea, coffee and death metal. Virgins welcome!
For further information, contact Rev. S. Trafford within.

Leaflet posted to Grove Road residents

> *'Behold, how good and how pleasant it is for*
> *brethren to dwell together in unity!'*
>
> *Psalms, 133, 1*

You have welcomed the SUNSHINE CONGREGATION into your midst! Now we would like to welcome you into ours! We extend a cordial invitation to all our new neighbours to join us for tea, coffee and 'home-made' cakes at 11.30 on Sunday after the morning service. Feel free to join us for the service as well and lend your voice to our singing!

Craig Scanlon (Reverend)

Classified advertisement

FOR SALE: Gelert Combat 40 litre rucksack. Olive green. Ventilated back, padded shoulder straps, waist belt and chest stabiliser straps, ice axe loops! Mint cond. Perfect for gap year! £15. No time wasters. Call Una Baines [number withheld for legal reasons].

Classified advertisement

FOR SALE: One copy of Koran, slightly thumbed. Also available, prayer mat, compass, halal cookbook. Contact Adam (formerly Anwar) at North London Church of Scientology [number withheld for legal reasons].

Phone call to the Noise Nuisance Hotline
(recorded for training purposes)

—Good morning, you've reached the Noise Nuisance Hotline, how may—

—Can you hear that?

—Excuse me, sir?

—I said, can you hear that?

—No, I'm sorry, I can't.

—Are you deaf? You're the Noise Nuisance Hotline for fuck's sake.

—Please, there's no need to—

—*Listen*, just listen, would you?

—I'm listening…Is that singing…? Are you in a church, sir?

—No, I'm across the bloody street from a chur—a *pub*.

—But that's…Hang on, I know it…'Come Holy Spirit, Dove Divine'. I do like that one.

—Jesus, not you as well.

—Excuse me?

—Look, there's a pub across the road that miraculously transforms into a church every Sunday morning. It's packed today. The entire bloody neighbourhood is in there. I'm surprised you can't hear it in the town hall. It's like some sort of mass…*brainwashing*. Anyway, I want you to do something about it.

—A church? I'm not sure we can.

—Of course you bloody can. *It's* a noise nuisance, *you're* Noise Nuisance, ergo DO SOMETHING!

—Really, there's no need to shout.

—Oh, but there is. I can barely hear myself think because of the FUCKING SINGING!

—But it's a church. Singing's what they do.

—It's not a fucking church. It's a fucking *pub*. You know, beer, pork scratchings, fist fights at chucking-out time. *That's* what pubs are for.

—But as Jesus said, 'Wherever two or three are gathered together in my name…'.

—Fuck, FUCK! Fucking…*Christians* everywhere! I thought this was supposed to be your day off. The *Sabbath*. *Jesus* Chri—Why do

I keep saying that? Forget it, right. Just forget I called. I'll go and fucking handle it myself.

—If you'd like to give me your name and address I can log your complaint, but if you continue to be abusive I'm going to end this call right—Sir...? Sir, are you there?

Item from Sunday evening news bulletin, BBC1
Earlier today the siege of a London pub ended when police marksmen shot dead a man they believed to be a suicide bomber. The man, whose identity has not been released, apparently walked into the pub during a Sunday morning religious service. He was wearing a rucksack and clutching a copy of the Koran. After the shooting, the pub was evacuated and bomb disposal experts destroyed the rucksack in a controlled explosion. A spokesman for the Metropolitan Police said that the shooting was regrettable, but that in the light of recent events the safety of the public was the overriding priority. He would not comment on reports that the rucksack had contained only a feather pillow, saying that it had been sent for laboratory analysis.

I Can Hear the Grass Grow

Rebbecca Ray

One night, Christine lost her fear and woke Doug up in the darkness. It was 4.13 a.m. – the quiet, red eyes of God stared out from her alarm clock – nothing else in the room was visible. She was forty-three. She had become desperate without noticing. It was frightening to realise that your needs could change so suddenly.

'Dougie...' she said. 'Dougie, I have to talk to you about something.'

'It's the middle of the night...'

'I know. I've been awake.'

He rolled over and put one hand on her arm – this was something she could always rely on him to do. He was a reliable person but, with no warning, she didn't want to rely on him any more. She wanted life to have no handholds. She wanted to lose her way.

Between the sheets, she took hold of Doug's fingers. 'Do you have fantasies?' she said.

She listened to his silence.

'What fantasies?'

'Sexual fantasies.'

He gave her no response.

Finally, she spoke again. 'I've been having fantasies. I can't sleep properly…and even in the daytime. I want to tell you,' she said.

His voice was full of sleep not sex. 'I've got to be up in three hours.'

'I know.'

For a minute, she lay quietly, but really the time for silence had passed already, while they were eating breakfast or while they were at work – she couldn't pinpoint when. 'I imagine…we're in a room full of people, some of them are friends, some of them are strangers. Sometimes we film it,' she said. 'We're there to lose all our inhibitions. We don't care about…the rules, it's not a dirty thing, we just care about pleasure. We all take off each other's clothes. We just care about being free. I like to watch them take yours off, you're wearing your blue suit. Two women undo your tie and shirt, they start running their hands over your chest, they touch your nipples. A man is kneeling in front of you and he unzips your fly…'

Somewhere in the loose dark beside her, she heard her husband draw a breath. It could have been excitement – or frustration with her – or sadness. She wasn't sure.

'…He reaches into your trousers and you're so hard, because there's three different people's hands touching you and if you closed your eyes, you wouldn't know which was which. People pull me over to you, so I can watch the man who's kneeling there put you in his mouth.'

Doug's breath came again but still Christine couldn't tell the difference – if he was now aroused or if distaste was the force behind the sound. It wasn't that she wanted to hurt him.

'Now the two women beside you, they undress themselves. I start touching one, her breasts. I rub my palms all over them while the other, she bends down and she puts her nipple against your mouth.

You start licking it, but you're helpless really because this man is sucking—'

'Christine,' he said quietly, 'stop.'

The night settled over them again. 'Why?' she asked, but he didn't answer her. So she went on, 'You're helpless because…you can't do anything except take it. He's got these strong hands, holding it. He opens his own fly and he starts to do it to himself at the same time. Both his hands are all slick with it. While I'm watching, the woman starts kissing me and another man, he pushes me down on to all fours so you can see him start to take me. He holds me open, but he's not pushing inside yet. He asks you to tell him when he can start, and I'm desperate because now the woman's getting down on the floor with us, kissing my breasts. I just want this man to start but you won't let him yet. You say to me, *Do you want him to?* And I say, *Please.* And you say, *Beg for it.* So I start to tell you…'

His silence was part of the bed, it was a piece of the room, some cornerstone.

'Why "stop"?' she asked him.

He opened his eyes and stared upwards.

'It's not wrong,' she said.

'I want more,' she tried to explain. 'It's not just sex.' It was everything. She didn't believe in freedom any more. She couldn't remember what she'd once wanted her life to be. She was afraid of the real world.

The next day, neither Doug nor Christine mentioned the occurrences of the night. Work began and ended at the same times as usual, but when Christine returned to the house, he wasn't there. Usually he arrived at least half an hour before her; she worked in Ealing unfortunately. Christine read a novel for twenty minutes, drank wine, planned dinner, and eventually she called Doug's mobile phone, but he had switched it off.

She'd never been aware of needing fantasies. They'd crept into her life unnoticeably, as if it had had a hole. They'd hovered in corners, they had sat in the kitchen when she made lunch on Saturdays. In truth, she didn't want them. She had never been a highly sexed person, she'd always been happy. Now normal things looked dim to her.

It had begun in the car. She and Doug had been driving home from his mother's and she'd been almost asleep, her face against the cool window, the traffic a reverberation in her thoughts – and an image had come into her mind. The image was of a girl with very curly blonde hair, a great head of it, and before the thought had been banished, this girl had been giving Doug oral sex. Sitting up in the passenger seat, she'd glanced at her husband but his eyes had been dead set on the road.

Perhaps they didn't have an active sex life any more. There were things that made it impossible sometimes, even when you didn't have children. For instance, she and Doug would go to dinner with friends on Monday, he might work late on Tuesday night, perhaps on Wednesday she would get caught up in *Newsnight* and by the time she looked he would be asleep. Thursday night he always went for drinks. And during the weekends, in those moments when sex might happen, quietness would sometimes fall instead, to make twenty years a barrier between them – as if none of those years had in fact been shared.

It had occurred to her that this might be the beginning of the end as far as their sex life was concerned, but it hadn't occurred to her that it might be so painless – just slowly submerged in the water.

Doug didn't get home until 1 a.m. and by that time she was drunk.

He came to stand in the living room and look in silence at the television while she stared up at him, at his expression – unsettled, unresolved. She waited for an explanation but none came.

'You enjoy yourself last night, then, did you?' he said finally. And, before she could answer him, he left the room.

'Doug…?' she said, 'Doug?', following him upstairs to the bathroom. She pushed open the edge of the door, allowing all yellow light to spill, showing him before the mirror.

'I have feelings too,' he told her, his toothbrush in one hand.

The next day they had plans. For the last few months, Christine had been organising their trip down to see the Eden Project. There are more than 100,000 different species inside its two great, static arks. Christine is very concerned with ecological issues – recycling has been made far easier now anyway. But generally she has become more liberal with the years, in opposition to the majority flow – where age brings greater financial security which in turn brings conservatism. Sometimes she and Doug look through political websites in the evening; also easier now that they have broadband.

The next day, however, when the morning came, Doug got out of bed with the alarm and dressed in his office clothes, despite the fact that he'd had the day booked off for months. Christine pretended to be asleep for a while, scared to speak to him, but it became obvious that he would leave in silence, so she finally sat up.

'I don't want to go on my own,' she said.

He didn't seem to know how to look at her though.

'I'd rather work now.'

They'd both planned to keep their phones off all day. Christine had been imagining the place – she had purposefully not got hold of brochures – she'd imagined wandering with him underneath the great growths of foreign trees, which would survive whatever happened outside their greenhouse. It had been a little like a science fiction film in her mind, or even *Charlie and the Chocolate Factory*. They have always been garden-lovers, park-goers.

Doug picked up his coat, his briefcase, he shrugged and did not look happy as he left the room.

Though Christine called him at eleven o'clock, just to see whether he had changed his mind, in the end the Eden Project went unvisited.

They were planning to travel the world, once retired, but she's found it harder and harder to picture recently. Instead she sees him investing in better personal organisers, she imagines sets of matching recipe books which she will look at with her tea. 'Why didn't we have children?' she wonders now. Maybe there'd been a spring missing from her biological clock. The thought of kids had only ever left her feeling scared. But if they had had them, the weekends might now be filled with comings and goings. For instance, they might have a Sunday lunch. Galleries and things. It isn't unusual not to want children now, though. The world is full already.

On Saturday, Christine went shopping alone and spent four hundred pounds in Agent Provocateur. She stood in front of the mirror with a candelabra on either side and saw her nipples in a peephole bra. She brought the things home and laid them out on the bed in their little nests of tissue paper. When Doug came back from The Gunners and saw them there, though, he just picked them up one by one and placed them in a pile on the ottoman. He sat down on the bed's edge, slowly took off his shoes and did not look around at her as she began to cry.

Why do we bother wanting things that we can't have? When we are adults and can see the difference easily. It doesn't make us happy to churn out these fantasies. It doesn't change our lives.

On Sunday afternoon, Christine confronted him. She sat beside him on the sofa and took the remote control out of his hand. They sat there mute, with *Points of View* mute too. It took a long time, just for him to turn to her.

'What?' he said.

'I'm sorry. I'm sorry if I made you feel bad. That's not what I wanted to do.'

'What *did* you want?' he asked her then. 'What did you expect?'

'I didn't have any expectations.'

'Do you want to have sex with other people?' he asked her, turning to see the TV screen as if its silent expressions were giving him an answer, not her voice.

'No, I don't want that.'

'Then what?'

She wanted to explain to him but did not know how. 'I'm standing outside the Eden Project,' she said, and laughed. 'I'm standing outside but there isn't any door.'

'That's a very cruel thing to say. That's what I am to you, is it? A wall.'

'Maybe that's what I am…Doug,' she said, 'I don't want to *live* in a fantasy…'

She wanted to tell him, though, how she felt possibilities narrowing, chances winking out. She wanted to tell him how normality had come like an ocean across her life. But he only turned and looked at her, as though there was no reason for drawing such clear lines to delineate sex or sadness – or the world – or any of these things.

About the Contributors

Steve Aylett is the author of fourteen books of satirical science fiction, including *LINT*, *Slaughtermatic* (for which he was shortlisted for the Philip K. Dick Award), *Toxicology*, *The Crime Studio*, *Dummyland* and *Shamanspace*. He also created *The Caterer* comic.

Matt Beaumont has written four proper novels and one really skinny one that you can still get for £2.99 or something. His next book will appear sometime in 2008. He's not yet sure what it will be called, so you'll just have to look out for the shiny, foil-embossed, John Grisham-sized MATT BEAUMONT, which he is almost certain his publisher will stick on the cover. You can find out more (though not much) about him at www.LetsTalkAboutMe.com.

Nicholas Blincoe was born in Rochdale in 1965. He is a novelist, screenwriter and playwright and lives in London and Bethlehem.

Clare Dudman realised she wanted to be a writer aged eight when her poem about a goldfish was critically acclaimed by her teacher and stuck on the wall. After some years as a research scientist and then a teacher and lecturer of both chemistry and English she won a couple of awards for her novels and a prize for a short story. She now writes full time.

Richard Evans has received critical acclaim for his science fiction thrillers *Machine Nation* and *Robophobia*, which take inspiration from the real-world development of androids and humanoid robots. The stories are topical, thought-provoking and lyrical, dealing with ethical questions concerning scientific progress, slavery and the nature of humanity. For more information, see www.richardevansonline.com.

Michel Faber is the author of six books, including *The Fahrenheit Twins*, *Under the Skin* and *The Crimson Petal and the White*. His greatest love, however, is not literature but music. He listens to records many hours a day, every day. Some of those records, inevitably, are by The Fall. He thinks their version of 'War' is even better than Henry Cow's. Drop round and he will bore you about Krautrock.

Niall Griffiths was born in Liverpool in 1966 and now lives at the foot of a mountain in mid-Wales. He has written five novels, numerous short stories, radio plays and reviews, and will continue to do so until he dies.

Andrew Holmes is the author of *Sleb*, *All Fur Coat* and *64 Clarke*, all published by Sceptre. He used to live with Genesis P. Orridge, and was once awarded an MBE by Mark E. Smith. His website is at www.64clarke.co.uk.

Mick Jackson was born in Great Harwood, Lancashire. His first novel, *The Underground Man*, was shortlisted for the Booker Prize, the Whitbread First Novel Award and won the Royal Society of Authors' First Novel Award. His second novel, *Five Boys* (2001), was runner-up for the Encore Prize. *Ten Sorry Tales* (2005), illustrated by David Roberts, is a collection of rather dark stories, possibly for children. Jackson is currently working on an animation project and a screenplay. He no longer keeps bees.

Nick Johnstone is the author of various books including *A Head Full of Blue*. His writing has appeared in the *Guardian*, the *Observer*, *Uncut*, the *Daily Telegraph*, the *Jerusalem Post*, *Dazed & Confused*, *Zembla*, *Melody Maker*, *Mojo*, *The Jewish Chronicle*, *Tank* and *The Times*.

Stewart Lee was born in 1968 and has been working as a stand-up comedian since 1989. He co-wrote and directed Richard Thomas's *Jerry Springer: The Opera*, and is the author of a novel, *The Perfect Fool*. He first saw The Fall at The Elephant Fayre in Cornwall in 1984 and *Hex Enduction Hour* is his favourite album of all time.

Kevin MacNeil was born and raised on the Isle of Lewis. His debut poetry collection won an international award for the best book of poetry published in Europe by a writer under thirty-five, and his novel *The Stornoway Way* was described by the *Scotsman* as 'the best Scottish book since *Trainspotting*'. His single 'Local Man Ruins Everything' (Fantastic Plastic) was Single of the Week on Steve Lamacq, in the *List* and in the *Guardian*. www.kevinmacneil.com

Carlton Mellick III is the Bizarro author of the cult novels *Satan Burger, Punk Land, Razor Wire Pubic Hair, The Baby Jesus Butt Plug, The Menstruating Mall* and several others. His short fiction has appeared in over a hundred publications, including *The Year's Best Fantasy and Horror 16*. He lives in Portland, Oregon, where he sings for the band Popes That Are Porn Stars. Visit his website: www.avantpunk.com

Rebbecca Ray is twenty-six. She lives with her husband, a South African artist, and is the author of two novels, *A Certain Age* and *Newfoundland*. Throughout her career in writing, she has continued to pursue an interest in waitressing. She hopes to progress to Silver Service in the future.

Nicholas Royle was born in Manchester in 1963. He spent his twenties and thirties in London writing five novels – *Counterparts, Saxophone Dreams, The Matter of the Heart, The Director's Cut* and *Antwerp* – before moving back to Manchester with his family in 2003, just in time to catch The Fall at the Bierkeller on Piccadilly. His favourite Fall album is *Slates*. His latest book is *Mortality*, a collection of short stories.

Matthew David Scott was born in Manchester in 1978. His debut novel, *Playing Mercy*, was published in May 2005 by Parthian Books and has been optioned for screen adaptation. His next novel, *The Ground Remembers*, is due for publication in 2008. He currently lives in Newport, South Wales.

Stav Sherez is thirty-six and lives and writes in west London. His first novel, *The Devil's Playground*, was published by Penguin in 2004. He writes regularly for the cult music magazine *Comes with a Smile* and is a feature writer for the *Daily Telegraph* and literary editor of the *Catholic Herald* (despite not being Catholic). He is currently finishing his second novel.

Nick Stone is the author of *Mr Clarinet*, a dark thriller set in Miami and Haiti in the mid-1990s. A Fall fan since 1983, when he belatedly heard 'Totally Wired', Stone liked to listen to the band most of all when he was getting ready for 76 of the 117 boxing matches he fought as an amateur. Had he turned pro he would have used 'Hit The North' as intro music.

Matt Thorne was born in Bristol in 1974. He is the author of six novels: *Tourist* (1998), *Eight Minutes Idle* (1999, winner of an Encore Prize), *Dreaming of Strangers* (2000), *Pictures of You* (2001), *Child Star* (2003) and *Cherry* (2005, long-listed for the Booker Prize). He also co-edited the anthologies *All Hail the New Puritans* (2000) and *Croatian Nights* (2005), and has written three books for children.

Jeff VanderMeer is a two-time winner of the World Fantasy Award, as well as a past finalist for the Hugo Award, the Philip K. Dick Award, the International Horror Guild Award, the British Fantasy Award, the Bram Stoker Award and the Theodore Sturgeon Memorial Award. VanderMeer is the author of several novels and story collections, including *City of Saints & Madmen*, *Veniss Underground* and *Shriek: An Afterword*. He currently lives in Tallahassee, Florida, with his wife, Ann.

Helen Walsh was born in 1977 in Warrington. She left school at sixteen and moved to Barcelona. She has written for the *Observer*, the *Guardian*, the *Sunday Times* and the *Telegraph*, had a column in *Arena* and was a regular contributor to the *Erotic Review*. Her first novel, *Brass*, won a Betty Trask Award and has been translated into nine languages. She is currently writing her second novel. She lives and works on Merseyside.

Peter Wild is the editor of this book. He likes The Fall a lot. Visit his website: www.peterwild.com.

John Williams lives and works in his home town of Cardiff, where he has set several books, including the Cardiff Trilogy, published by Bloomsbury. The Puritan Guitars' single '100 Pounds In 15 Minutes' has recently been re-released on a compilation called *Messthetics Greatest Hits: The Sounds of DIY 1977–80*.

Acknowledgements

The editor would like to thank: Mark E Smith and The Fall for the music, Arts Council England for the generous support, Pete Ayrton & everyone at Serpent's Tail. Call-outs, big-ups, without whoms, etc: Martin Worthington, Will Carr, Pru Rowlandson, Rebecca Grey, Ruthie Petrie, Paul Wilson, Neil Porter, all at Drumbeat, Michel Faber, Matt Thorne, Andrew Holmes, Helen Walsh, Scarlett Thomas, Niall Griffiths, Jeff VanderMeer, Steve Aylett, Sara Gran, Gary Ramsay, Mike Young, Stefan, Conway, Clayts, Graeme Larmour, Michael Wild, Andrew Lane, Peter Brumby, Sarah Hymas, Susan Tomaselli, Heidi James, Louise Jury, Hayley Cavill, Tim Lee, Christian Lewis, Karen Duffy, Dan Thomas, Anthony McKenna, Stephen Donlan and (of course) Louisa, Harriet, Samuel & Martha.